The Civilization of the American Indian Series

WHY GONE THOSE TIMES?

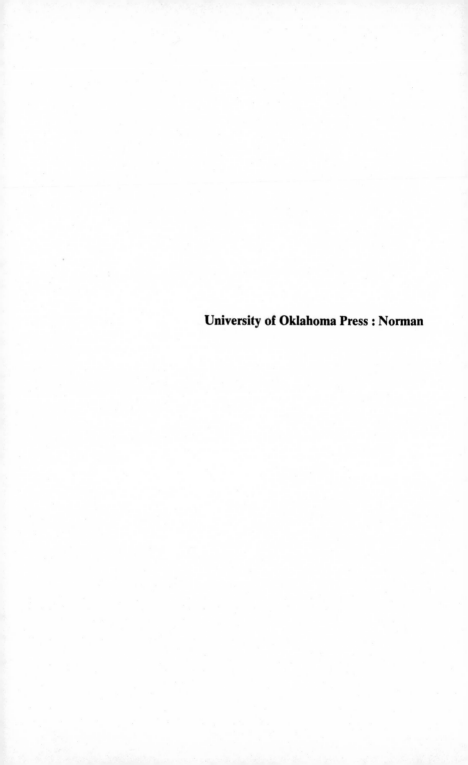

University of Oklahoma Press : Norman

WHY GONE THOSE TIMES ?

Blackfoot Tales

by James Willard Schultz (Apikuni)

Edited by Eugene Lee Silliman

Illustrated with paintings and bronzes by
Charles M. Russell

Library of Congress Cataloging in Publication Data

Schultz, James Willard, 1859–1947.
Why gone those times? Blackfoot tales.

(Civilization of the American Indian series, v. 127)

1. Siksika Indians—Social life and customs.
I. Russell, Charles Marion, 1865–1926, illus.
II. Title.   III. Series.
E99.S54S34   1974   398.2'09701   72-9262
ISBN 978-0-8061-3545-8 (paper)

Copyright © 1974 by the University of Oklahoma Press, Norman,
Publishing Division of the University of Oklahoma. Manufactured
in the U.S.A. First edition, 1974.

EDITOR'S INTRODUCTION

This book is about a people and a time unfamiliar to most Americans. Few realize that the not-so-distant ancestors of the Blackfoot confederacy now living on reservations once controlled the destiny of the northwestern plains. In the eighteenth century this powerful confederacy, aided by the acquisition of the gun and horse, spread its rule over southern Alberta and northern Montana. Shoshonis, Crows, Flatheads, Kutenais, and other tribes, as well as white fur trappers and traders, came to respect and fear Blackfoot country. Not until the Baker Massacre of 1870 and the extermination of the buffalo in 1883 did the power of this mighty people ebb. But this book is not a history of those eventful two centuries; such a book has already been written.[1] Because the stories in *Why Gone Those Times* are about individual feelings and experiences they offer insights into the life and character of the Blackfeet that history books do not convey.

The recorder of these stories was a trader who lived in intimate contact with the Blackfeet for the greater part of his life. Born in Boonville, New York, in 1859, James Willard Schultz was a rebel-

[1] John C. Ewers, *The Blackfeet* (Norman, University of Oklahoma Press, 1958).

lious child, preferring the freedom of the world outdoors to the conventions of society. At the age of seventeen he was permitted to go to Montana, and as he later wrote, "The wild, free life of the West had so entranced me that I could not go back." Under the employ of an able Indian trader named Joseph Kipp, Schultz spent the next six years trading and living with the Blackfoot Indians as they followed the buffalo from the upper Marias River to the Musselshell River in central Montana. During this time he married a Piegan[2] woman, Natahki, or Fine Shield Woman. When the buffalo were gone, they established a ranch on the Blackfoot reservation, though he preferred to spend his time guiding hunting parties into the Rocky Mountains and writing stories and articles about the Blackfeet for the popular outdoor magazine of that day, *Forest and Stream*. The editor of the magazine, George Bird Grinnell, incorporated many of these tales into his book *Blackfeet Lodge Tales*. The most notable material Schultz submitted to that magazine was an autobiographical series in 1905–1906 entitled "In the Lodges of the Blackfeet." Published as a book under the title *My Life as an Indian*, it has become a western classic.

Not long after Natahki's death in 1903, Schultz moved to southern California. He continued to write, and his many serials that appeared in *Youth's Companion* and *American Boy* were published in book form by Houghton Mifflin. In 1930 he collaborated with Jessie Louise Donaldson in writing *The Sun God's Children* and a year later married her. From 1915 on, he returned almost every summer to the Blackfoot reservation to renew friendships. His death in 1947 ended the long career of a man who wrote with love and insight about a culture which now belongs to our past.[3]

---

2 The three subdivisions of the Blackfoot confederacy were the Piegans, Bloods, and Blackfeet.

3 More biographical information may be found in Jessie Donaldson Schultz, "Adventuresome, Amazing Apikuni," *Montana: The Magazine of Western History*, Vol. X, No. 4, (1960), 2–18; Harry C. James, "Apikuni as I Knew Him,"

This anthology, Schultz's thirty-ninth book, has its origins in the earlier collection, *Blackfeet and Buffalo* (Norman, 1962), edited by Keith C. Seele. My enjoyment of that book led me to search the newspapers and magazines mentioned in *Blackfeet and Buffalo* for more short stories. It was soon apparent that a treasury of Schultz stories lay "undiscovered" in not readily accessible periodicals. Believing others would enjoy the material I had found, I began preparing the stories for republication in book form. Nine of the following stories were obtained from Schultz's papers and effects on deposit in the Montana State University Special Collections Library in Bozeman. Schultz's widow, now Mrs. H. L. Graham, has kindly given permission to publish this collection of stories.

The paintings and sculpture of another Montana frontiersman, Charles M. Russell, illustrate this book. Like Schultz, Russell was a restless youth who preferred the world outside the schoolroom. Russell's parents satisfied his yearning to visit the wild west by packing him off to Montana Territory in 1880 at the age of sixteen. While a cowboy in the Judith Basin, he began painting Indian and cowboy scenes, many later to be given away or traded for drinks and groceries. Most of Russell's Indian scenes depict the Blackfeet, probably because he lived among them the winter of 1888–89. After his marriage in 1896, Russell settled down as a full-time artist in Great Falls. With his artistic development came fame and higher prices for his paintings. Before his death in 1926, he was the highest-paid living American artist, a tribute to his uncommon genius and talent.[4] Schultz and Russell knew each other, but Russell never illustrated any of Schultz's books. In this volume the works of these two great Montanans—James Willard Schultz, master of the pen, and Charles M. Russell, master of the brush—are finally brought together.

Eighth Brand Book of the Westerners, Los Angeles Corral (Los Angeles, 1959), 191–206.

4 Two well-illustrated biographies of Russell are Frederic G. Renner, *Charles M. Russell* (Fort Worth, 1966); and Harold McCracken, *The Charles M. Russell Book* (Garden City, New York, 1957).

It should be understood that Schultz was a storyteller, not a historian. He did not carefully study, as a scholar would, historical records, journals, and reports in order to reach objective, documented conclusions. Rather, as a sympathetic listener, he recorded the stories and oral traditions of an Indian culture before its demise. To this man whom they trusted, the Blackfoot warriors and elders opened their hearts, telling of their adventures and tragedies, of their beliefs and fears. From these stories emerges a realization that although the Blackfeet were different from the white men who overpowered them, they were real human beings with all the complex personal and group traits that are often not ascribed to "savages." Only stories told by Indians can effectively convey their emotions, religious beliefs, fears and loves. It is my hope that this anthology will help the reader to empathize with the Blackfeet and understand how the Indians saw life. Toward this end lies the greatest value of this book.

Two final points should be made to the reader about this collection. These stories are reprinted exactly as Schultz wrote them. Consequently, there are some old spellings and constructions. In the footnotes I have used asterisks and other symbols to indicate Schultz's original footnotes. Numbered footnotes are my own explanatory additions.

An expression of gratitude is due the following people for their assistance in the preparation of this anthology: my wife, Nancy Mitchell Silliman, and her parents, John and Viola Mitchell; my parents, Minott and Marjorie Silliman; the widow of James Willard Schultz, Mrs. H. L. Graham; Montana State University Special Collections Librarian, Minnie Paugh; Montana Historical Society Librarian, Harriett C. Meloy; and the late Keith C. Seele of the University of Chicago.

The Charles M. Russell illustrations are reproduced through the courtesy of the R. W. Norton Art Gallery of Shreveport, Louisiana.

EUGENE LEE SILLIMAN

CONTENTS

ILLUSTRATIONS

WHY GONE THOSE TIMES?

1.

The Buffalo Hunt

BUFFALO HUNT. From a painting by Charles M. Russell, 1897.

(Courtesy R. W. Norton Art Gallery, Shreveport, Louisiana)

1.

The Buffalo Hunt

My people said that of all the professions, that of war was best suited to one of my temperament, and I agreed with them. Therefore it was intended that I should go to a military school, preparatory to entering West Point.

But my lungs were not so sound as they should have been, and our family physician said that I must go West and live on the high, dry plains for a time. I went, well provided with letters to the members of a great fur-trading company at Fort Benton, Montana. One of them, dear old Kipp,—or Berry, as the Indians called him,—was appointed my guardian.

I was to stay on the frontier a year. I remained there, except for occasional visits East, for so many years that I do not like to count them. I went, a boy of seventeen. I am white-haired and wrinkled now.

There were no railways in Montana in those early days. Except Fort Benton, there was no settlement save Helena, Virginia City, and one or two other mining-camps in the mountains. On the great plains were various tribes of Indians, millions of buffalo and other game.

Published in *Youth's Companion* (November 3, 1910).

My friend and guardian, Berry, followed the buffalo with the Blackfeet, here one year, there another, as was determined by the shifting of the herds, and his trade with the people amounted annually to thousands of fine buffalo-robes, beaver-skins and other pelts. Through him I came to know the Blackfeet, and to love them. I learned their language, lived with them, hunted, and warred with them against other tribes, and was adopted as a member of the tribe. So I do not write of those old buffalo days from hearsay, but from actual experience.

It was Chief Running Crane who gave me my name, Ap-pe-kun-ny—Spotted Robe. I lived for months at a time in his big lodge of eighteen skins.

The first winter of my residence on the Montana plains passed, the buffalo shed their heavy coats, and "new lodge time" came— the season when the short-haired buffalo cow-hides were most easily converted into soft leather.

Our trading post was in the Judith Basin, not far from where the town of Lewistown now stands, and the Blackfeet, three thousand people in five hundred lodges, were in camp near us. All the winter and spring buffalo had been plentiful in the vicinity, but for some cause which no one was ever able to learn they had suddenly grazed away to the eastward, and scouts reported that the nearest of the big herds was in the vicinity of the Musselshell River, near its junction with Big Crooked Creek.

Thither the Indians decided to go, as nearly all the families wished to make new lodges, and Running Crane asked me to join him in the big hunt.

"Don't you go," said my friend Berry. "There isn't as dangerous a locality in the whole country as that is. Where the Musselshell flows into the Missouri there is a good ford, and war parties from all the different tribes, Sioux, Cheyennes, Crows and the north Indians, are constantly passing. Just you stay here with me and keep your hair on."

"Though the enemy be as plentiful as grass leaves," said Running Crane, "no harm shall come to this white son of ours.

Whenever were my people not victorious over the warriors of the enemy?"

In a way, that was not an idle boast; but he might have added that even the victorious may suffer heavy loss.

I went with my Indian friend; but there came a day and an hour when I wished that I had remained at the post.

To me, not even the sight of a multitude of buffalo, the plains dark with them to the horizon, was so impressive as a view of three or four thousand Indians and their twelve or fifteen thousand packed and loose horses trailing across the country from one camping-place to another. They formed a slender column miles long, the pack and *travail* horses following a three-rut trail deeply worn in the earth, the various bands of loose stock prancing and playing to the right and left of it, as they were herded along by the young boys.

What a medley of color there was in the trappings of the horses, the costumes of the riders, the painted rawhide pouches, sacks and other receptacles in which were stored the food and finery and other property of the people!

And the people themselves! Hilarious youths and maidens, mischievous urchins, staid mothers with infants clasped to their breasts or perched at their backs, wrinkled and bent old men and women peevishly quirting their stolid mounts, proud warriors and still more proud and dignified chiefs and medicine-men, riding in advance of the long column, discoursing of bygone hunts and battles, and of the strange doings of the gods.

More than once in the course of a day's march I would ride to one side and dismount and watch the great caravan go by, and then I would hurry on and regain my place at the side of my good friend, the chief.

Skirting the foot of the Moccasin Mountains and the Black Butte, we saw innumerable bands of antelope and deer and elk, and here and there a few buffalo, mostly bulls. The hunters had no difficulty in securing an ample supply of meat for the great camp. Daily Running Crane and I would make a detour to one

9

side of the trail, or ride far ahead, and kill an antelope or two, or a deer or elk, or perhaps a fat young bull buffalo for our lodge.

Travelling by easy stages, on the afternoon of the fourth day we came to the mouth of Big Crooked Creek, and went into camp along the border of the Musselshell. Big Crooked Creek is the modern name of the stream that Lewis and Clark named Sak-a-ja-we-ah, in honor of that intrepid Indian woman to whom was largely due the success of their expedition.

Ever since early morning we had been passing immense herds of buffalo that ran off out of sight in the broken country. Material for the new lodges was assured.

The great camp was now under what may be called military rule, enforced by order of the chiefs by the "In-ah-kiks," an order or fraternity of young men which had several subdivisions.

That all might have an equal chance in the great hunt, the country was to be scoured by sections, the hunters starting each morning in a body to run a certain herd selected by the scouts. Should any one go off by himself to hunt, thus disturbing and scattering the game, the In-ah-kiks would in reprisal destroy his lodge and property.

A big herd of buffalo south of Crooked Creek and west of the Musselshell was the first to be attacked, and early in the morning Running Crane and I, with the several hundred other hunters, set out for the chase, each one riding his best horse, bareback, and stripped to the least possible weight.

Besides myself, a very few of the men were armed with .44-caliber repeating rifles. The rest carried muzzle-loaders, smooth-bore and rifled, some of which were flintlocks. Some had no other weapon than a bow and quiverful of arrows, but at the close range of a buffalo run this was terribly effective. Riding up beside one of the huge animals, the hunter would drive an arrow clear to the feathers into it, and often, if no bone was struck, quite through its body.

After perhaps a half-hour's ride we sighted the buffalo—four or five thousand of them—in a basin several miles in extent and

10

much broken by slender, flat-topped buttes on which was a scattering growth of dwarfed, wind-twisted pines. We were far too many to approach the animals in a body, and after a brief consultation, about a third of our number circled off to the west, another third to the east, leaving the rest of us to rush the herd when they should come in to the flanks of it several miles farther on.

We had dismounted behind a low ridge which screened us from the watchful eyes of the old sentry bulls, and while we waited, earnest prayers were offered by the medicine-men for our success in the coming run, and the gods—the sun and Old Man— were besought to protect us from all danger.

We waited there nearly an hour, and then a couple of young men who had been peering over the ridge called out to us to mount; that the other parties were ready.

In another moment we were over the ridge, quirting our horses, urging them to their utmost speed. Yet they did not need it; a trained buffalo horse became madly enthusiastic the moment that he was given free rein, and laying his ears flat to his head, he dashed after the fleeing animals with such determination that no bit could check him, much less the leather thong the Indians used in place of one.

But he could be guided. He would swerve to the right or left simply from the pressure of the rider's knee, and when the hunter selected some certain fat cow, would use all his energy to run up alongside of it, so that the shot could be given. But no horse could long keep the pace of the frightened buffalo, although at the start and for a mile or more he could outrun them. Their muscles seemed to be tireless, and once started, a run of ten miles and more at top speed was no task for the animals.

At the start we were three hundred yards or more from the nearest of the buffalo, which were well scattered over the plain in groups of various size, and singly. Some were feeding, some lying down; numbers of the funny-looking, red-colored calves were playing tag; solitary old bulls stood, head lowered, pawing

11

the fine, white alkali earth, sending the dust skyward in slender columns like smoke from chimneys.

As they became alarmed at our rush, they did not, as would deer, scamper away each in his own direction; instead, they formed into a compact herd, and then went southward with a deafening thudding and rattle of hoofs.

Fan-like, we spread out and attacked their rear, those riding the faster horses pressing on into the midst of them. I was one of these. I had done it often before, each time telling myself that I would never do it again, for the danger was great. But always excitement would get the better of my discretion.

Try as they would, so densely were they massed, the animals we rode beside could not crowd more than a gun-barrel length or so away from us, and those we passed closed up the narrow lane we had made. In front, behind, on all sides was an undulating sea of brown humpbacks, black, sharp horns and gleaming coal-black eyes. If a man's horse fell with him in such a place there was nothing to save him from the sharp hoofs of the dense mass behind.

Selecting only the biggest, fattest cow buffalo, I simply poked my rifle out to one side or the other—an aim was not necessary—and pulled the trigger.

Nine times I fired in the course of a ten minutes' run, and then something attracted my attention that drove from my mind all further thought of a big killing.

Happening to look ahead, I saw that the other parties of hunters had each massed as large a portion of the scattered herd as we, and each one of them was coming quartering toward us at tremendous speed. When they should all meet, I for one did not wish to be there. I glanced at the other riders near me; they, too, were checking up their now tired horses, all but one man, named Two Bows, and were letting the buffalo pass them. In two or three minutes we were again at the tail of the herd, where I shot one more, making an even ten.

Two Bows was a noted warrior, a very successful hunter, but he was not popular with his people. He loved too much to brag of his deeds. He was a very reckless man, taking all sorts of risks, and it was really wonderful how he had managed to come through some of them unharmed.

He himself asserted that it was because of a certain under-water animal that had appeared to him in a dream, and said, "When in danger, when in doubt what to do, call me and I will help you. Call me four times: once from the north, once from the south, and from the east and the west, and wherever I may be, I will come to your aid. Failing not to call me, nothing can harm you, and you shall live to be white-haired."

What the Blackfeet dreamed, that they believed really occurred. They thought that when asleep their shadows (souls) actually departed from the body, and went forth on strange adventure.

So in all his recklessness Two Bows was sustained by his unquestioning faith in the animal of his dream. Where we had withdrawn, he rode recklessly on, urging his horse into the very center of those rushing streams of buffalo, and discharging shaft after shaft from his bow as he went.

The three bands met. Imagine it if you can—something like five thousand buffalo, five million pounds of impetuous flesh and bone, rushing to a central point. They packed together so densely that not a few of the smaller ones were trampled to death. The terrific pressure forced others up on their hind feet, and they pawed the air and the backs of those next them, trying to climb out of the press. There was a deep thunder of groans and grunts mingled with the clash of horns and rattle and pounding of hoofs.

When they met, Two Bows was in the very center of the jam, and suddenly we saw him, horse and all, actually tossed up in the air by a huge bull.

"He dies!" cried Running Crane, who was at my side; and so I thought.

The horse fell and disappeared. Two Bows, however, was more fortunate. In falling, he clutched the long, shaggy hair of a bull, and raising himself, secured a firm seat astride its hump.

13

Intensely frightened at its strange burden, the bull bucked and jumped, and unable to free itself, surged forward with prodigious force and speed. At the same time, the now united herd began to break up and stream madly in all directions from the common center.

As usual, the old men of the camp, on superannuated ponies, and the women and children on fat, lazy *travail* mares, had closely followed the hunters, in order to cut up and pack home the game. They could now be seen madly fleeing in all directions. I could plainly hear the shrill "Na-ya-yah!" of the women and the screaming of the children. But our main interest was in Two Bows.

With all his faults, none disliked him so much that they wished to see him die, and with one accord the hunters pressed forward to rescue him if possible.

Soon clear of the herd, the bull fled eastward toward the Musselshell with far more speed than our tired horses could attain, and we would soon have lost sight of it and the rider altogether had it not stopped now and then to try to shake or jar Two Bows off. I have seen some ludicrous things in my time, but that huge, unwieldy, long-whiskered bull trying apparently to imitate the lithe, lightning-like antics of a wild bronco is fixed in my memory.

We soon realized that Two Bows had no weapon of any kind. Had he possessed even a knife, he could have drawn it across the sinews of the bull's neck. He dared not jump, for once on the ground, he would be at the mercy of the infuriated animals. We followed, several hundred of us, sometimes gaining, sometimes losing ground.

"I-kak-i-mat!" (Keep up courage!) we cried, from time to time, as if the poor fellow could hear us! Down into the breaks of the river we rushed, across deep converging coulees, through thickets of berry and rose brush, through groves of low-branched pine, and out on the level bottom at last.

Here the bull started bucking and circling again, and we rapidly approached him. If only one of us could get near enough for a certain shot, Two Bows would be free. We were near enough now to see the man's face; it looked ashy; the eyes were fairly bulging, and watched us with a great appeal for help. Running Crane, I, and a dozen others in the lead, were closing in, calculating when best to aim the delivering shot, and then, like a flash, the animal was off again, straight across the wide bottom toward the river, which there flowed under a cut bank at least thirty feet high.

"He's going to jump!" "He's going off it!" I heard on all sides of me, and then, with a last, long leap, the bull and its burden disappeared.

A moment later we were at the edge, looking down, and again we were too late. The shallow water was flowing over a quicksand in which the bull was floundering, and we got just a glimpse of Two Bows as the frantic animal rolled upon him and forced him down into it.

Someone fired and killed the bull; others hurried to collect brush driftwood, anything to sustain one's weight, and they hurried out to the place.

Well, why should I describe the rest? The next day the body of poor Two Bows, wrapped in many a robe, was lashed to a platform in a cottonwood-tree, and beside him were placed his weapons. Two horses were killed there, that his shadow might have shadow steeds to ride to the Sand Hills—shadow land— and for many and many a night thereafter we could hear the wailing of the women.

2.

The Peril of Lone Man

TRACKS TELL TALES THAT
RIVERS MAKE SECRETS. From a
painting by Charles M. Russell,
dated 1926.

(Courtesy R. W. Norton Art Gallery, Shreveport, Louisiana)

The Peril of Lone Man

As the country merchant loves to ride out beyond the bounds of his own town and look over the broad fields of the farmers, yellow with ripening grain ready for the reaper, so the old-time Indian trader loved to look upon the big camp of the plains people, red with drying meat and white flesh side of newly stripped hides ready for tanning into robes. But I fancy that in the heart of the Indian trader there was a kindlier feeling, less of a spirit of grasping than these same merchants have. The Indian trader was an anomaly. If he charged his customers enormous prices for his goods, he also gave to the needy and to his friends with a prodigal hand. Generally his interest in the welfare of the people to whom he had become attached was greater than his desire for gain; and so it came to pass that when the buffalo were finally killed off, not one in fifty of these men could show much of a balance on the credit side of his ledger. I merely mention this to explain why, as we rode into the edge of the Blackfoot camp one autumn afternoon in the long ago, my old friend Berry exclaimed: "Plumb red and white, isn't it! My! but they're happy."

And so the people were; from several quarters of the great

Published in *Forest and Stream* (December 28, 1907).

camp, above the shouts and laughter of playing children, could be heard the beating of drums; and voices raised in gambling, and feast, and dancing songs.

Passing along between the lodges, women ceased from their occupation to look up at us with smiling faces, and make some joke about our coming; and here and there a man shouted out: "Our friends have arrived. You shall feast with us."

And yet most people believe that the Indians are a silent, taciturn people! Well, they do appear to be so before those whom they instinctively know despise them.

We rode on and dismounted in front of Lone Man's lodge; a youth sprang to take charge of our horses, and we entered the home of our friend. "Welcome, welcome," he said heartily, motioning us to seats on either side of him, and then shaking hands with us, his comely, intelligent face alight with pleasure. One by one of his three young wives came in, three fine looking, long-haired, clean and richly dressed sisters. They, too, were glad to see us, and said so, as they began to prepare the evening meal. Again the door was drawn back and our saddles, guns and bridles were brought in by the youth and piled in the empty space.

It was a fine lodge, that one of Lone Man's; about 22 feet in diameter, of good height, made of twenty new, white soft tanned cowskins artistically cut and sewn together. All around close to the poles was a brightly painted lining, between which and the outer covering the air rushed up and out through the top, carrying the smoke of the cheerful fire along with it. Here and there were luxurious buffalo robe couches, with painted willow back rests covered with buffalo robes, and in the spaces between them were piled set after set of bright, pretty-figured parfleches, containing the stores of clothing and finery of the family. Suspended above the head of our host, securely fastened to the lodge poles, was a long, thick buckskin-wrapped roll, containing a medicine pipe. At each end of it were some red-painted, long-fringed, rawhide sacks filled with various sacred things. Our friend was a medicine

22

man. Once, when very ill, he had paid fifty horses for the pipe, and through its miraculous power, the Sun had listened to his supplications, and restored him to health. The sick now came to him, and he unrolled the sacred bundle with the prescribed ceremonies and songs, painted the sufferers' faces with red symbols of the sky gods and prayed for their recovery as the fragrant smoke of tobacco and burning sweet grass arose.

We exchanged such news as we had to tell, while the roasting of fresh buffalo tongues, the frying of thin flour cakes, and making of coffee progressed. In those days Lone Man was one of the few Blackfeet who cared for bread and other white man's food. Meat of various kinds, prepared in various ways, and without salt, was all the most of them had. Meat was ni-tap'-i-wak-sin: real food. Flour, beans, rice, corn and the like they called kis'tap-i-wak-sin: useless food.

Some visitors came in and we repeated what we thought would interest them, and told why we were there: to learn how they were going to winter; if in one locality, or in moving about. We had our own view of the matter; we wanted them to remain where they were, at the foot of the Snowy Mountains, and I may as well say here that before we left camp they promised that they would. So we built a substantial trading post there, and had a very good trade.

To look at our good friend, Lone Man, as he sat there in the glow of the little lodge fire that night, laughing and joking, and at his three unusually handsome wives, happy in ministering to the wants of their husband's friends, one would not have thought that they had ever known trouble; but they had. For years a grim spectre had hovered over them. Death in the form of some unknown enemy, in most unexpected ways, at the most unusual times, had more than once nearly overtaken Lone Man, the popular, the kind, the helping friend to the poor and afflicted. Why he, of all men, rich and kind and generous, should have an enemy, and that enemy a member of his own tribe, was a mystery which

23

had never been solved. He had never quarreled with anyone. Not a man nor woman was there in all the tribe at whom the finger of suspicion could be pointed.

The winter previous to this time Lone Man had paid us a somewhat long visit, and one night he told us in detail the story of his escapes from this mysterious foe. "It began," he said, "the very day after I married my first wife, when I was feeling happier than I ever had before, and I had always been a pretty happy youth. I was very proud, too, that morning. Why should I not have been, with just the prettiest girl in camp riding by my side— well, maybe not any prettier than my Pwai-o'-ta and my youngest woman, Pus-ah'-ki. You remember how they looked in those days, don't you? Such smooth-cheeked, bright-eyed, quick and graceful girls as they were. And don't you remember their hair, how the long braids of it almost touched the ground as they walked along?

"We had eaten our first meal together, Si'-pi-ah-ki and I, and then we rode out to round up my herd of horses and drive them into water. I held my head pretty high as we passed on between the lodges. Many a young man, I knew, was gazing at me envious- ly; nearly every one of them at one time or another, had tried to get this girl to share his lodge, and I, I had got her. Had I not good reason to be proud and happy? Of course I had, for she cared for me as much as I did for her; she also was happy.

"We rode out across the sage and greasewood flat bordering the river, then up the valley's slope on to the big plain, seamed with deep, brushy coulees putting in to the river. Away in the distance was my herd, and we went toward it, riding along a narrow ridge between two coulees. We were talking and laughing, never thinking of any danger, when suddenly a gun boomed behind us, and I fell from my horse. I don't remember feeling the bullet strike, nor falling. I merely heard the gun. When I came to myself there was a terrible pain in my head. The bullet had struck just here, above this temple, and glanced off, not doing any dam- age, except to cut the scalp and let out considerable blood. But

24

the pain was terrible. I saw that I must have lain there for some time, because the sun was now quite high above the edge of the world. When I opened my eyes Si'-pi-ah-ki bent over and kissed me. She had my gun on her lap, and sat facing the direction from which the shot had come, the coulee on the down river side of the ridge. 'Oh,' she said, 'I thought at first you were killed, and I wanted to die, too. But I felt for your heart and found that it was beating. I pressed your wound as I knew the skull was not crushed. So I just picked up your gun and watched for the enemy to show himself.'

"Now was she not brave? Most women in her place would just have screamed and ridden away as fast as they could urge the horse; would have been so frightened that they would not have known what they were doing. She had seen no enemy, had heard nothing. Our horses were grazing not far away. I tried to rise, and fell back, dizzy. 'Lie still,' she said, 'someone will be coming this way before long, and we'll get help.' Sure enough a rider did appear, coming out from the river on another ridge, and Si'pi-ah-ki arose and waved her robe. He whipped up his horse and came quickly; and when he learned what had happened he hurried back to camp for aid. A big crowd of men returned with him, also my mother with a travoi, on which I was taken in to my lodge. My friends searched the coulee and found no signs of a war party, only the tracks of a man leading down it to camp. The tracks were fresh, made that morning, and they were the imprints of parfleche soled moccasins! He who had shot me then, was some one of our own people. Many men had gone out afoot after their horses, but no one had been seen to return afoot; all had returned riding, driving their herd before them. And that was all. 'Look out,' the people said to me. 'Watch sharp; some one in this camp is your enemy.'

"I couldn't believe it. I thought that some friend had fired in our direction just to scare us, and that, seeing what he had done, he had fled from the place and sneaked home.

"Four nights later, I learned that I was mistaken. I awoke

suddenly with a sort of fear in my heart; with the feeling that some terrible danger threatened me. There was no moon. I glanced up through the smoke hole; there were no stars; the sky was clouded over and 'twas very dark. I lay on the outside of our couch, Si'-pi-ah-ki on the inside. I heard a faint rustling; she was sleeping, and motionless. 'It is a dog.' I thought, 'lying just outside against the lodge skin.' And then all at once I knew what it was; again I heard the rustling noise, and, dark as it was, I saw the white lodge lining rising, rising, very slowly a very little way at a time. My gun was by my side. I noiselessly cocked it, took aim where I thought this enemy of mine was lying, and fired. The flash of the powder revealed both lodge skin and lining raised and a hand, grasping a shining knife. Then all was dark again, and mingled with Si'-pi-ah-ki's frightened screams, I heard the thud, thud, thud, of retreating feet. My shot aroused the camp. Men rushed here and there with ready guns inquiring what had happened. My woman built a fire; we took lighted sticks and examined the ground outside; there was no blood, nor anything save a pulled up lodge pin and the still half-raised skin. 'Who, who was this enemy,' we asked, 'who so desired our death?' Why did he try to kill me? What harm had I ever done to any of my people that must be paid for with my life?

"I was never spoken of as a coward. I had proved more than once in battle with the enemy that I was a pretty good fighter; but now I felt afraid. It is very terrible to feel that some one is trying to bring about your death. Thereafter I never went alone anywhere. When I hunted, my cousin Red Plume always accompanied me. I got a youth to care for my horses, and that was a great pleasure I had to give up, for nothing is more pleasant than to round up your band and drive them in to water, listening to the thunder of their hoofs, watching them play, their fat, sleek, hard bodies shining in the sun. Also, more than all else, I feared the night; the darkness. When we went to bed, first we put out the fire, and then pretending to occupy one couch, we would quietly step over and take another one. We couldn't talk to each other any more at night; not even whisper; and that was hard to two young people who love and have so very much to say to each other. I got two big dogs and kept them always tied except when we moved camp, and I made them savage. Always, they slept inside, one by the doorway, the other by our couch.

"A winter and a summer passed, and then my father-in-law died. So, as my perhaps-to-be wives* no longer had a home, I took them. I had always intended to do so in time. They wished it, their older sister wished it, and so did I. We were four happy persons. My enemy had not troubled me for a long time, and I looked forward to a life of peace. Also, I became somewhat careless. On the very night that the two new wives came to my lodge, away out beyond the confines of camp there came to our ears the sound of shots and the cry of the enemy, an Assiniboine war party some of our young men had discovered as they came sneaking in to steal our horses. Like every other man, I seized my weapons and ran toward the place. From the time I left my lodge I heard someone running behind me, but I had no thought of danger until, twang! went a bow string and an arrow pierced my left shoulder, burning my flesh as though it was made of fire. I could not use my left arm at all, but, turning, I raised my gun with my right arm as quickly as I could, and fired at the person I could but dimly see running from me. The flash of the gun blinded me for a little time, and when I recovered from it, there was no one in sight, no longer any sound of running feet. I turned and crept homeward by a circuitous way, moving very silently through the tall sagebrush. I had no place out in the fight beyond, not with one of my own people waiting for just such a chance to shoot me in the back. Again I had a terrible feeling of dread, and that, with the loss of blood from my wound, overcame me. I managed to reach my lodge, and fell within the doorway as one dead.

* The younger sisters of a woman a man married were his potential wives. If he did not wish to marry them, he had the right to choose their husbands. (Schultz's note. Throughout the book Schultz's notes are indicated by symbols, editor's notes by numbers.)

27

"Before I came to life they drew the arrow from my shoulder, so I did not feel that pain. It was just an arrow; plain and new, and straight, without one mark to designate its owner. And it had a terrible barbed point; they had to push it on through and break it off in order to pull out the shaft.

"I lay ill and low hearted for some days. The chiefs held a council, and the camp crier went about telling loudly their words: 'This is to the cowardly, mean dog who seeks the life of a good man. Let him beware; let him cease his wrong doing, for if discovered he will be given to the Sun; he will be bound to a tree and then left to starve and thirst until his shadow passes on.'

"Little good that would do, I thought. Sooner or later, at some unguarded time, he would succeed in his attempt, and my shadow would go on to the sandhills, not his. More closely than ever I now kept watch for him; more carefully than ever my women and my friends guarded me from possible surprise. How I longed to meet him face to face, to fight him with gun, or knife, or club, or even with bare hands. I planned what I would do if I ever got him in my power, how best to make his dying a long day of great suffering.

"You can understand how unpleasant a camp life is to an active man. How, instead of sitting idly in your lodge you long to mount a horse and ride out over the plains; if not to hunt, why just to ride and see the plains, and the mountains rising from them, and to watch the game and birds; to see the cloud shadows sweep over the big land; to feel the wind, made by the gods, gentle or fierce as their heart happens to be at the time. And I couldn't go and see it all, live it all, as others did, when they pleased. I could only go when someone was willing to accompany me. During many idle days I did much visiting, and gave many feasts myself. One by one I considered every man of our people as that enemy of mine. And see, not one of them all but gave me friendly smiles and greeting, and yet some one of them wanted my life. Time and again my women talked over those who had desired to marry them, who made proposals to their parents for them. There had been many, it is true, but not even among them could we point to one as possibly this enemy. Every one of them was married, and certainly content and happy.

"Two winters passed. In all that time nothing occurred to disturb us, except that I felt sick, having pains in my stomach, in my head, and often, when starting to rise from a seat, I became blind and dizzy, and weak, and would just fall back in my place. This sickness grew worse and worse. We called in doctor after doctor; men and women who had a great favor with the gods, who had medicines that cured all ills. But neither their prayers nor their bitter drinks did me any good. I lost my desire for food. I became weaker and weaker. I hated to die. I was still young; my women loved me. I loved them. I wanted to live and be happy with them, but most I wanted to live because some evil one so desired my death.

"One day there came some visitors from the North Blackfeet camp, and I gave them a feast. They remarked upon my thinness and ill health, and I told how I was afflicted. 'Why,' said one, 'there is a way by which you can recover. Our people have a sacred pipe which always cures this kind of sickness. It is now owned by Three Suns. Go you at once and get it; the value of it is great; no less than fifty horses, but what are horses compared to health?'

"Instantly I determined that I would have the pipe, but outwardly I made excuses. Said that I was too ill to travel; that I had tried everything, and had concluded that there was no cure for my trouble. I had made my plans even before I spoke. The very next night Red Plume carried out such things as were needed for the journey. Saddles, robes, a couple of parfleches filled with various foods, and cached them in a coulee some distance from camp. The next night he had two of my best horses there, and when the fires had gone out and the people slept, Si'-pi-ah-ki and I stole out to the place, and were soon mounted and heading for the mountain trail leading to the north. My other women were to live in Two Plume's lodge during my absence. Of course we were excited as we started out, and I felt quite strong; but long, very long before

29

daylight, I became weak and dizzy. By this time we had got to the foothills, the children of the big mountains, and riding to the top of one we dismounted to rest, securing our horses in a little pine grove on its side, concealing ourselves in the tall green bunch grass. My woman placed the robes for me, covered me from the dew, and I slept, she herself taking my gun and sitting by my side, watching, listening, for any danger.

"I was awakened by the sun shining in my face. Si′-pi-ah-ki bent over me with that patient, mother-like smile I had always loved to see, and that never failed to cheer. 'Why yes,' I answered her question, 'I feel much better. I will be able to ride a long ways today, but first we are going to eat, then you will sleep while I keep watch.'

"She descended the hill to the creek, and came back with a bucket of water and we had our morning meal. I had kept watch for some time when I saw a lone horseman far out on the plains, in the very direction we had come. I thought at first that he was hunting; someone from our camp in quest of meat. But no, there were buffalo in sight not far to the north of him and he did not turn toward them. Instead he came steadily on, right on our trail, plain to be seen in the green grass of early summer. I awakened my woman. 'There he is,' I said, pointing. 'There is our enemy. At last the day has come when we shall see his face, when either he or I will die. I am glad.'

"He was still far out on the plain. 'When he comes near,' I said, 'I will steal down to the brush there, where we crossed the little creek, and as he rides down the bank into it I'll shoot him from his horse.'

" 'Yes,' my brave woman agreed, 'and I'll hide on the other side with a big club, and this knife of mine. He won't think of anyone there, and if you should miss him, why, I can do something I hope. But you will not miss, such a good shot as you are. He will just tumble off his horse into the water. And if we cannot kill him, if he should kill you, then, my husband, our shadows will go together to the sand hills, for I will kill myself.'

"I noticed that our pursuer often stopped and turned his horse and looked back, and all around, and then he would start on again swiftly. 'He is afraid of being seen on our trail,' I said. 'I hope that nothing will prevent him from coming on.'"

"But there did, and it was a great disappointment. Some riders appeared off to the south of him, and he turned at once and disappeared in a big coulee which ran down into the Two Medicine River. We saw no more of him for some time, and then, away further down, we saw him leave the valley and strike across the plains toward Badger Creek. There was no use of our remaining on the hill any longer. We mounted and continued our journey.

"In good time we came to the Blackfeet camp, and to Three Suns' lodge. The old man received us kindly, and when I told him why I had come he gave me the sacred pipe without hesitating at all, agreeing to send his son and another young man back with us to receive the fifty horses I gave him. We stayed there some time, he praying for and teaching me the ceremonies of the pipe, until I knew them well. Then we returned home and met with no incident by the way worth telling. I had steadily grown stronger. Little by little my sick spells wore away until I felt as I do now, perfectly well and strong. Also, I now had good, instead of bad dreams, one especially quite often. 'You shall survive the attempts on your life,' my secret helper told me. 'You shall outlive your enemy.'

"This gave me courage, a strong heart, and I went oftener out on the hunt, and to just ride around. Never carelessly though, never alone. For three winters I was not troubled, as I learned, just because I was so watchful. The very first time I did take chances this happened: We were nearly out of meat, both lodges of us, so Red Plume and I went out after some. It was a cloudy spring day, warm, still, but the clouds were above the mountain tops, and we decided that rain would not fall, not until night at least. We had been encamped a long time at that place down on the Bear (Marias) River in the Medicine Rock bottom, and game had moved out some distance from the valley, scared away

31

by the hunters. We rode away southward up the Dry Fork, and it was nearly midday before we sighted game, several bunches of antelope, then a fair-sized herd of buffalo. These last were feeding on the south side and on top of that long flat butte, the one rock walled at its eastern end. We rode up a deep coulee on its north side, then climbed it, and found ourselves right among the animals. We chased them across the flat top of the butte, killing only one cow, Red Plume only wounding the one he fired at. That wasn't enough meat, and we loped our horses on down the steep and rocky slope. There the buffalo had the advantage of us of course, as they could descend a hill more than twice as fast as the best horse could. Down on the flat it would be different; there we could regain lost ground and complete our kill. But I never got there. My horse fell and sent me rolling until I brought up against a boulder. I wasn't hurt, only scratched in places, nor did the fall break my gun. But it was different with the horse. One of his fore legs was broken, and the ball that was intended to bring down meat sent his shadow to the sand hills. Red Plume was lucky. Down on the level he killed three fine young bulls. He is a fine shot on horseback and a very quick reloader. The three animals lay within the length of a hundred steps. He felt as badly as I did over the loss of my horse. It was one of my best runners, and he often rode it himself. 'Well,' he said, 'what is dead stays dead. We cannot help it, so let us determine what is best to do now. I think that we had better skin our kill, cut up the meat, and then, taking just the tongues and a few ribs, ride home double on my horse. I'll come back tomorrow with some of the women after the skins and everything.'

" 'I don't like to ride double,' I told him. 'I never did, even when I was a boy, if you remember. It is still a long time until dark, so just ride in to camp and lead out a horse for me, while I stay here and do the skinning and meat cutting.'

"He objected. 'Not that I mind the ride,' he said. 'Think of yourself, that enemy of yours may be even now somewhere out this way watching us.'

32

"We argued the matter for some time, but I had my way. Not long after Red Plume left the wind began to blow and then it began to rain. I kept on with my work, however, and skinned and cut up the animals. By that time I was very wet. I covered the meat with three of the skins and then crouched down under the other one, but I could not keep warm, and I was very uncomfortable. Finally, I could not stand it any longer, and throwing off the cover I arose and started homeward. The rain was falling harder than ever, the wind blowing more fiercely. I was nearly blinded by the water, but splashed on faster than ever, expecting to meet Red Plume about half way out, and go on in to the cheerful fire awaiting me just as fast as I could make my horse travel.

"The trail on the Dry Fork is pretty straight, cutting the bends of the valley. Sometimes it runs beside the stream and again up and across a point. All at once I began to be afraid. 'This is a good place for that enemy of mine to waylay me,' I thought, trying hard to keep the water out of my eyes, and scan every place ahead. I know now that my secret helper was trying to warn me of danger, but I could not quite believe it. 'In such a storm as this,' I tried to make myself believe, 'he would not be out, and anyway if he were he could not know that I am hurrying home afoot over this trail.' Well, for all my arguments I couldn't feel easy, and so, when a gun in some bushes off to the left of the trail banged, and flashed red, and I felt a bullet tear through my thigh, I wasn't a bit surprised. There was a small thicket right there on the right of the trail, and I tumbled into it purposely. The shot had not knocked me over, but I acted as if it had, hoping that this man, who wanted to kill me, would show himself and give me a chance to kill him. I no sooner fell into the brushes than I straightened up and looked out through the screen of thick leaves. I looked and looked. No one appeared. I heard no sound but the wind and the pattering rain, and the rush of the rising stream. My wound began to be very painful. Considerable blood was running from it, but not enough to make me believe that a vein had been cut. I pressed both holes tightly with my thumb and forefinger, and kept very still except

33

that I could not help shivering, nor keep my teeth from chattering. I felt easier at heart than I had, anyhow. My enemy had done all he could this time. He would not dare approach my hiding place, and Red Plume could not be far away. When he came we would at least learn who this coward was. He did come before I expected him, leading a horse for me, riding a fresh one himself. I tried to rise, but the effort was too painful. So I shouted, and he rode up and dismounted at the edge of the brush. I explained what had happened, where I thought my enemy was concealed. 'No,' he said, 'he couldn't be there. A little ways back I saw some fresh horse tracks across the trail, going in the direction of the lower ford of the river.'

" 'Then go,' I said. 'Ride as fast as you can. Overtake and kill him or trail him into camp and learn who he is.'

"He did not speak, helped me to rise, and lifted me up on to his horse. As soon as I took my fingers from the wound it bled as freely as it had at first. He stuffed some tobacco into the holes, tore his shirt into strips and bound it. 'You just hang on, if you can,' he said at last, 'and I'll lead the horse. I am going to see you home as quickly as I can get you there.'

"It was dark when we got in, and I had become so weak that I was reeling in the saddle like a drunken man when they lifted me off and laid me on my couch. That very night I had another good dream. Again my secret helper encouraged me. 'Be firm-hearted,' he said. 'You shall see the green grass of many summers. You shall be happy here long after your enemy has become a shadow in the sand hills.'

"So I did take courage, and when my wound healed I went about again with caution as usual. All this happened before you came to us. You know all about the other times that this dog has tried to kill me."

"And of course you now know that he can't kill you," I said, when he had concluded his narrative.

"Of course I do," he acquiesced. "My secret helper is certainly of the Sun. I can depend on what he tells me."

This night, as we sat in our friend's lodge, I thought again of the many attempts that had been made to murder him, and of the man who so desired his death. I longed to know what his motive was, and I wished very earnestly to see him brought to justice. Such a deadly hatred of one man for another, and the persistent attempts of the one to kill the other, by stealth, are not uncommon with white people, but a similar case had never been known among the Blackfeet, nor in any other Indian tribe so far as I have been able to learn. There have been deadly strifes and murders, but never in an underhand way such as were these attempts to murder Lone Man.

We were invited to several feasts that evening, and passed about a half hour with each host. At 9 o'clock or a little later we were back with our friend. "We will smoke another pipe or two before retiring," he said, drawing the board before him and beginning to cut and mix the l'herbe and tobacco. The door curtain was drawn aside and an old, old, bent and wrinkled and gray-haired woman entered and dropped to her knees clasping and unclasping her shrunk and withered hands.

"Welcome, old woman," said Lone Man, stopping his work and looking at her sympathetically, knife poised above the little heap of the mixture. "Speak, what can we do for you. Will you have food—tobacco?"

"Oh, chief," she whined, "oh, great and generous heart, as you love your pretty wives I pray you to have pity. Listen: My grandson, Running Eagle, is more sick than ever this night, and near to death. In his long, long illness he has tried many doctors, has paid them all his wealth, but none has helped him. I beg you to take down your sacred pipe, and pray for him. He has nothing to give you, his last horse has gone to those doctors. Great chief, generous heart, have—pity—pity on—"

She broke down and sobbed as only the old and weak can sob.

"Don't cry; don't cry," said Lone Man. "Of course we'll take down the pipe; he shall smoke it; we will pray for him. Go quickly and tell him to come in."

"Ai yah!" the old woman cried. "He can no longer walk. He is not even conscious. He must be carried—"

Lone Man's wives looked up at him questioningly. He nodded his head and they arose and went out, and presently returned with other women, carrying the sick man on his robe couch. They laid him down on the left of the fireplace, between it and one of the women's couches. He was terribly emaciated; had evidently long suffered from some internal trouble; cancer of the stomach, perhaps; certainly not tuberculosis. He seemed to be sleeping.

Lone Man and his head wife hurriedly painted their faces with that dull red earth, the sacred color, and then Si'-pi-ah-ki carefully took down the sacred roll, the sacred sacks and placed them in front of their couch. The woman drew a live coal from the fire, took from one of the sacks a pinch of sweet grass and dropped it upon it. As the sacred, perfumed smoke from it arose they rubbed their hands in it, to purify themselves before beginning the ceremony. The woman then removed the wrappings all but the last one of the pipe—really a pipe stem, any bowl being used that would fit it.

Now Lone Man took the red paint his companion handed him, and bending over the sleeping man painted on his face the symbols of the sky gods. On his forehead the sun, on his chin the moon, on his cheeks a star. He moved restlessly several times while it was being done.

A number of songs were now to be sung before the last covering could be removed, and the gorgeous stem, beaded and feathered and hung with colored hair, exposed, and lifted from its place. The first was the Song of the Robe. I have heard people say that Indian songs are "mere discordant ki-yi-ings." Those who said so had themselves no knowledge of music. To them anything classical would have been wholly unappreciated. I say that there is genuine music in many Indian airs. This Song of the Robe, for instance, is a grand and solemn thing expressing the veneration and adoration of the human soul for the infinite, and it is as truly pleasing to the educated ear as is any part of the Messiah.

36

They began it, and the sound of their voices aroused the sick man. He opened his eyes and they widened in terror as he beheld our host sitting there near him. "Stop! stop!" he cried, half raising and supporting himself by one frail, trembling arm, and raising the other as if to ward off some threatened blow. One of the women, his wife, reached over and attempted to lower him back on his couch.

"Let go of me," he shrieked. "Take me out of here; away from this terrible pipe which has brought this sickness upon me."

"Oh, be still, my son," the grandmother wailed. "He knows not what he says," said his wife, sadly. "Do not listen to him, Lone Man."

"I do know what I say," the sick man cried. "I am dying, and I'll tell it all. I am beaten, and I acknowledge it. I am the one who so often tried to kill you, Lone Man, and I would have succeeded had you not got that terrible pipe. Its power has been greater than mine; it has protected you and saved you from each of my attempts. Take me out, you women, and let me die elsewhere unless he wishes to kill me here."

"Tell me why you did it," said Lone Man, bending forward and speaking in a kindly voice. "What have I ever done to you that you should want my life?"

"What did you do? Why, you got the women that I wanted. I loved them. I have always loved them. If I could have killed you I might have got them. Take me out of here, you women, at once."

"Friend," said Lone Man, "I forgive you. We will forget what you have done, and now we will try to heal your trouble. If my medicine has brought this upon you we will ask it to restore you to health. Si'-pi-ah-ki, once more the song."

The woman stared at him in amazement. "What!" she cried, "you ask me to sing and to pray for one who has so wronged us, who made us live in fear for your life, and grief for your suffering all these years? I refuse."

"Yes, yes," cried the other wives. "Her words are ours. Oh, do not aid him."

"Let us be kind," said he. "If I have forgiven him, surely you may too. Si'-pi-ah-ki, as you love me, listen to what your kind heart tells you. Now again, the song."

They sang it, both with more fervor than before, and the sick man dropped back upon his couch and closed his eyes. One after another they went through the songs. Then Lone Man lifted the stem and, holding it aloft, prayed earnestly for the recovery of Running Eagle, and for good health and long life, peace and happiness for us all. It was a very impressive scene.

At last the ceremony ended. The sick man had roused up and drawn a few whiffs of smoke through the sacred stem, and muttered his prayer of supplication to the gods. The women arose and carried him out to his lodge. Silently the women prepared their couches, made a bed for Berry and me with some extra robes and our blankets, and silently we all laid down to sleep. "And yet," said Berry after a little, as though concluding a conversation, "white people say that Indians never forgive an injury!"

"They pass judgment on many matters," I added, "about which they have no knowledge."

Running Eagle died the next day.

3.

Little Plume's Dream

SECRETS OF THE NIGHT. Bronze
by Charles M. Russell, 1926.

*(Courtesy R. W. Norton Art Gallery,
Shreveport, Louisiana)*

3.

Little Plume's Dream

One spring the Blackfeet were camped on the Judith River, which in their language is named the Yellow Stream. Game was getting rather scarce in the vicinity of camp, so it was determined to move camp to Armell's Creek, another tributary of the Missouri, some thirty miles east. At that time I was living with Little Plume, a young warrior of thirty years or more, very brave and a great hunter. He was of a cheerful disposition, always laughing and joking; but the morning we were to move camp he seemed to be unusually quiet. He got up and had his customary plunge in the river, and ate his breakfast, speaking very little, and seemed to be in deep thought. After a time he got out his war sack, and selecting a bunch of choice eagle's tail feathers—very highly prized by the Blackfeet for decorative purposes—he went out and gave them to the sun; that is, he made a prayer to the sun for health and safety, and concluded by tying the bunch of feathers to the branch of a tree as an offering to the powerful god. Soon the lodges were taken down, everything was packed up and loaded onto the horses, and the march began. In those days a tribe of Indians on the march presented a stirring scene. Most of the

Published in *Forest and Stream* (October 13, 1894).

riding horses were decked with fancy beadwork and bright saddle trappings; the pack horses carried queer-shaped sacks and pouches of rawhide, which were painted with quaint designs in bright colors. The horses which carried the property of the medicine men, sacred and mysterious bundles, were always white, and their manes and tails were painted with vermillion. The medicine pouches, made of white rawhide, were beautifully painted, and the long fringes of buckskin depending from them nearly swept the ground. The costumes of the people added not a little to the brightness of the scene. The older people often wore a buffalo robe or sombre-colored blanket, but the young and middle-aged men and women wore fancy-colored blankets of every conceivable hue; and as they trooped along laughing and chattering, their long hair flying in the breeze, they were an interesting sight. At the head of the column rode the chiefs and head men, followed by the women and children; behind them and on the flanks rode the great body of the warriors driving the loose horses before them, and of these there were many hundred.

As we rode along this bright spring morning, Little Plume informed us that he had had a very bad dream. He said that a little old white man came to him and cried out "Beware! You will be in great danger tomorrow."

"How?" asked Little Plume.

"I may not tell you;" replied the white man. "All I can say is, have courage, do your best and you may come out all right."

I had never argued with these people about their beliefs. In fact, to get at their inner life, to learn their innermost thoughts and ways, I pretended to be a true disciple of their religion. I made them think that I too, was a sun worshiper and a believer in dreams and signs. Often I would recount to the old men some dream I pretended to have had, and ask their opinion as to its portent. So when Little Plume recounted his dream to me, I said: "My friend, this is truly a fearful dream. How did the little old white man look?"

"He was very small and thin," he replied, "and his face was very smooth and white."

"Well," said I, "if I were you I would be very careful today. Stay close to camp, also don't ride any wild horse or fool with your gun. You can't tell what danger your dream has warned you of. There are more ways of being killed than by the enemy. Your horse might fall and crush you; your gun might go off accidentally; a rattlesnake might bite you. Oh, yes, you must be very careful."

"I am not, I never have been," replied Little Plume, "a coward, you know my record in war; it speaks for itself. But I hate these warning dreams. You are told that something is to happen to you, but do not know what it is; and that makes the heart uneasy. You can not eat or talk of anything. Always you are on the watch and fear you know not what."

About 2 o'clock we reached some pine buttes, and while the camp halted to rest a little, Three Suns, the head chief, Little Plume and I rode up to the top of one of the buttes to take a survey of the surrounding country. Only a few miles distant was the valley of Armell's Creek, very broad and level and bordered by high hills and bluffs. Here and there along the stream were small groves of cottonwood and poplar, and on the hills grew scattering pines. But what interested us most was the game. I got out my glass, a powerful telescope, and by its aid I could see countless herds of buffalo and antelope. Some few of these were between us and the creek, but the main body of them were on the plains west of it. For at least thirty miles, as far as the eye could reach, the prairie was fairly covered with buffalo.

"This is a rich country," I remarked, as I handed the glass to Little Plume. "We will soon be feasting on boss ribs."

"I'm glad of that," said Three Suns, "I'm tired of elk and deer meat," and he went on to speak of the buffalo, saying that they really were the life of the Indian, that they were the food, shelter and raiment of the people.

Little Plume, who in the meantime had been sweeping the

43

country with the glass, here exclaimed that there seemed to be a commotion among the game far down the valley. Some buffalo and antelope had been frightened and were running toward us.

"Well," said Three Suns, "that is nothing strange. You know Running Rabbit's camp (another Blackfoot chief) is between us and the Big River (Missouri), and very likely they are camped somewhere about here."

"No," replied Little Plume, "I don't think it was they who frightened the game, for they would be on horseback and we would see them. I feel quite certain that some war party on foot is sneaking along up the creek and that they are what scared the game."

"You may be right," said Three Suns, "and it's best to look out. We will herd the horses in for a night or two and keep a strong guard on the watch. Now, then, we ought to be going. I think we shall camp pretty well up on the stream in order not to disturb the game until we are ready to make a big killing. Let us make to the left of that sharp butte over there (pointing to one southeast of us) and keep straight in that direction until we strike the creek."

So we mounted our horses and descended, and shortly the march was resumed. In an hour or two we reached the creek and our lodges were pitched on a level bit of prairie handy to wood and water. One of Little Plume's wives (he had five) caught a young antelope which had evidently been born that day and brought it up to us, saying, "See what a beautiful little pet I have found."

"I am just hungry for some young antelope boiled," said her brother, who was standing nearby, and seizing it, he drew his knife and with one slash ripped it open and threw it upon the ground. The poor thing lay there gasping, and we could see its heart still beating but growing fainter and fainter. It was a brutal act, and I felt like giving the young scamp a good thrashing, but held my peace. The woman roundly berated him, and from the way Little Plume looked I thought he, too, was displeased.

After a hearty meal and a good smoke, Little Plume saddled up a fresh horse, and saying that he was going out on the hills to take a look at the country, rode away. I was tempted to go with him but the day had been a very warm one, and I hardly felt like exercising any more, so I stayed in the lodge and smoked and read (I had quite a bundle of books with me) until it was too dark to see the print. When it was quite dark and Little Plume did not appear, we began to grow quite uneasy about him and after a while the women began to cry and scream that he was killed. I tried to quiet them by saying that he might have found Running Rabbit's camp and concluded to stop there for the night. But it was of no use. So to get away from the doleful noise they made I went outside. Suddenly I thought I heard a call far out on the prairie, and listening intently I heard it again but could not make out what was said. A young man who was standing by heard it too and ran out in that direction. He soon returned, out of breath and so excited we couldn't understand what he said except "Little Plume —almost dead—take him horse." Immediately there was the greatest excitement in camp. Little Plume's wives and female relatives began to mourn, and cry; men came from all directions with drawn weapons, crying out for revenge, and the young man who had found Little Plume leading the way, we all went out. When we got up to him we were agreeably surprised to hear him say, though in a very weak voice: "I'm not going to die yet. Put me on a horse and I can ride to camp. I've killed one Sioux." At this there was a wild howl of joy and all began to shout out his name, and those in the camp hearing it, joined in, all crying out in their loudest voice "Little Plume wa! hai! Little Plume wa! hai!" meaning the victor. It is the proudest moment of a Blackfoot's life when he thus hears himself extolled by the people.

It did not take us long to get him to camp and in his lodge, and stripping off his leggings we found that he had been shot in both legs; through the calf of one and thigh of the other. No bones were broken, but the muscles were badly lacerated and there had been considerable loss of blood. I washed the wounds and dressed them with such simple remedies as I had, and after a light meal, our hero was fairly comfortable. Late that night after everything had quieted down, he told me the story of his adventures.

"You remember," he said, "that my dream warned me I would be in danger today. He spoke truly; I have had a very close call. All day I have felt uneasy, and the signs have been bad. When my brother-in-law ripped open the young antelope and we could see its heart beating, I felt sure that something was going to happen. Then when I rode away from camp I had gone only a very short distance when the ravens began to circle close to me, and that was still another bad sign. I ought not to have gone out, but I thought I would only go a little way, just to see how the game was, and lay out a place for the big hunt tomorrow. I went down the valley quite a little piece, and then started to ride to the top of the bluffs so that I could get a good look at the surrounding country. I was riding quartering up the ridge which is broken by deep coulees, when I saw four buffalo bulls coming toward me up the hill. No other game was close to me, so I drew my horse back out of sight, got off, and crawling to the edge of the coulee, watched for them to come within range. When they were so close I could see their eyes I fired at what I thought was the fattest one, and over he went. The rest ran off. All this time I felt very uneasy. I kept looking up at the top of the hill, then down below. My heart felt heavy, yet I could see nothing to be afraid of. I left my horse and went down and began to cut up the bull. The ravens came all around me, flying close to my head, and calling out, and some lit on the ground so close I could see their eyes. I took out the tongue and then skinned down one side and took out the entrails. Then I got so uneasy I couldn't stand it any longer, and, leaving the tongue and all, I went back to my horse, and had put my foot in the stirrup to get on and ride home, when the thought struck me that I was a foolish coward. I thought of all that fat meat lying there which my children would be so glad to have, and I went back and began to cut off and tie in shape to pack some of the best parts. As I was working away I got very uneasy again, and would often stop and look all around. And I thought I saw something

46

appear for an instant on the edge of the hill above me, but concluded it must have been a raven just flying out of sight. I stooped over to tie some meat, and when I rose up again I saw five Indians where I thought I had seen the raven, and just as I saw them they fired at me. I ran for my horse, and just as I reached him he fell over dead. They had killed him so as to give me no chance to escape. My heart failed me when I saw this, but I ran to a coulee which partly concealed me, and fired three shots at the enemy who were rushing down the hill. That stopped them, and they went out of sight in a coulee. Soon I could see them crawling and sneaking above and below me, and saw they were trying to surround me, so I jumped up, and yelling as loud as I could I ran straight back toward camp. One of the enemy was right ahead of me, and he rose up and fired, but didn't hit me. I stopped and fired, and he threw up his hands, dropped his gun and fell over. I had more courage when I saw this, and felt strong. I ran on as fast as I could, and the enemy followed, shooting pretty often. Every little coulee I came to, I would crouch down and fire a shot at them, which would make them drop down. Then I would run on again. We kept up a running fight this way for quite a while, when a shot struck me in the calf of the leg. It didn't hurt much at first, but I could feel the blood running down into my moccasin. The next coulee I came to I fired twice at them, tore off a piece of my shirt and ran on. At the next coulee, after firing at them, I tied up the wound as well as I could, and ran on again. They didn't seem to want to catch up with me, but kept a good long rifle shot behind. I suppose they thought by keeping a long way off and shooting pretty often, they would get me after a while without much risk to themselves, but as I ran I kept dodging this way and that, and gave them a pretty difficult mark. I was getting pretty well toward camp and was running up a hill, when a shot struck me in the thigh, and over I went. I thought then my time had come, but I managed to roll into a little washout. Then I sat up, and fired twice at them. They had started to run toward me, but that stopped them, and they went 'way back and started to climb to the top of the hill. I knew if they should get up there that they would surely kill me, for they would be in easy range and could see me plainly from there. I prayed then. I didn't quite give up. I called on my dream white man for help. I had only three cartridges left, and thought I would save them for the last round. As I was looking up over the edge of the coulee I saw them stop climbing. Soon one of them made a sign to me and motioned me to go home, and that they would go to their home. I didn't answer at all. I just took aim and fired once at them. They turned and ran back the way they had come. I am not sure what made them do this, but think when they were getting near the top of the hill they either saw our camp or some of the people riding about, and thought they would be safer to get back toward the Missouri. As soon as I saw them going I fixed up both of my wounds as good as I could, and using my gun for a crutch hobbled toward camp. I thought I never would get here. Toward the last I had to crawl a little way at a time, and when you heard me call I was so weak I could have gone no further."

"Well, my friend," said I, "your dream gave you a true warning, didn't it?"

"Yes," he replied, "it did. What powerful medicine that little old white man is. I wonder what kind of a white man he really is!"

The next day a large party scoured the country in search of the war party (supposed to have been Sioux), with whom Little Plume had the battle, but could not find them. Where he shot one of them they found where he had fallen. The grass was covered with blood and all trampled down. Undoubtedly his comrades on their retreat had taken him away and buried him, or perhaps sunk the body in one of the deep holes of the creek.

4.

To Old Mexico

ATTACK ON THE PLAINS. From
a painting by Charles M. Russell,
dated 1899.

*(Courtesy R. W. Norton Art Gallery,
Shreveport, Louisiana)*

4.

To Old Mexico

It was a cloudless day in August, many years ago. The sun beat down unmercifully upon a hot, dry plain, where the Blackfeet were encamped. It was so hot that even the keenest hunters had not the energy to mount their runners and ride forth to the chase.

Under one of the raised lodge skins an Indian trader reclined upon a couch of robes, lazily smoking. The people of the lodge were out gossiping, all but an old, old man, who, like the trader, was thoughtfully smoking. He had been blind for many a year; his thin hair was white. His skin was streaked and furrowed and wrinkled with age; his form bent and withered; he was the oldest of his tribe, and had seen nearly a hundred winters come and go on these northern plains. His thin, low voice broke in upon the trader's reverie.

"White man," he said, "are you still here?"

"Yes," the trader replied. "Yes, I am here; what can I do for Hollow Horn?"

"Hand me my medicine sack; the large one which is hanging up. I will show you something, and then tell you a story. This day

Published in the *Great Falls Tribune* (March 4, 1900).

reminds me of a journey I once took to the south, where every day was like this, only hotter."

The trader arose and handed him the painted and fringed cylinder of rawhide. Hollow Horn deftly opened it and began to draw forth various packages and parcels, until he found the one he was seeking, which he tossed across the lodge.

"Look at that," he said.

The trader unwrapped its covering of buckskin and found that it was a long, slender lance head of gray steel; stamped on the socket were the words: "Antonio Perez, Sevilla, 1723."

"Why," he exclaimed, "it's a Spanish lance head and very old. Where did you get it?"

"I will tell you," the Indian replied. "It is a long story and a very strange one; but strange things happen. Perhaps we should not say that anything is strange, for is it not all ordered by the gods?"

"Long ago," he said, "when I was a youth, we were hunting one summer along the Yellowstone. One evening, when the sun was nearly set, the people saw something coming toward the camp, and at first they could not make out what it was; but after a little they saw it was a man, limping along very slowly by the aid of a staff. Some of the young men were for rushing out and killing him; but my father, the chief, forbade them.

" 'Let him come,' he said, 'he can do us no harm; we will find out who he is and maybe learn news.'

"So everyone stood and waited, and the man came on, very slowly and painfully, nearer and nearer. He came to where we all stood watching, and the people drew back this way and that, leaving my father to face him. He was naked except for a long ragged shirt he wore; his long, thick black hair, his beard and mustache, were matted like a bull's full of grass and burrs. His eyes were wild and rolled like those of a wounded wolf when it is brought to bay. He was thin, so thin and lean that the bones seemed ready to burst through the skin; his feet were sore and bleeding; a wound in the thigh dripped blood down his leg. He did not appear to see us, but kept limping on, shaking his head, looking wildly this way and that, and muttering to himself.

" 'Where are you going?' asked my father, stepping up and placing a hand on his shoulder. The stranger gave a shriek and fell senseless to the ground.

"It was many days before he recovered and it was nearly a year before he learned our speech. He said he came from the far south, where the weather was always warm, where all kinds of berries and things grew the year round, where snow was never seen, except on the tops of the highest mountains. His people were white men, but of another race than the trappers we had seen. His father had died, leaving him and his brother large square lodges made of stone, and great riches of various kinds. This brother had always been very mean and cruel, and as soon as the father died, he began to plan to get all that the old man left. One night the great chief of that country came to the lodge of the brothers for a feast, and on his way home some men sprang out of the bushes by the trail and would have killed him but for the warriors who were with him. Then the bad brother went to the great chief and said: 'I know who did this wrong; it was my brother and six of his friends and relations.'

"The chief's warriors seized them all, threw them into a strong stone lodge and told them to pray, for when the sun rose the next morning they would be shot. But there were those who knew the bad brother had lied, and pitied them; in the middle of the night these good friends let the prisoners out, gave them fast horses, weapons, food and robes and sent them away.

"Day after day, moon after moon, they rode, ever to the north. One night they camped by a swift, deep stream. Some of the prairie people must have seen and followed them, for as they sat about the fire toasting some meat the air was suddenly filled with arrows, and all of the stranger's companions fell over with scarcely a cry or a struggle. He, too, was hit, deep in the thigh, but pulled the arrow out, and with one jump went over the high bank into the rushing stream. He floated and swam a long way with the

55

current and then, crawling out on the shore, started to cross the valley out to the rolling plain. When he left this stream the next morning he traveled two days without finding water or anything to eat, and then he must have gone crazy, for the next thing he knew he was in our lodge.

"Well, when he had told his story, my father asked him what he intended to do; if he would return to his country, or remain with us. He said he could never go back, much as he wished to, for the great chief would kill him; so he would stay with us as long as he lived. That pleased my father; he gave him my sister for a wife, a lodge, rich clothing, good weapons, and many horses. He named him Spai-yu, which is the word for his tribe of white men.

"So the years went on, and I grew up to be a tall, strong young man. One day we were riding together ahead of the great camp, which was moving from the Belt Mountains to the big falls on the Missouri, when he said to me:

" 'Brother, something is continually pulling at my heart to return to my country. Not to stay, but just to punish that bad brother of mine. I have tried hard to resist this, for the sake of my wife, but I can do so no longer. I must go. Will you take the trail with me?'

"Of course I would, and 400 warriors came with us.[1] We traveled very slowly, as we had a long ways to go and wished to keep our horses always strong and fat. Sometimes we camped two or three days at a time, when game was plentiful and the grass good, hunting while our animals rested. One day we saw in the distance what looked like a great flat rock, upon which people were moving about, and Spai-yu told us it was made of mud by the people who lived in it. As we rode nearer, those of the strange builders who were not around on the plain climbed up sticks to the

---

[1] Other expeditions to the Southwest by the Blackfeet are on record. One of the early explorers to visit the Blackfeet, David Thompson, was told in 1787 that a large war party of Piegans traveled far south and attacked a Spanish pack train laiden with silver. *David Thompson's Narrative of his Explorations in Western America, 1784–1812*, ed. J. B. Tyrrell (Toronto, 1916), 370–71.

top of the walls, and then pulled up the sticks. But we paid no attention to them for we could not climb up where they were, nor would they come down to fight us. Spai-yu said that he had heard they were very rich, and we agreed to try to capture some of them on our return.

"I think it was two moons after we passed the great mud lodge when Spai-yu told us one day that we had but a little way farther to go. We were glad. For a long time we had been traveling through a country where everything was dead and dry except the prickly pears, which were here of great length and peculiar shapes. The land was full of rattlesnakes, of lizards as big as otters, and poisonous bugs and spiders. But now we had come to where there were forests of beautiful and strange trees in the valleys and along the foothills of the mountains; and there were many trails running this way and that, beaten wide and hard by frequent travel. At last, one evening, we came to a low ridge covered with trees, and he told us to camp, for on the other side of it, in a broad, open valley, was his home. By many a campfire on the way we had planned just what should be done, and now, as we lay in the brush, without fire or shelter, we talked it over for the last time.

"With the first light of morning we saddled up and rode to the top of the ridge, where, looking out through the trees, we saw the great stone lodge, surrounded by a beautiful grove. Presently the people came out of their lodges and went to work.

" 'Now my friends,' said Spai-yu, 'we will charge; remember what I have so often told you: No women are to be killed; you will know my brother by his light red hair, and must not touch him; leave him to me.'

"The next instant we were off; quietly at first, but as the nearer workers saw us and ran for their lodges, we gave the war cry and rode like the wind. Many of the people gained the lodges before we did, and from doors and windows fired guns at us. A few fell; the rest of us pushed on, jumped from our horses, and rushed in; the larger part of our band had gone to the upper lodges, and I

57

was with Spai-yu and the rest before the stone lodge. A lot of men were in front of the great doors, and they all had guns and pistols and were shooting at us. It was but for a second, though, and then the most of them lay dead where they had stood, and we rushed inside after the few who had fled. The red-haired one ran into a great room at the left, Spai-yu and I at his heels. Spai-yu said something and struck the sword with his war club so that it flew away to a distant corner, and at the same time the bad man recognized his brother, fell on his knees, and I knew that he was praying for his life. I looked at Spai-yu; he was smiling like a little child, which was his way when very angry. All the rest of the men in the lodge had now been killed by our companions, who came crowding around us. I had killed two myself; from one of whom I took this lance—it had a good staff then—and from the other I got a fine gun.

"Spai-yu put his hand to his chin and stood a long time silent, while still the brother begged.

" 'No,' he said at last, 'I will not kill him; if I did my vengeance would be all over, and I would have no great pleasure in it. I wish it to last a long, long time. I want to see him suffer. Tie him strongly; we will take him back with us.'

"When we had done so our leader bade us take everything we could find that we cared for, and others he sent up the valley to drive in the great herds of horses. We got great plunder from the stone lodge and from the dwellings of the workers. Then we all caught fresh horses and started back on the long journey homeward, driving the great herds before us, many of them packed with rich plunder. So we traveled on, on, to the north over the trail we had come, never stopping even to bother the people of the mud lodges, for we had everything we wanted and were hurrying to get home.

"Every night about the campfire Spai-yu had his brother sit before him, and he talked bad words to him; laughing pleasantly all the time. And the bad one said nothing in reply. He got very thin, and would eat but little, and we saw by his face that he suffered in his heart.

"At last we came to the Yellowstone. It was now winter and we had passed there on our way south early in the spring. The river was frozen over and we were crossing on the ice, having made a dirt trail over it from bank to bank. Nearly all had crossed, when all at once the ice gave way and men and horses were plunged into the cold water, among them the bad brother, who was tied to his animal. We rushed to the place, but ere we reached it the swift current drew them under, and we never saw them again. Our people, though, easily swam to the edge of the hole and were pulled out.

"In a few more days we came to the camp of our people on the Missouri, and there was great rejoicing over our return. What became of Spai-yu? He lived with us many a year; and then came the traders building forts along the river; his wife died about that time, and he went to live with them. One day the Sioux attacked a fort where he was stopping and he was killed in the fight."

5.

The Loud Mouthed Gun

THE AMBUSH. From a painting
by Charles M. Russell.

(*Courtesy R. W. Norton Art Gallery,
Shreveport, Louisiana*)

The Loud Mouthed Gun

Of all the noted story tellers in the Blackfeet camp, away back in the buffalo days, I loved best to listen to old Red Eagle. That he was my wife's uncle, and therefore very friendly to me, perhaps had some influence in my preference. But, anyhow, he was a born story teller; he got in all the little details that enhance the value of a tale, and he always told one that was worthwhile.[1]

It was on a winter evening when the great Blackfeet camp was trailing the buffalo around in the Bear Paw country—yes, we were camped on Cow Creek in the winter of 1877–78—that he told me the story of Is-so-kwo-i-ni-ma—The Loud Mouthed Gun, the very first gun that the Blackfeet possessed. That I have the story right is certain, for here before me on four leaves of my old note-book is the memorandum I jotted down about it at the time.

Well do I remember that evening. There were only the four of us in the lodge. Old Red Eagle and his wife on their buffalo robe couch at the back of the lodge, and Natahki and I on the soft

Manuscript in the Special Collections Library, Montana State University, Bozeman.

[1] A mountain, creek, glacier, lake and pass in Glacier National Park now bear the name of Red Eagle, a tribute to this venerable Blackfoot.

robe guest seat on their right. The little fire in the center of the lodge burned brightly and noiselessly, and lit up the fine and impressive features of the old man and his faithful old wife. And oh, such kindly faces they were. And how they did love each other, that old couple; always they sat as close together as any young bride and groom.

Said the old man as he knocked the ashes from his black stone pipe and laid it away: "Apikuni, my son, did you ever hear of the loud mouthed gun?"

"No, but I shall be glad to hear," I answered, and he took a drink of water and began:

"This is the story of the gun as my grandfather told it to me— and as his father told it to him."

"In the very long ago the Blackfeet did not own the country in which we are camping this night. It was then Crow country. The country of the Blackfeet was far to the north; from the Saskatchewan south to Milk River, say, and from the Rocky Mountains eastward five or six days journey on horseback. On the north and east the tribe was hemmed in by the Woods, and Plains Crees, and on the south the Crows held their own against it.

"Once, in a time before this time I shall speak of, the Crees and the Blackfeet were on friendly terms; but they fell out about a woman and there followed bitter war between them. And so it was that one spring a large party of young Blackfeet warriors started out for a raid in the Plains Crees country. Before they left —of course—they had a medicine sweat bath, and an old medicine man prayed for them. And as they were leaving camp he gave them this warning: 'Remember that the Crees have one strong medicine man. His is the thunder medicine. Look out for him.'

"The war party travelled eastward for many sleeps, and then, one day discovered a not large party of Crees ahead, bound, evidently, for a raid into Blackfeet country: 'Ha! They are not so many as we, and anyhow the Blackfeet are the best fighters. Come on, let's charge them,' said the leader.

"He had no sooner said the word than the charge was started, and as soon as the Crees saw the Blackfeet they turned and ran, and took refuge on the top of a round, but not high nor steep hill. Arrived near the foot of it, the Blackfeet counselled together. They could, of course, surround the hill and just wait until the enemy would be forced from want of water to come down and fight on level ground, but most of the party were too impatient for that and it was decided to rush the place from all sides. As they stood talking they noticed that one of the Crees had something in front of him that glittered in the sun like ice and certain rocks, but they paid little attention to it, and moved quite up to the foot of the hill, from there to separate and make the charge. And then, suddenly, at the top of the hill there was a boom of thunder, a puff of smoke, and with a yell of pain one of the Blackfeet fell over dead: 'The thunder medicine man,' his comrades cried, and ran and took shelter in a timber belt on the north side of the hill. There they counselled again, getting so angry at the death of their friend that they made a rush up the hill as fast as they could go. And again thunder boomed at the top and another of the party fell. They dragged him down into the brush. He was dead. There was a small hole clear through his body: 'Friends,' said the leader, 'it is no use for us to try to take that hill. Up there is the thunder medicine Cree that we were warned against.' And at that they hid their dead and took the back trail home.

"Arrived in camp they told what had befallen them, and then the chiefs and medicine men at once called a big council. They at first doubted the news brought them. One of the camp sun priests had a thunder medicine, but all he could do was to pray to the thunder bird and ask it to bring the rains, that the berries might grow plentiful and sweet. It did not seem possible that any one could actually handle thunder, and kill with it. Everyone of the returned party insisted, however, that their description of what had happened was wholly true, and realized that, unless the Blackfeet could wrest this powerful medicine from the Crees, the tribe would be driven from the country: 'We must, regardless of our lives, make one great effort to secure that medicine,' the head

67

chief said. 'No doubt the war party carrying it is now on its way here. As you love your women and little ones, your old fathers and mothers, go forth you fighting men and take it, or die.'

"The warriors took his words. They made preparations; the medicine men prayed for them; they went eastward in different bands to look for the party of Crees.

"Surely the sun heeded the prayers of those ancient medicine men. One of the Blackfeet parties discovered the enemy. They were in a thicket of willows beside a little stream, and were cooking meat of a buffalo they had killed. The Blackfeet sneaked as close to them as they could, and when discovered, made the rush. Boom! went the thunder medicine, and a man fell. Arrows flew and more of the Blackfeet dropped; but the rest kept on and overpowered and killed all of the Crees, and one of the victors, a young man, secured the thunder instrument and everything else that its carrier had on him. Oh, how proud they were, how glad. And yet, how afraid! They had in their hands the thunder instrument, a dread medicine that they did not understand. Some of the party were for leaving it right there; many of them would not even touch it; but the young man who had captured it was brave: 'I shall carry it, and all that goes with it,' he said, 'and if it kills me, why, then, I die.' And he picked up the gun and they started home. It was very heavy, this ancient piece, and one other of the party assisted him, the two carrying it turn about.

"Arrived home, the young man gave the gun to a very wise old medicine man, and there was such a rush of all the people to see the strange thing that a whole day was required to display it. Then the medicine man, the chiefs, and the young man who had taken it, made a thorough examination of the thing, and some round strange-kind-of-rock balls in a buckskin sack. There was also some dried, fine black paint—powder, of course, in an iron bottle. Thinking it bad medicine, they threw it away.

"This gun was very long and heavy, and the muzzle of it was bell shaped. It was a flintlock, and its trimmings were highly polished brass. There was with it a long, iron forked rest. Well, as

I said, the old medicine man, the others looking on, made a thorough examination of it, not only that day, but for many days thereafter, but never could find out how to make it thunder. The balls were what made holes in people when it was fired, but what made the balls go? When one was rolled down to the bottom of the barrel, it would simply roll out again when the gun was inverted. At the first examination of it, the old man cocked the hammer, and then accidentally pressed the trigger. Down came the hammer on his thumb and bruised it severely. 'Ha! That has something to do with its thundering, and he tried it again, this time with the pan shut. Sparks flew when the flint struck the pan, and he jumped and dropped the gun, expecting the thunder to boom. But it didn't; that was all he could do with the gun: just make it spark. It was a great disappointment. But anyhow, the thing was great medicine, a precious thing. The old man rolled it in fine furs and kept it with his other medicines, and tried to dream how to use it, but never could get the right dream. Every few days he would take it out and examine it all over. Nothing ever happened. And so passed several winters.

"Yes, several, I know not how many winters passed, and then, on a day in the early summer this same young man who took the gun, he had been named because of it Na-mak-an, with others went on another raid into the Cree country. They had no sooner got well within it when they met a party of Crees, and attacked them, and were fired upon by no less than four thunder instruments. They were so surprised—two of their number were killed —that they had hardly sense to turn and run: for some time they just stood and stared, open mouthed, and never moved until the Crees charged. Then they did run, and travelled back to the Blackfeet country, and to camp as fast as they could.

"The news that they brought was again almost unbelieveable. It struck terror to the hearts of all the people. Why, with four thunder instruments the Crees could do as they would with the Blackfeet. Again the chief called a big council, and the men talked and talked: 'If we only knew how to use the one thunder instru-

69

ment we have,' said a warrior, 'it wouldn't be so bad. Try. Try again, you medicine men, to get a revealing dream about it.'

"Because of his capture of the gun, Na-mak-an had been made a chief, and now with authority he spoke up: 'Dreams will not come,' he said. 'We are to the Crees what dead leaves are to the wind. I propose to go make peace with our enemies, and learn how to use the thunder instrument we have.'

"His words brought instant relief to the council: 'Yes. Yes. Why didn't we think of that before? It is the one thing to do,' they cried, and went their ways after naming those who should go on this peace mission.

"Na-mak-an led the party of fifteen. They carried rich presents for the Cree chiefs: fine war bonnets, tanned bighorn skins, beautifully porcupine quill embroidered moccasins, bunches of the valuable eagle tail feathers, and a large quantity of na-wak-o-sis: a plant the Blackfeet grew for smoking before they got the white man's tobacco.

"Proceeding very cautiously into the Cree country, they at last found the big camp of the tribe and openly approached it, singing the peace song and making signs for peace. The Cree chiefs, seeing them coming, advanced without weapons, met and embraced them, and invited them to the lodges. There they rested and were feasted, after which they distributed the presents they brought. These were not at once accepted. They were laid aside upon the ground, and the Cree chiefs counselled together. It was not long, however, before their talk ended, and the head chief addressed the Blackfeet: 'We accept your presents,' he said. 'Brothers, we are glad you have come to us this day. It is a good day. The sun is shining and is glad to see us sitting here in friendship instead of fighting to take one another's lives. Return to your people and tell them that we too desire peace. But first rest with us while we prepare presents for your chiefs.'

"So all was well, and they remained for some nights in the camp enjoying many feasts and dances. And they learned, to their great surprise, that the thunder instruments were medicine contrivances of white men. The white skins, said the Crees, had a strange, square, log lodge away eastward on the Assiniboine River,* and it was from them that they obtained the weapons, giving for each one fifty beaver skins. And then they showed the Blackfeet the few they had—five in all, and taught them how to load and fire. And best of all, they gave Na-mak-an enough powder and ball for a hundred charges for the weapon he had taken from them. Well satisfied, the Blackfeet returned home, many Cree families going with them for a visit. So was a peace made that lasted for many winters.

"Na-mak-an and his men arrived home late in the evening, and in the old medicine man's lodge took the loud mouthed gun and showed a wondering crowd of chiefs and head warriors just how to use it. He even loaded and fired it, outside the lodge, and women and children, and even some men, ran in every direction when it boomed. The old medicine man at once named its different parts. He called the hammer its jaws, because they firmly gripped the sparking flint. The pan was named the ear, and the ram rod was the throat, because it was held in place under the barrel by throat-like brass loops. The barrel itself was the loud— or big mouth.

"And, strange to say, now that the old medicine man understood the death making instrument, important, revealing dreams came to him about it. His dream medicine—his secret helper gave him these rules about it: It was never to be taken from its embroidered case except to be actually used. It was to be hung outside the lodge, every pleasant day, before sunrise, and taken inside every evening after sunset. When being taken on a war expedition, on the day before the start the leader of the war party must carry it completely around the big camp, all his men

* In the winter of 1743 the Sieur de la Verendrie had a post on the Assiniboine River, in what is now the Province of Manitoba, Canada. I doubt not that the Crees obtained the "Loud Mouthed Gun" from him. The Blackfeet tradition has it that this was the only bell muzzle gun they ever saw. They have no end of stories of infinite detail about the raids upon which it was taken.

71

following, dressed in their war costumes, and singing certain songs which the dreams had also revealed, dreams sacred to the gun.

"War! Ai! Now came war. The Blackfeet had often invaded the country of the Crows, even to the Yellowstone and beyond. They had seen its many rivers and streams, valleys, its mountains and plains, all alive with all kinds of game, and in season red with sweet berries, and they knew that it was a far richer, a far more kindly country than that of theirs in the north. They wanted it. They had for countless winters tried to take it, but ever the Crows had managed to hold their own. But now, with this medicine, loud mouthed gun, what might they not do?

"The chiefs called a great council and made talk for strong war against the Crows; the warriors all agreed to it and made preparations for the start. After taking medicine sweat baths, after many prayers and sacrifices to the sun, after the loud mouthed gun had been carried by Na-mak-an the complete circle of the camp, all the warriors following and singing, the start was made for the south. Hundreds and hundreds of warriors went; only enough men were left to guard the camp.

"Southward they travelled day by day, to Elk River, to Old Man's River, to Belly River, to the River of Many Dead Chiefs, to Little River, to Cut Bank River, and there they found signs of the enemy and halted, and scouts were sent forward on discovery. During their absence Na-mak-an, with his medicine pipe, and the loud mouthed gun, and a young man for servant, moved to some little distance from the party. There, by himself and in quiet, he prayed to the sun for success against the enemy and tried to get revealing dreams. He did get them; his secret helper told him that his expedition was to be successful. The servant carried the news to the waiting party and made glad their hearts. They were eager to go on.

"The scouts returned after an absence of four nights, and went direct to Na-mak-an in his alone sleeping place. Said the leader of them: 'We bring you good news: the Crows are encamped on

72

the next stream to the south.' It was the one that the Blackfeet afterward named the Two Medicine Lodge River.

" 'In what shape are they—what is the position of their camp?' the chief asked.

"Said the scout: 'Their lodges stand at the edge of a wide long grove of cottonwoods in a big wide bottom. Just above the camp is a long high cliff, and at the foot of it is a very large impounding place built of drift logs and brush. As we were watching from a distance, the Crows decoyed a big band of buffalo to the cliff and scared them over it to their death. Those not killed by the fall were unable to get out of the impound and were shot down with bow and arrow.'

" 'I like not that big grove of timber,' said Na-mak-an. 'It would be a place of refuge for the Crows and in driving them out of there our loss would be heavy. What kind of country lies below the camp?'

" 'A wide, long, level bottom with a spring creek flowing through it. And at the lower end of it, and to the north, is a low pass with a high butte in it, and on either side coulees and broken hills.'

" 'Ha! That is better. There will we fight them,' said Na-mak-an. In the breaks there a part of us will hide. With a few men I will lie on top of the butte with the loud mouthed gun. Still others shall attack the camp, and retreat, decoying the Crows to the butte.' And with that he gave orders for the advance as soon as the sun should set.

"It was the next day. The sun was well up. Women in the Crow camp were everywhere busy drying buffalo meat, tanning leather and soft buckskins. Men were generally making new arrows, and flint arrow heads. Everything was very quiet. Then, suddenly, came running into camp from below a couple of men: 'Ho! the enemy comes,' they cried. "A big crowd of the enemy is coming up the spring bottom, and they are loudly singing their war song. The Blackfeet are coming.'

"The alarm spread quickly to the very upper edge of the camp.

73

The Crow warriors, every one of them, grabbed up bow and quiver and shield, many putting on their war bonnets, and rushed down around the point of the grove and Blackfeet, about fifty of them, advancing, and they laughed as they sprang to meet them. Fifty men against the whole Crow camp. What fools they were. Not one of them should escape.

"But the Blackfeet had well calculated their approach. They had not come too near, and they were just as good runners as were the Crows. They turned and ran, ran as fast as they could, down the bottom, up in the pass, and to the top of the butte. The Crows, a multitude of warriors, ran after them, gained upon them toward the last, and swarmed up the front side of the butte. Then it was that Na-mak-an, with big mouthed gun loaded with four balls resting in its fingers, took good aim at the thick of the crowd and pulled the trigger. Whoom! it thundered, and vomited heavy smoke, and five of the enemy— dead and crippled—fell. The others, all those hundreds of warriors, halted, started, questioned one another, could not understand, believed—as was long afterward learned— that thunder itself and a flash of lightning had struck their comrades: 'Advance. Advance. It will not happen again,' cried their chief, and again they made a rush, even to short bow range of the top. They used their bows; the air was full of arrows, and the Blackfeet fired arrows down at them, and men on both sides fell. Na-mak-an, alone in front of his men and at great risk to himself, knelt behind the reloaded loud mouthed gun, waiting, waiting until the Crows should come quite close and see the medicine thing he pointed at them. An arrow struck him in the shoulder; he did not flinch. He waited a little longer and then fired, and three men fell. And this time the Crows plainly saw what was killing them: the Blackfeet had thunder, and lightning medicine, had the power of the gods themselves. With hoarse cries of fright they turned and fled—fled for their lives, and out from the coulees poured the great body of the Blackfeet warriors and chased them up the flat, overtaking and dispatching many. They did not follow them clear to their camp. They had no mind to fight them in their grove. Soon they went back down the flat, joined Na-mak-an and the men with him, and all together went over to the river to rest and eat.

"That very night the Crows fled southward, and never again did they set up their lodges on the Two Medicine Lodge River. Na-mak-an and his men leisurely followed them, to Birch Creek, to the Teton, to the Missouri, and drove them across that big stream, from time to time on the way frightening them with the thunder of the loud mouthed gun. And there, at the Missouri, well satisfied, with what they had done, the Blackfeet turned and went home to get the camp and occupy the country they had taken.

"That was but the beginning of raids with the loud mouthed gun. It was carried again and again against the Crows, and they were driven to the Yellowstone. It terrorized the Flatheads; the Kootenai; the Assiniboines and other tribes. It was great medicine. And then, one day, when taken out to war and fired in battle, the barrel burst, and seriously injured Na-mak-an. The fight was won, however, and as soon as the chief could travel the party went home. Again the old medicine man took the gun: 'It can never thunder again,' said he, 'but it is still strong medicine. I shall keep it as long as I live, and I want it buried with me.' As he said, so was it done.

"Remaining friendly with the Crees, the Blackfeet soon got other guns from them and with the weapons held what they had gained. Long afterward, even after all their enemies became equally well armed, they held, and still hold the great country they gained with the loud mouthed gun. Ai, my son, it was great medicine.

"Kyi, my son, I have finished. It is time for sleep."

And so saying, old Red Eagle smilingly waved us the good night sign and we went out into the night and home.

6.

Trouble for the Gros Ventres

WHERE FOOLS BUILD FIRES.
From a painting by Charles M.
Russell, 1919.

*(Courtesy R. W. Norton Art Gallery,
Shreveport, Louisiana)*

Trouble for the Gros Ventres

Turning again the leaves of my worn old notebook of that winter of '77–'78 on Cow Creek, I find the following under date of December 24:

The night before Christmas. The Monroe families, good Christians they are, all busy today with preparations for tomorrow, and Kipp and I are invited to the big feast to be held in Grandfather Monroe's lodge.

Trade fair today. 67 robes and some antelope, deer, wolf, and elk hides. Cold as the weather is, Red Eagle's daughter has the white buffalo hide on a stretcher and is chipping it. I watched her for a time this morning. Before getting up on it with her little elk horn, steel bladed hoe, or chipper, she made a short prayer which I was close enough to hear: "Oh, sun, I am indeed pure; I am worthy to prepare this sacred robe for you," she murmured. "Have pity on me. Continue to keep me in good health and strength that I may make the robe fit for your acceptance."

And then she got up on the stretched hide, the frame of lodge poles was raised about two feet from the ground, and went to

Manuscript in the Special Collections Library, Montana State University, Bozeman.

work. She used the tool just as a carpenter does an adze, and at every stroke took off a thin shaving of the frozen, board-like hide —the inner, or flesh side of it, of course. Eventually the hide will be reduced to half its thickness, and then tanned with a mixture of liver and brains. Chipping a hide is very hard work; the hardest of all the labor performed by Indian women. However, they take their time about it, working an hour or so, then resting a couple of hours—or more, and so on until the task is completed. The harder a hide is frozen, so that it does not give before the stroke of the chipper, the easier becomes the woman's task.

Bucknum was the story teller this evening, he giving us the promised further adventures of himself and Murray Nicholson.

"After our first winter in the country," he began, "Murray and I boarded a steamboat and had a look at the upper river. We were ten days or more from Fort Benton, and were sorry when the trip up ended. If there is anywhere more weird and wonderful scenery than that of the Upper Missouri, from the mouth of Milk River, say, up to the mouth of the Marias, just you tell me where it is. Why, looking from a distance at the sandstone rims of that deep old gash in the plains, you just have to rub your eyes and wonder if you are awake, or dreaming. You can almost swear that what you see are ancient towns and castles, battlements and donjon keeps, inhabited by mailed knights, and archers, and beautiful captive women waiting to be rescued. Well, you needn't laugh, you Kipp, I once read a book about all that kind of thing, and the pictures in it were just like the wind and rain carved cliffs of the upper river.

"Well, Murray and I liked the upper country so much that we never went back to Fort Union. Fort Benton, with its fine bunch of real men held us for a couple of months, and then we outfitted and dropped down to the bottom just above the Hole-in-the-wall, for the winter. We took with us old Seviere Amiotte, even then so badly crippled with rheumatism that he almost had to be waited upon. But he knew the ways of the country and was sure a big help to us. He taught us to trap beaver, and he got the Gros

82

Ventres to camp close by for a part of the winter and trade with us, we having brought down from Fort Benton a good supply of trade goods on his promise that he would get rid of them for us. What with wolfing, beaver trapping, and trading, we made fine clean up that winter. Over five thousand dollars clear.

"It was astonishing to me how Murray took to the Gros Ventres. From the day they first came to camp by us, he was with them at every opportunity, sizing up their customs, and, with the help of old Seviere Amiotte, learning the language. He is one of the very few white men who ever mastered the Gros Ventre language. As you all know, one must have, so to speak, an unhinged jaw and a double twisting tongue in order to get off its sputtering words.

"Well, we wolfed, and trapped, and traded at the Hole-in-the-wall for several seasons, and then, at the request of the Gros Ventres, moved to the north side of the river, right below here at the mouth of this very Cow Creek. By the first of November we had our cabin—three rooms—up, and every thing in good shape for the winter. The Gros Ventres then came in from Milk River, and our trade for prime robes, and small skins began.

"Life in camp and with us in the cabin ran along smoothly until December 24, just eight years ago today, to be sure, and then came trouble for the Gros Ventres. On that evening, as Murray, and Seviere and I sat before the fireplace of our living room, there came hurried taps on the door and a woman's wail-cry in Gros Ventre, begging us to let her in. I answered the call, and when I opened the door two women rushed in so suddenly as to nearly knock me over. I recognized them: one, a handsome young girl of sixteen or seventeen, named the Red Star, the other her mother, wife of a chief named Fire Carrier. They had been almost daily visitors for several seasons, and did our washing, made our footwear, leggins, and buckskin shirts, and generally cleaned up the rooms.

"They now quickly brushed past me, and, wild eyed and well nigh breathless, rushed across the room to Murray, the mother

83

crying—as Seviere afterward explained to me: 'Help us, Kills Alone, help us. Fire Carrier has not returned to us. He is somewhere out on the plains, and the hunters report fresh signs of Assiniboines. None of them will go with us to search for him, but you will, oh Kills Alone, powerful white chief that you are. Oh, come! Let us hurry.'

" 'What—do you ask me to go now—now in this cloudy night?' Murray asked. 'Why, woman, that would be foolish; a crazy thing to do. We could find no trace of your man. If there be enemies about they would have every advantage of us; we would be stuck full of arrows in no time.'

" 'Yes, that is just what they said at camp,' the woman said, 'but we thought that you would be braver than the Gros Ventre men; that you would live up to the name the Crows gave you. See, we are only women! But we are not afraid to go. If you will not go with us, we shall start out, start now, alone.'

"Well, Murray and Seviere both argued with them, but they wouldn't listen to reason, and finally old Seviere said that sooner than let them go out alone on the plains, he would lock them up in the trade room for the night. The threat brought them around quickly enough, and, saying that there were nowhere men neither white nor Indian, with pitying hearts, they sat down by the fire, and throwing their robes over their heads, cried dismally until we could stand the sound of it no longer. The crying of Indian women is about the most terribly melancholy, nerve racking sound in all the world.

" 'Come, we are going to take you home,' Murray told them at last, and without a word they went with the three of us across the bottom to camp. There we found excitement enough. Three more hunters, men who had gone out in the morning with Fire Carrier, were also not returned, and other hunters, coming home late, had heard considerable firing at dusk away up in the heads of the breaks of the river to the west of Cow Creek. Still others reported the tracks of a large mounted war party away up the creek, and heading toward the very breaks in which the firing had been heard. There could be no doubt as to who they were: Assiniboines, of course. No other people would venture out on the war path in the dead of winter."

"Ai! That is true enough," old man Monroe exclaimed. "They are brothers to Cold Maker. Blizzards do not daunt them. They choose the worst winter weather in which to prowl around."

"You remember the time they tackled us on Rocky Spring ridge; the time they killed Buckshot and Narcise," said Kipp. "Well, there we were snowbound, and the thermometer was certainly less than forty below zero. They attacked us just at dawn, and fought so hard that it was all we could do to rout them, they leaving four of their dead around us. We examined them. Thinly clothed they were, their leggins just cowskin, their wraps just common blankets, and still they had been unaffected by the terrible weather. They could have had no fire, there was no timber or brush within forty miles of that place; they must just have burrowed into a snowdrift when they were tired and needed sleep."

"Sure thing. That's just what they did," Bucknum agreed, and went on with his story:

"At this time, as luck would have it, only a small part of the Gros Ventre camp was with us, the greater part of the tribe having pulled out south of the river for a few days hunt in the thick of great herds of buffalo. They had for the most part left their women and children, and old people, three or four each with one of his wives, taking together one lodge for the hunt. There were not all told twenty able bodied men left to go in search of the missing men. It was agreed that we would all pull out together in the morning, as soon as there was light enough for us to see the way. The two women were to be watched, but they had promised to remain in their lodge, and we went home and to bed.

"When we were ready to start the next morning, Fire Carrier's wife and daughter appeared on horseback to go with us, and with them were three or four other women: 'What do you think this is —a summer berrying party?' an old warrior asked them. 'Now, go put your horses out—every one of you and stay quietly in your lodges. Where we are going is no place for women. Mind, now, not one of you may accompany us: men are for battle; women's duty is to stay in the lodge and raise children, strong, brave children for future defenders of the tribe.'

"And with that we left them, and the crowd of other women, and their children, and old people, all in charge of Seviere Amiotte, and rode away up Cow Creek for a few miles, and then turned west along the plain where it broke off into the washes, and cliffs, and long and well nigh impassable badland jumble of the Missouri valley slopes. We had not gone very far, however, when two riders were discovered on our back trail, trying their very best to overtake us. Thinking that they were the bearers of news we slowed up, and presently discovered that they were women. On they came and presently Fire Carrier's wife and daughter drew rein in front of us, and said nothing, nor even looked at us. 'Well, what is it—what want you?' someone asked.

" 'We are going with you,' the mother answered.

" 'You shall not.' 'Go back at once.' they were quickly answered, but they only stubbornly shook their heads, and held their ground. Valuable time was being lost. One old fellow called upon the sun to witness the obstinacy and foolishness of women. Others begged them to go back, and one angry young man threatened to drive them back with the whip. The mother rode straight up to him and said, or, rather, hissed—and maybe her eyes were not shooting fire! 'You threaten to strike me! Me, a medicine lodge woman, a woman who has declared herself before the sun. As you do to me, oh sun, I beg you do the same to him!

"Well, sirs, when she said that you should have seen the young fellow wilt. He just too quick drooped over the saddle and pulled his horse around. Said Nicholson: 'Let the women come. They shall ride with me. Lead on. We are losing fast this early daylight.'

" 'Oh, Kills Alone! You are generous to us,' the mother cried.

" 'He alone understands our hearts and pities us,' said the daughter, as she rode up beside him as we started on.

"In an hour's time, perhaps, we approached the breaks where the shooting had been going on the evening before, and presently struck the trail of the war party that had been seen on Cow Creek the previous morning. By the way the grass was trampled—there was no snow on the ground except in coulees—we judged that no less than thirty riders were in the outfit.

"The trail ran straight toward a timber fringed break that headed much farther out in the plain than any others in sight, and suddenly ended about half a mile from it, or, rather, split up into individual horse tracks, all suddenly diverging like the ribs of a fan. The meaning of this was plain: here the party had discovered enemies, Fire Carrier and his companions, no doubt, and had spread out to attack them. We put quirt to our horses and rode straight for the break head, and there found Fire Carrier's horse dead and stiff, the saddle still on it. At sight of the animal the women became frantic, and dashed into the pines and brush at the head of the break, while our party examined the plain on each side of it, and found, as we expected, tracks of the war party's horses on each side, overlooking the ever deepening break. A hundred yards down it the women called, and three or four of us, including Murray and I, joined them. There was a little snow here in the pines, and in it a confusion of horse and moccasin tracks, but we were not long reading the tangle: four men afoot had fled on down the break; other men on foot had come down both slopes, and seized and led out the three horses that Fire Carrier's friends had here abandoned. The women wanted to go straight down the break in the trail of four men, but Murray insisted that they go back with us to open ground.

"Divided now into two parties, we followed the two trails of the war party down the ridges dividing the big break from the smaller one on each side of it, getting ever into rougher and rougher badland until it seemed that our horses could go no farther. There were here and there broken rock—almost cliff-like formations that the animals staggered, and stumbled, and pitched down, at the great risk of crushing us. But the war party had gone down the breakneck places and we just had to follow.

"Far ahead of us, and of the west of our party on the opposite ridge, was now a scout, running here, crawling there, and sneaking from shelter to shelter, ever on the watch for sight of those we followed. A man in each party of us led their horses. We were several hours, no doubt, getting down from the head of the break and ridges to within a quarter of a mile of the river bottom at the foot of them, and it was not until then that the scout ahead of our party—on the west ridge of the deep wash—suddenly came running toward us making the sign to halt, and soon as he saw us obey he turned and ran back, and from a clump of junipers looked down at what we could not see—the Missouri and its bottomlands below. A minute or two passed; Murray and I and several of the Indians had dismounted, and were starting on foot to join the scout and see for ourselves what he had discovered, when, from some place down by the river there came to us faintly the sound of many shots, and, fainter still, the war whoops that are always a part of an Indian fight.

"We ran then, as fast as we could, and joined the watcher at the junipers, and from there saw close below us the white, frozen ribbon of the river, its brown, dead grass bottoms, and the groves of bare limbed cottonwoods lining its shores. The bottom directly below us, at the mouth of the big break we were following, was several hundred acres in area, and about as broad as long. At its upper end was a grove of perhaps twenty acres, and at the upper end of that rose a lone steep butte of broken lava, perhaps a hundred feet high. Well, on the rough summit of this butte we could see an occasional puff of smoke, and hear the following boom! of a gun. And under it, from the shelter of the timber at its base, came the confused rattle of many guns; but nowhere was a man in sight. It was all plain enough to us, however: the four Gros Ventres were on the summit of the butte, and the Assiniboines, below, were attacking them—from shelter: 'Trust an

Assiniboine for every time getting the cinche, or not fighting,'
said Murray.

"The question now was how we were to rescue the Gros
Ventres. We saw the other bunch of our party on the ridge across
the big wash; like ourselves they were halted, and a few of them,
ahead, were with their scouts down at the fight in the bottomland.
Murray consulted those with us, and then one of them signalled
the other party to ride down into the wash and meet us there. They
signed back 'Yes. It is good,' and we were presently altogether in
the now wide, sandy bottom of the wash, and in the soft, dry,
unfrozen sand we found the footprints of Fire Carrier and his
three companions. When the two women saw them they gave
thanks to the sun; here their loved one had passed, as yet unhurt.
They begged us to hurry and rescue the besieged from their
perilous position. Murray and I wondered why, in the darkness of
the night they had not tried to travel toward camp, instead of going
down the wash, and up onto the lava butte? It was a question, as
you shall see, that was never answered.

"What were we to do? The Assiniboines plainly outnumbered
us. They were in good cover—would undoubtedly discover us
should we venture to approach them across the open bottom, and
from their places of concealment in the underbrush of the grove,
mow down half our number at the very first round. Various plans
for the rescue were quickly proposed, and as quickly turned down
by Murray, whom these Gros Ventres had learned to trust, and he
in turn offered a plan that was answered by unanimous 'Ah.' 'Ah!'
'Ahs' of approval. It was this: across the bottomland to the river
the flood waters of the big wash had cut a deep, wide channel. We
were, he said, to ride down the wash to the edge of the bottom,
there leave our horses and the women, and then afoot sneak down
the dry channel to the grove, and surprise the enemy, as, all unaware of our approach, they would be busy trying to dislodge the
four men on the butte.

"We started, Murray in the lead, and soon came to the edge of the bottom. There we all dismounted, and Murray and I, with several of the Indians, climbed up from clay shelf to clay shelf of the dry channel and looked across the bottom at the butte. From its summit still came an occasional shot; the Gros Ventres still held their position. Back we slipped into the wash, and, leaving two men with the women and horses, sprinted down it to the lower edge of the grove. There we climbed out and began to work along through the trees and brush toward the Assiniboine position.

"Before we had proceeded half way up the grove a sudden outburst of shouts and yells on the butte, and, through the bare tree tops, glimpses of the Assiniboines rushing the summit, warned us that we were come too late; that for Fire Carrier and his companions the end had come. To prove it, the firing and yelling suddenly ceased. All along the four Gros Ventres had fired sparingly, and the probability is that they perished from lack of ammunition.

"At the very moment the fight on the butte ended we saw ahead of us a number of the Assiniboine horses; and, now that they could not rescue their kinfolks, some of our Gros Ventres made a rush for them, and mounted, and started straight for the place where we had left the women and our own animals. In vain Murray and others tried to prevent this, urging that we must all stand together. They went, nor once looked back. The Assiniboines saw them the moment they left the timber and came rushing down the butte and to the other bunch of their horses tethered not far from its base, and in a moment or two those who had mounts were out in the bottom in hot pursuit, while the others came crashing through the brush toward us, hoping, no doubt to find a horse or two left. Instead of that they found us. Us and our bullets. Three or four of them went down as our guns popped, and the rest took to their heels; and such is the skill of the Assiniboines in getting into cover that they just melted out of our sight.

"Several of those with us, of course, made a rush to count coup, to take the weapons of the enemies we had dropped, and they did so despite Murray's yells to them to come back: 'We have to hurry to save the women and our horses,' he cried. 'Now, then, out of the timber we go.'

"Out we ran, and from the edge of the grove saw our deserting Gros Ventres sprinting across the bottom, pursued by twice their number of the enemy. We kept on running, although there was no possible chance for us to reach the mouth of the wash in time to do any good there, and the Assiniboines we had sent skurrying in the timber now appeared and began firing at our retreating backs. It sure was one grand mixup. Murray was boiling mad, and so was I: 'If ever we get out of this scrape,' he puffed as we ran side by side, 'we'll never again go into a fight with the Gros Ventres.'

" 'The fools, why don't they swing around toward us? It's the only possible chance for them, and the women,' said I, and as we ran on we began making signs to them to come toward us. They finally realized what they were doing, that they were leading the main body of the Assiniboines right to the women and to our horses, but it was not us who made them see their mistake; it was the women themselves, and the two men we had left with them. They had seen our signals, thought we were calling them, and out of the wash they came on their horses, driving the loose animals ahead, and made straight across the bottom toward us, and were soon joined by the outfit flying before the Assiniboines. While still some distance in the rear, the latter were now able to turn short off to the right and gain several hundred yards. We ran faster than ever, if that were possible, we met, the whole party of us, once more together, away out on the open bottom, and by the time we managed to catch our frightened horses the mounted Assiniboines, and those following us afoot from the timber, were close enough to begin firing at us. Two of our number went down.

"Well, sirs, there followed a fierce old fight for a few minutes. Three more of our Gros Ventres went down, and I saw five of the enemy keel out of the saddle. Then it was, when the rest showed no signs of retreating, that Murray and I rallied our wavering

91

party, he calling out: 'Take courage! Charge. Defend the women.'

"As we were starting I saw Fire Carrier's woman spring to the ground and snatch up the Henry rifle of one of our dead; in another minute she was right up with us, right on Murray's left, riding her horse for all he was worth and sure doing some yelling. I shall never forget how she appeared—I never saw another so fierce a looking woman. Her long hair had become unbraided and streamed straight back in a thick, black cloud. Her blanket was down and her almost sleeveless gown revealed bare, firm, round arms, and hands tensely gripping the rifle. Her eyes were fire; and oh, how she did yell as now and then she fired at one of the enemy.

"For a moment or two the Assiniboines came at us fiercely as we were riding at them. One more of our men went down, and several of the other side, and at that the rest broke, and made for the breaks, and closest after them was Murray, and next the woman. They two had by far the swiftest horses and soon out-stripped the rest of us; and the way they overtook one after an-other of those Assiniboines, and left them dead and dying was something never to be forgotten. They scattered before their determined pursuit like so many mice before a cat; we gave her credit for two of them, and I have never blamed her for it. The death of her man had for the time being changed her whole nature: she was crazed with grief and scarce knew what she did.

"We did not follow the remaining Assiniboines into the breaks. Those on foot had skurried back into the timber, and we didn't exactly care to go in there. We did, however, gather our dead and, following the river, take them home for burial. The next day rein-forcements from the buffalo hunters searched the country for what was left of the Assiniboine party, and never found it. Of course, all praise was given Murray for the outcome of the fight, and at a big feast in the head chief's lodge he was given a new name: 'Mad Wolf.'

"It was a few nights after the fight that Fire Carrier's widow and daughter came to our living room as we sat before the fire, the girl dressed all in her best finery. They sat long, saying not a word, and suddenly the girl with a little cry ran and knelt beside Murray as he sat in his comfortable chair: 'Well, what is it?' he asked, gently laying a hand on her shining, smooth black hair.

"For a moment she did not answer, and then, suddenly faltered: 'Why don't you marry?'

" 'Ho. For good reason,' Murray answered. 'No one will have me.'

" 'You haven't asked me,' she said, and at that old Amiotte gave me a sign and we went into the trade room for a while, leaving Murray and widow and daughter together for a time.

"So it was that Murray got Red Star, and as you all know, she sure made him a good wife."

7.

The Black Antelope

THREE GENERATIONS. From a
painting by Charles M. Russell,
1899.

*(Courtesy R. W. Norton Art Gallery,
Shreveport, Louisiana)*

The Black Antelope

Christmas day of '77 broke blizzardly on Cow Creek. Outside, the wind slatted the hard frozen snow crystals against the lodge skin like so much sand, and made the ears of the smoke hole drone drearily. It was late when we one by one rolled out of our blankets, and washed, and took the plates of food and bowls of coffee which Kipp's mother set before us. During the morning only three or four women came in to trade—small skins for coffee, sugar, and so on. The afternoon was still more monotonous. Little Plume was our only visitor, and he brought us assurance that the blizzard would soon be over: old Red Eagle, and other sun priests, he said, were again making medicine for a chinook, and would no doubt drive Cold Maker back to his own North Land.

At sundown came the summons we were impatiently awaiting —the call to the Christmas feast in old Hugh Monroe's (Rising Wolf's) lodge. We hurried over there, Kipp and his mother, Bucknum and I, and found all the other guests awaiting our coming. The party included the old man's sons—John and Francois,

Manuscript in the Special Collections Library, Montana State University, Bozeman.

with their wives and children; Jackson, the grown grandson; old man Revois and wife, Red Eagle, and the young married couple who kept house for our host. Gladly would his sons have had him live with them, but his was an independent nature; he preferred a home of his own; a lodge where he alone was master.

The women of the three families, assisted by Revois' wife, had worked hard to prepare the feast for us. There was plenty of boiled fat boss buffalo cow ribs; stewed dried camas roots (traded from the Flatheads); choke cherry pemmican; dried depouille, or back fat; Labrador tea, from the muskegs of the Far North; and that peculiar bread of the Red River half bloods, called "gollette." It is made by mixing flour, marrow grease, salt and water to a very thick dough, and then beating the dough with a club for several hours before cooking it in thin cakes before the fire. It is a very light, wholesome bread, and rather rich. As a present for the children we had brought over three or four cans of so-called jelly. Anyhow it was very sweet, and was appreciated by the old—as well as the young ones. The people of the plains have an inordinate love for anything sugary.

We all enjoyed this Christmas dinner. Naturally, I contrasted it with the dinner my own people were probably eating at that very moment: roast turkey, of course, and mince pie, and other usual Christmas dishes. The diners there, all dressed in the accustomed ceremonial way, were seated at a table covered with snowy cloth and glittering with silver and cut glass. We were seated on buffalo robe couches strung around the circle of the lodge, and eating from tin dishes. And I was glad that I was there in the lodge, instead of in our dining room away back there in "the States." One couldn't there sit down to boss ribs, pemmican, depouille and gollette with men who were actual pathfinders in this still wild west.

The feast over, and Red Eagle lighting the big stone pipe, came the time for the evening story: "Grandfather," said Jackson, "once in the long ago I heard you tell the story of the Black Antelope, but I have mostly forgotten it. Let us all hear it now."

"Ha! The Black Antelope!" old Rising Wolf exclaimed, in Blackfoot, and Red Eagle, quickly passing the pipe, straightened up on his couch, clapped his hands together with a loud spat, and echoed, "The Black Antelope! Ai! That *was* a medicine animal. Ah, but the trouble it caused. Go on, Rising Wolf, brother, tell these young ones all about it."

"Ai! That I will," Monroe readily answered. "Let me think. Well, I can't remember just how many winters ago it was; forty and more, I guess. We, the Pikuni—or, as the whites say, the South Blackfeet—were camped on the Marias River at the mouth of the Dry Fork. It was late spring; there had been plenty of rain; the grass was thick and green all over the plains; the antelope, the bucks, were already fat—they get fat soonest of all the animals, you know—and so the hunters were killing great numbers of them until the buffalo, and the elk and deer should in turn take on fat.

"It was my father-in-law, Lone Walker himself, who was head chief at that time. We thought much of each other. Naturally, I could not frequent his lodge, son-in-law and mother-in-law may not meet, you know, so he used often of an evening to visit me. Well, one night as he sat smoking beside me there came in a youth named Wolf Eagle. I greeted him, gave him a seat on my left, and Lone Walker passed the pipe. The guest smoked a few whiffs, passed it back, and then said: 'Chief, I went to your lodge; they told me you were here. I have a favor to ask of you: let me tell it before any other ears may hear it. I know that your good son-in-law here will not repeat my words.'

" 'Ai. He is close-mouthed; he keeps secrets,' Lone Walker answered, 'so, let's hear what is this favor you want from me?'

"Then said Wolf Eagle: 'Chief, I have found a black antelope.'

"We stared at him. Lone Walker shook his head: 'You have been seeing wrong,' he said, pityingly. 'White antelope there are, occasionally, just as there are white buffalo. But a black antelope! No, my son, no. Never such an animal roamed the plains.'

" 'I don't blame you for saying that,' the young hunter an-

101

swered. 'None of the people ever have seen a black antelope; none of the ancient stories even mention one. Yet, as true as I sit here, I have seen one. Not only today, but for four days past. It is as black as a dead coal from the fire, and as wise as it is black. I am a good hunter, for four days I have tried to kill it, but try as I will it is ever too cunning for me. I tell you, chief, the animal really is.'

" 'Well, I take your word for it that the black antelope is,' Lone Walker agreed, and by his tone—by the soothing voice he used—I knew that he thought as I did, that the youth was crazy. 'And now that I agree with you,' he went on, 'what is this favor you want from me?'

" 'It is this,' Wolf Eagle quickly answered. 'The animal is always on, or near, the east end of the big ridge south of here, the one between the forks of the Dry Fork. I ask you to have the camp crier go the rounds and tell the people that you forbid them hunting there. I found this black—this medicine—antelope, so it is but right that I alone should hunt it—and kill it, if I can do so.'

" 'I am sorry I cannot do that,' Lone Walker answered. 'You know as well as I do that general hunting cannot be forbidden except at times when much meat is needed, and a great herd of buffalo is near camp. Then, of course, for the benefit of all, a certain time is set for running it, and until that time, no hunter is allowed to leave camp.'

" 'But you are a great chief; the greatest chief our people ever had, the youth plead, 'surely, you have but to say do this, do that, and the people must obey.'

" 'My son, a chief is a chief only because of his justness, his fairness to all the people,' my father-in-law explained. 'Should I do as you ask I would be neither of those things. The game animals are scattered in this season of green grass. I have no right to shut off any part of the surrounding country from the hunters, and so lessen their changes to get food for wives and the little ones.'

"Wolf Eagle sighed, and sank tiredly back on the couch. We waited some little time for him to speak, expecting more argument, or, perhaps, angry words. But no. He had sense; he was reasonable. What he said was: 'I was a fool to ask that. I might have known you could not do it. I will go now.'

" 'Let me ride out with you tomorrow and see the animal?' I asked, as he arose and started toward the doorway.

" 'Ai. Come with me,' he answered, and the door curtain flapped down and he was gone.

" 'I pity him; he certainly is crazy,' said my father-in-law.

" 'But I shall go with him tomorrow. I may be able to make him see that this black is yellow and white,' said I.

"It was no more than daylight when Wolf Eagle called me, and we were first out of camp. We rode up the hill at the upper end of the big bottom, and then across the plain straight toward the east point of the long ridge, almost a half day distant. Thus we cut the big bow of the Dry Fork, between the forks of which my friend assured me the black antelope would be grazing.

"We arrived at the west fork sometime before noon. It is not a stream, you will remember; only a wide, treeless and brushless coulee in which is here and there a pool of water. We approached it carefully, I using my spy glass often, but neither in the coulee, nor on the ridge was there a black antelope. Real antelope there were, four or five bands of females and their young, and apart from them, singly, and in small bunches, grazed numerous bucks. We left the west fork and started up the south, and main fork, in which water was still running. The trees and willows along its banks concealed us well enough. At the edge of every little grove and brush patch we took a good look ahead and all around, before crossing the open spaces. There was much game in the valley, and some of it we could not help frightening, here a bunch of buffalo, there some antelope. Always they made for the high plain, on the one side, or the big, and in places, rock-walled ridge on the other, and so did not alarm the bands that were some little distance ahead of us.

"We went on and on, slowly and ever on the lookout. The sun climbed to the middle, and went past it and down towards the Back-bone-of-the-world. It was half way there from the middle when we came near the beginning of the rock-walled narrowing of the valley and stopped in the upper edge of some high willows for a look ahead. I was levelling my spy glass at some antelope away up on the big ridge when Wolf Eagle suddenly cried out: 'See. See. There it is, the black one, there on the slope.'

"I turned and saw at once a dark animal where he pointed, and brought the glass to bear upon it for a better view; and what was now clearly revealed made me gasp; my heart throbbed so hard that the glass wobbled in my hands. Wolf Eagle was right. It was a black antelope; a big buck, and coal black. I was so overcome at the sight that I had to lower the glass; to rest until my hands stopped shaking. Wolf Eagle gave a low laugh; he enjoyed my surprise; and he uttered no taunt. What he said was: 'I am glad we have found him. I was beginning to fear that he had left this part of the country.'

"The strange animal was grazing about three long rifle shots from us, on a long slope running down from the plain on the east side of the valley, and I at once noted that we could not from any direction get nearer to it than we were right where we were. There wasn't a coulee in the slope in which to sneak, nor was there sagebrush or other cover to shield our approach. Again I raised the glass—I was steady handed now—and had a long look at the animal. Except in color it was not different from any other of its kind, although it seemed to be more alert than most bucks. It would hurriedly snatch a bite of grass and instantly raise its head, and look all around, and turn and look again, and often stare in one particular direction a long time, imagining that it saw something approaching to do it harm. It would then stamp the ground with its front hoofs alternately, the round patch of long hair on its rump—that should have been white—would fluff out, and with a forward thrust of the head it would whistle loudly. Yes, it was the most nervous, the most quick-to-take-alarm-at-nothing animal that I have ever seen.

" 'You notice the place it has chosen for the day: that we cannot from any direction get within range of it,' said Wolf Eagle.

'Well, that is what it does every day. It never grazes anywhere near a coulee, nor brush, nor a rim of the plain.'

" 'But it drinks—twice, at least once a day it must go to water. We can lie hidden in the brush and watch, and, when it enters the valley, sneak as close to it as we please,' said I.

"Wolf Eagle laughed. 'Twas the kind of laugh that has in it no sound of joy: 'Huh!' he exclaimed. 'Think you I have not tried that? The black antelope comes not to water in the daytime. It drinks only at night. It is great medicine and perhaps does not drink at all.'

"We moved farther back in the big, thick willows and dismounted, tethered our horses on short rope, and went back to the edge of the brush and sat down. The black antelope was still in the center of the wide, long slope, not grazing now, but not lying down with full stomach to re-chew its food. It was chewing it though, with the glass I could see the working of its lower jaw, and it was as uneasy, as alert as ever, often turning, and turning again to watch the country in every direction.

" 'Is that what it always does?' I asked.

" 'Always. I have never seen it lie down,' Wolf Eagle answered.

" 'There is some way to get it,' said I, 'no matter how medicine an animal is, man is the smarter. Now, we could, of course, get it by calling out all the hunters tomorrow and making a surround of its grazing place.'

" 'I believe that it would even escape a surround. And anyhow I do not want it tried. I myself want the black one. I must have it,' said he.

"We sat there a long time, watching the black one and trying to plan some way to kill it. We at last decided that the one thing to do was to attempt to decoy it within rifle range. That needed preparation. We went back to our horses and sneaked down the creek the way we had come, without alarming the animal. On the way home we killed a buck antelope, and took its head-skin and horns along with the meat and hide. During the evening Wolf Eagle made a decoy cap of the head part of the kill, strengthening

105

it with small bent willow sticks, and stuffing it here and there with grass.

"When I told Lone Walker that evening that Wolf Eagle had seen straight, that I myself had been watching a really black antelope all the afternoon, he was so surprised that at first he had not a word to say except to mutter several times: 'A black antelope. Son-in-law, it can't be. Something is wrong. Are you sure that some kind of an affliction has not attacked your eyes—as well as the eyes of this young Wolf Eagle?'

"And when I told him that my eyes were as good as ever, he doubted me: 'This bottom here is an old camping place,' he said. 'Here, before us, camped many a time the Crows, whom we finally drove from the country. Here many people have died at our hands, and their ghosts linger for revenge. No doubt one of them has stricken you and Wolf Eagle. I will give orders for camp to be moved tomorrow before more harm comes to you.'

" 'Not tomorrow,' I told him. 'Go with Wolf Eagle and me tomorrow, and if you do not with your own eyes see a black antelope, I will admit that I do not see straight.' He agreed to do that.

"The three of us looked out from the willows where Wolf Eagle and I had remained so long on the previous day, but the black antelope was nowhere to be seen. We pointed out for Lone Walker the place on the long slope where it had grazed and watched, and he admitted that at the distance, even without my spy glass, one could certainly tell the color and shape of an antelope, or even something much smaller; a coyote, for instance. 'However, I do not believe that what you saw there was a black antelope,' he concluded. 'The evil ghosts have surely touched your eyes.'

" 'Wait here for me. It is better for one, than for two or three to go on discovery,' said Wolf Eagle, but Lone Walker would not agree to that. If there was anything to be seen, he wanted to see it without delay. We rode on up the valley to the stone-walled narrows, there dismounted and tied our horses, climbed to the top of the right hand wall, at the last very slowly and cautiously, of course, and little by little made the last of the raise and looked out on fresh country. Our search was ended. There across the canyon from us was the black antelope, again grazing on a wide, smooth, couleeless, brushless slope. I was the first to see the animal, and without a word I pointed at it. Lone Walker gasped, reached out his hand toward me, and I handed him the spy glass. He leveled it, adjusted it, and squinted through it a long, long time; and finally, lowering it, and blinking, he said: 'Unless the ghosts have also touched my eyes, that animal across there actually is a black antelope.'

" 'You know that your eyes are as good as ever they were,' I told him. 'I can prove that they are: look at the rocks in the opposite wall. Do you not see the different colors of them—gray, yellow, brown and black?'

" 'Ai! That I do,' he readily answered. 'Yes. It is, it is truly a black antelope. This is wonderful. Strange. Undoubtedly great medicine. We must have the animal. I care not who kills it, but for the good of the tribe we must have its skin for sacrifice to the sun.'

"After some further talk and planning, Wolf Eagle slipped away from us to attempt to decoy the antelope, taking with him his antelope head cap. From the mouth of the canyon-like narrows he went straight out from the valley under cover of the steep break-off of the flatish slope on which the black one was grazing. When right opposite the animal he climbed to the edge of the break, and raised just enough above it to show his headpiece. He did it so naturally that anyone not knowing differently, would have been sure that a wary buck antelope was peeping up over the break to see what was ahead of him.

"Well, the black one sighted the top of that lifelike head, its well set horns and forward thrust ears, as soon as it showed above the rim of the slope, and made one big leap away from it, then stopped and turned to look again, and the head was gone. He stared and stared at the place where it had been, looked all around in other directions and stared and stared again, often angrily

107

striking the ground with a fore foot. 'Perhaps,' he thought, 'I just imagined that I saw something over there.'

"But, no. Again the top of the head appeared above the thick-grassed slope rim, and disappeared, and again appeared. The black one advanced one step, two steps toward it, and Lone Walker and I, watching, held our breath. Again the head went out of sight, and the black one advanced not one, but four or five steps. 'The decoy works! The decoy works,' I whispered. 'Wolf Eagle is surely going to bring the black one within range of his rifle.'

"And I had no sooner said that than the head again rose in sight, and, with a leaping backward whirl, the black one fled from it with that swiftness that only an antelope can attain. So quick were his leg movements that we could scarcely see the four feet touch the ground: he seemed rather to soar like a huge bird instead of run. And he ran circling, instead of straight away, so as not to at once, strike too abruptly the crest of the slope, and the danger that might be hidden there. Yes. He chose the route that enabled him to ever see far ahead, and, so running, passed quartering over the top of the slope, and presently re-appeared on the other side of its break-off in line with the mouth of the canyon. And there, with stamping feet and tossing head, he snorted and snorted at Wolf Eagle, slowly and sadly making his way down to the horses. There we met him, and sat down.

"Lone Walker got out his pipe and filled the small black bowl, and I lit it with my sun glass. We did not talk much: we were too badly disappointed to talk; and as soon as the pipe was smoked out we got on our horses and rode home. Arrived there we found the camp all excited, and the hunters cutting out their best horses for next day's use. A dozen of them hailed us, surrounded us, all trying at once to tell us that Weasel Tail had that very evening seen a black antelope away up the Dry Fork. It was running when he saw it, as though something had given it a terrible scare, and was keeping on the east rim of the valley, some distance below the rock wall narrows. All the hunters were to start out after it at daybreak.

"Here was bad news, especially for Wolf Eagle. He groaned, and drooped over. 'That ends it. Some great misfortune is coming to me,' he said.

" 'No, this doesn't end it,' Lone Walker cried. 'I shall call a council. We will talk this matter over and see what can be done for you, you, the discoverer of this medicine animal.'

"A little later the chiefs all met in my lodge, Wolf Eagle and I present, and we told them all about the black one, and our attempts to kill it. They asked many questions, offered many plans to outwit it, and together were deciding that the one thing to do was for all the hunters to make an unbreakable surround of its always open grazing place, when Wolf Eagle begged for one more day in which alone to attempt its death: 'I found the animal, it is no more than right that you grant this I ask,' he concluded.

"Then up spoke a blind old man, Otter Cap, a medicine man of great power. 'Young man,' he said, 'let me ask you something: Have you ever seen the black one with real bucks?'

" 'No, I have not,' Wolf Eagle answered, 'he has always been alone, and nowhere near any of his kind, neither bucks, nor does and their young.'

" 'Ah! I think that explains it,' said the old man. 'The black one is an outcast because of his color. Real colored bucks have ever fought him, and whipped him until he has not the least bit of courage. He runs as soon as he sees one of them. That is why he ran from your decoy cap today. Now, then, all you chiefs, listen. As this young man says, it is but fair that he have one more chance to alone try to kill this medicine animal. Give it him. Let him paint his decoy cap black. My medicine tells me that by so doing, success will be his.'

"Only one or two of the chiefs made any objection to this, and they soon were brought to agree to the plan. The council then broke up and scattered to their homes. Wolf Eagle went from lodge to lodge for black paint, and soon collected enough to change the color of his decoy cap. It was agreed that he, Lone Walker, and I should again start out together in quest of the black one, all the other men of the camp following at some distance behind, in case they would be needed to make a surround.

"Friends, we did not find the black one that day, nor the next, nor the next, and then, the hunters of the camp becoming impatient, another council was called and permission was given all to hunt when and where they chose for the black animal. Many days passed, and none saw the animal, and it was believed that he had left the country. But, somehow, Wolf Eagle and I thought different. Our opinion was that in the country around the forks of the Dry Fork the black one had been born, had always lived, and that we would there find him again some day. After a time the hunters ceased going out in that direction, for during their quest of the animal they had made game scarce there. But Wolf Eagle and I kept going, one day to the west fork and the butte, the next day up the south fork, and on a day of the next moon we found what we sought: There, right on top of the end of the long butte the black one was grazing. Leaving our horses we sneaked as near him as was possible, and then Wolf Eagle allowed him to glimpse his back head cap. He jumped and whistled, just as he had done before, and then, little by little, came toward us. How our hearts beat then. Would he come near enough for a fair shot at him? Oh, how Wolf Eagle prayed. And so did I. And, although the day was cool, so great was our desire that perspiration streamed down our faces. And, yes. He did come near enough. No doubt he thought he was approaching a brother. Perhaps, like him, his twin brother—or sister—had been black. Anyhow, he came near, we fired together, and he fell with two balls in him. And at that we ran to the body, and beside it embraced one another.

"We did not take the meat. That, of course, was sacred to the sun. But we took the hide with feet and horns complete, and that evening set the camp wild at sight of it.

"So ends the story, friends, of the black antelope."

"Ai! Ai! And we gave it to the sun at the medicine lodge in that very moon," old Red Eagle added, "and oh, what luck it brought us for all the summer. Always our war parties returned successful, and happiness and plenty were ever in the camp."

8.

The First Fire Boat

INDIAN HEAD. From a painting
by Charles M. Russell.

*(Courtesy R. W. Norton Art Gallery,
Shreveport, Louisiana)*

8.

The First Fire Boat

On Christmas day, 1877, in the Blackfoot camp on Cow Creek, Montana, the Blackfeet medicine men, or sun priests, made medicine to end the fearful blizzard that had held the country fast in its grip for many days, and lo! that very night there came out of the west a warm chinook wind that drove old Us-to-yi-stam, (Cold Maker) back to his Arctic home. Of course all the medicine makers took credit for the weather change, but in most of the lodges it was generally conceded that my old friend, Red Eagle, with his powerful medicine pipe, and his prayers, was the principal cause of it.

December 26 broke warm and sunny. The hunters scattered out for the buffalo herds, and my friend Charles Bucknum, long delayed by the blizzard, hitched up his four horse team and pulled out for his place down on the Missouri. Apsi and I rode down Cow Creek to examine our wolf baits, and found so many dead wolves, coyotes, and foxes around them that we wondered if we could ever skin them, even with the help of his mother and

Manuscript in the Special Collections Library, Montana State University, Bozeman.

sister. In their present hard-frozen state, of course, it was impossible to do anything with them.

We returned to camp early, and after a hearty meal and a rest, I went in the evening to visit old Red Eagle. I found quite a gathering in his lodge, congratulating him upon his success in bringing the warm chinook wind. He was very modest, however, and as soon as was possible turned the talk to the one subject interesting old men: reminiscences of their youthful days. Several stories were told by one and another of the visitors, and then old Red Eagle wound up the evening with one that I thought good enough to note down. Said he:

"I was a young man at the time; sixteen or seventeen winters, perhaps. Our camp was away down on the Missouri. It was berry time, and we were preparing to set up the medicine lodge. A woman of my clan, the Small Robes,[1] had made the vow to the sun, and we were encamped on a big bottom of the river suitable for the great offering to the sun and the ceremonies attending it. Other clans of the people were scattered out on the plains and in the hills north of us, getting the balance of the berries and buffalo tongues necessary for the occasion. They were, however, soon due to join us, and the sun woman began her four days fast."

Here, turning to me, he explained: "Apikuni, for four days before the sacred lodge is put up, the sun woman has to sit in her lodge on a buffalo robe from dawn to dark, and during that time

---

[1] The Small Robes, named for the smaller buffalo robes they wore, were the largest band of the Piegan Indians, numbering 150 lodges or more. Because of their numerical strength they kept aloof from other Piegan bands and even dared to make peace with the Flatheads—traditional enemies of the Piegans. The Small Robes visited the Flathead camps in the Bitterroot Valley and permitted the Flatheads to accompany them on buffalo hunts in the plains country of the Piegans south of the Missouri River. But the smallpox scourge of 1837 and an attack by a superior force of Crows in 1845 reduced the ranks of the Small Robes to about 30 lodges. By 1944 only two families of Small Robes were left. See John C. Ewers, "Identification and History of the Small Robes Band of the Piegan Indians," *Journal* of the Washington Academy of Sciences, Vol. XXXVI (1946), 12.

she cannot touch the ground, nor eat, nor drink. After dark, of course, she is allowed to go about as she pleases."

"Yes, I know it," said I, "don't you remember that I have seen several medicine lodges put up?"

"Ai. So you have," he answered, and went on:

"Well, on the first day of the sun woman's fast some young men were on the bluffs at the upper end of the bottom, and, looking away down the river they saw there a thick, black smoke rising. At first they paid no attention to it, thinking that it was the smoke of a fire in the grass of a bottom, or in a grove. But after a time they noticed that the smoke was coming nearer, and then they did pay attention, for the smoke was steadily coming nearer. 'How is this?' one asked. 'Smoke cannot move against the wind, and the wind is blowing straight down the river.'

" 'Oh, well,' another answered, 'Probably down there the wind is blowing in a different direction.'

"But now they suspicioned; they had the uneasy feeling that something was wrong, and they remained there on the bluff and watched, and the smoke came nearer and nearer, until, at last, they knew that it was travelling against the wind. Then, while several of the youths remained on the bluff, others hurried down to camp and gave the alarm.

"They were only laughed at: 'What—smoke travelling against the wind?' said the wise ones, 'Impossible. Clear your eyes and look again.'

"But they were so earnest about it, so insistent, that finally one of the warriors—more to satisfy them than anything else—accompanied them to the top of the bluff. Arrived there he saw the smoke. He watched it. He saw that it was even as the youths had reported: it was coming against the wind. And such a strange smoke it was: a thin, round column of smoke, rising fast above the timbered valley. 'This,' he said, 'is perhaps something for us to fear. Anyhow it must be looked into.' And he, himself hurried down to camp to call the chief, the medicine men, and all who would, to the bluff.

117

"They went quickly enough then, and saw that the youths had been right in the first place. There was the black smoke, a strange shaped smoke, and without doubt it was coming up against the wind. The tall, dense groves of cottonwoods in the valley prevented them seeing the river, but apparently this smoke, as it advanced, was following the course of the winding stream; it wove along up, now on one side of the valley, now on the other side, and again came on for a time in a straight course. The chief and medicine men consulted together and agreed that the steadily approaching smoke might be the sign of some dread calamity about to visit the people. Thereupon they all went down to camp to call the warriors together, to tell them to get out their bows and shields, and be prepared to fight.

"All this commotion in camp alarmed the women and children, of course, and the sun woman as well; alarmed her so much that, despite her vows, her sacred duty, she got off the buffalo robe, she stepped upon the ground and ran out of her lodge. And she no sooner appeared than the people began to upbraid her: 'Now see what you have done!' they cried. 'You are on the ground.' 'No doubt you have broken your vows in other ways!' 'You, and you alone are the cause of this coming trouble.' 'Of course the sun is angry at us.'

"And then, as they scolded her, came the sound of some monstrous beast drawing long, loud breaths: 'Whuh-h-h! Whuh-h-h! Whuh-h-h!' Oh, it was a fearsome sound.

"And then came worse to the ears of the people: loud yells, undoubtedly made by one voice, but so loud, so hoarse, so deep that it seemed that none but a man as big as a mountain could have uttered them. That was enough for everyone, even the warriors and the chief himself. The horses had been driven in. The lodges now began to come down. Women everywhere were packing, the men for once helping them saddle their animals. And as they worked, there suddenly came in sight around the bend in the river a monstrous thing. A long, broad, high beast of some kind that spouted smoke from its tall, black top piece. A beast

118

that had queer legs behind; a hundred legs that went round and round, kicking up the water and pushing its big body swiftly up the stream, keeping in its deepest part. And on the beast stood horses. Yes. And men too. All this the people saw. One look at it was enough. They fled, some, even women and children on bareback horses, and such was their haste that half the lodges, and more than half of the property of the different families was left right there. Up over the bluff they went, and northward on the plain.

"Well, ai, well do I remember how we all felt during that dreadful time. The Blackfeet, you know, are not cowards. They do not run from their enemies. But this was different. We were fleeing from—just what we did not know, except that it was great medicine.

"As soon as we got out on the plains messengers were sent to the other bands of the tribe to tell them about the terrible beast that had come into the country, and before night they were all with us. We travelled all that night. And ever the women and children, the aged, all the helpless, were in the advance, the whole fighting strength of the tribe behind. And from every butte, from every rise of ground along the way, men watched to see if that which we feared was pursuing us.

"The next day, the women and children being unable to go farther, we made camp, and from a nearby butte the warriors watched by turns, keeping their eyes ever upon our back trail. The medicine men tried to get a dream about this thing but all failed; no dream would come to them. Two old men got into a quarrel as to what it was, and fought fiercely. All blamed the sun woman; her husband disowned her; no lodge, not even that of her parents, would give her shelter, but food she had as needed.

"Now, let me go back in my account of all this. About a moon previous to this time the Crows had made a raid on our horse herds and driven off about a hundred head. That number was of no consequence, of course, but among those taken was a certain black race horse owned by Two Owls, and that did matter. It was the swiftest horse ever seen on the plains, and we were depending upon it to win when, in the coming fall we should meet the Pen d'Oreilles and race horses with them. Therefore more than a hundred of our warriors started at once for the Crows to try to take it from them. They knew where to look for us upon their return; it had already been decided where the medicine lodge should be held.

"Our warriors were successful; not only did they get the black racer, but more than two hundred horses with it, and after a fight with a number of Crows who pursued them, all went well on their homeward trail. They came at last to the breaks of the Missouri, a day's ride above our encampment on it, and there determined to cross, as at that place was a good ford. Driving the big herd before them they rode down the breaks to the small bottom at the foot of the trail and were there preparing to rest when around the near, and sharp bend below came this terrible beast that we had seen, breathing hard, kicking the water at its hind end with a hundred legs, and then suddenly letting out one after another of its more than powerful yells.

"What a scatterment there was then, my friends. The great herd of horses bolted in all directions, and the warriors, never at all paying any attention to the animals, not even the black racer, themselves raced back up the trail, and reaching the plain, made a straight run for the place appointed for them to find us. There, at the to be medicine lodge bottom they crossed the river, although it was a wide and dangerous place, and what did they find! Deserted lodges. Parfleches full of food; of wearing apparel; robes; and generally most of the property of our clan. The sight of it all made them sick. Naturally, they thought that the great beast in the water that they had seen, had devoured or captured us all, and they began to mourn for their loved ones. But presently one of them found our trail and they all set out upon it, up the bluff, and then out across the plain as fast as they could go.

"It was late in the day that we, worn out, were camping there on the bare plain. Lone Walker, chief of the tribe, and also of our clan, was himself one of the watchers on the butte. There were many with him: medicine men, great warriors, all who were at the head of the people. Tired they were, their eyes red and smarting from want of sleep, and in their hearts what anxiety! There, close at the foot of the butte, there slept their tired loved ones. What if the great, loud yelling beast should come? The very thought of it sickened them. The medicine men prayed and prayed the sun for mercy, and all the warriors prayed with them.

"Hai-ya! In the very midst of the prayers there appeared a great cloud of dust far back on the trail we had made, and by the very shape of it the watchers knew that it was not made by buffalo. At sight of it their heavy hearts became more heavy. When, after a time, it was seen that this dust cloud was coming straight along on the trail, they despaired. Said Lone Walker: 'Medicine men, warriors, my children all, there is no hope for us. Yonder comes the yelling monster. Let us now go down and dig pits and fight our best, and die as Blackfeet should die.'

"So, down the butte they ran, and with knives, and buffalo shoulder blades, and hands, dug shallow pits across the trail at a little distance from camp. The work, the talk, of course aroused the sleepers; and when the women learned of it they were all for going on again. But no, Lone Walker commanded, no: 'It is useless,' he said, 'to attempt to escape by flight. We will end it all right here.'

"There were still several watchers on the butte, and about the time the pits were finished one came down and reported that the dust cloud was coming close, but that it did not now at all resemble the smoke that the beast in the river had given forth. 'Oh, well, that proves nothing,' said an old medicine man, 'a powerful, fast moving thing such as that is can give out any kind of smoke it wishes to.'

"Said Lone Walker: 'Everything is finished here. We have now only to wait. I will go back on the butte, and return at the proper time.'

"So back he went and sat there, watching closely the oncoming

121

dust cloud, and after a time, before any of the other watchers could see what caused it, he cried out: 'Ha! It is not the river beast after all. That dust is raised by horsemen. Run, one of you, and tell the people so.'

"A little later all the watchers could see that it really was a horseback party raising the dust, and still later they made out that the riders were their own people. No other than the party that had gone against the Crows. At that they all ran down to camp, and soon afterward the party came in. But they did not come shouting the victory song; all could see that they were frightened men; nor, at Lone Walker's command, did their women and kinfolks begin shouting their names in praise. This was too serious a time for anything of the kind. They rode slowly and quietly into camp on worn out horses, and their first question was: 'Did the strange, smoke spouting monster in the river do you harm?'

"At least that was what the leader of the war party asked Lone Walker; and he replied: 'It killed none of us. We flew as soon as we got sight of it, and here we are, prepared to fight it the best we can. When we saw the dust raised by your animals we thought it was surely the smoke of the medicine beast.'

"The leader then told how it had suddenly appeared around the bend as his party was about to ford the river. How it had frightened the horses as well as himself and the men. The black horse, he said, was among those abandoned. And this was more bad news. Said Lone Walker: 'We must call a council right away, consider all this, and determine what is to be done.'

"The council was held that evening, while many warriors kept watch on the back trail. It was conceded by all that some move must be made at once. That the medicine lodge must be built, else the sun would forever abandon the people, and that another woman must make the vows, as the one who had made them had stepped upon the ground on the very first day of her fast. As to her being blamed for that, opinion was divided; some believed that she was the cause of the appearance of the dreadful thing, others thought that she had had nothing to do with it, and that, when all

122

the camp was fleeing, there was nothing for her to do but get out with it.

"Again, as the war party had seen the monster some distance above the medicine lodge bottom, it was possible that it was going straight up through the country; possibly to the Back-Bone-of-the-World, and beyond. Anyhow, something must be learned about its movements, and more learned about the thing itself. Volunteers were called for to go and trail it up, and return at once with what news they could give. Tired as he was, the war party chief said that if he could only rest until daylight, he would himself head the scouting party. This was agreed to be the best thing to do, and the council broke up.

"Headed by the war chief, the little party started early next morning upon its quest of the river monster. Cutting across the plains to the river, and striking it where the thing had last been seen, they were glad to see the big band of captured, and abandoned horses grazing in the bottom, and on the hills across from them. They crossed over on the ford, rounded up the whole band, including the black runner, and drove it to the north side. There they caught up fresh animals, the chief taking the black, and rode with caution up the valley.

"On the third day out from the camp on the plains, they discovered the smoke of the monster away up the valley ahead, and at once took to the hills. From a high point they looked long at the smoke, now heavy, now light, found that it was neither moving up, nor down the river, and taking courage they went on, and on, ever along the heights, until they came opposite it and saw that it was at a ford, a shallow ford that they knew well. It was out in the middle of the river, and, although now and then its hundred pushing legs went round and round at tremendous speed, it did not go ahead at all: 'Ha!' the chief laughed. 'Our people need not have abandoned their camp, nor we our horses. The thing can't travel on land. See: It is trying and trying to push itself over that shallow crossing, and cannot do so.'

"And, even as he spoke, fresh black smoke spouted from its

123

tall, black head piece like a burnt pine tree trunk, its hundred pushing legs suddenly whirled the other way, and it floated down stream, and then over to the north shore, where it stopped. There, owing to a heavy growth of timber, they could not see it: 'If it remains there until night,' said the chief, 'we will go down and see just what it is.'

"Some of the party objected to that. Said one: 'We have learned that it cannot travel on land, not even in shallow water. Our people are safe from it. Let us go home.'

"Said another: 'Let us not even approach the strange medicine thing. There is no knowing what it may do to us. Strange medicines are dangerous.'

"But the chief would not listen to them. He was himself a medicine man. He had his medicine pipe with him. He got it out and they all smoked it, and prayed, and were encouraged, and at night, on foot, they stole down from the heights.

"Across the bottom they went, then through the grove, slipping slowly, quietly from tree to tree, and, finally, creeping along on hands and knees, they came close to the bank, and it.

"There was now no smoke rising from the monster, but all along its side were windows, just like those they had seen in Fort Union, and within, through these windows, they could see light, and in one place people—white men, sitting and eating, and talking and laughing. This, then, was a white man's contrivance. And realizing that, they lost all fear. It could not be medicine, for white men have no medicine. The thing seemed to be both a house and a boat. There were loads of stuff on it: Boxes; barrels; brown cloth bales; just such things as they had seen the Long Knives hauling up the river in boats and unloading at the Fort. Long, long they looked, and then withdrew as quietly as they had come. And when they had got out on the bottom, said the chief: 'It is both a boat and a house, and by some means, I know not how and don't care, the white men make it go. Now for a little rest, and then we will go relieve the anxiety of our people.'

"In three days time they arrived safely in camp with the band of Crow horses. And when they had told just what they had seen, how the people did laugh. Laugh at themselves and their terrible fright. And then they moved back to the river and held the medicine lodge. And later, when they saw another of the river travellers they did not run. They knew what it was; nothing but a fire boat, as the war chief named it."

9.

The First Elk-Dog

WATCHER OF THE PLAINS.
Bronze by Charles M. Russell,
1902.

*(Courtesy R. W. Norton Art Gallery,
Shreveport, Louisiana)*

The First Elk-Dog

Natahki washed and wiped the supper dishes and put them away in the big parfleche that was the receptacle for our meager outfit of cooking utensils: "Kyi! Let's go over to Uncle Red Eagle's lodge and ask for a story," she said, and her proposal struck me just right. We covered our lodge fire and hurried through the raging blizzard across the big camp to the old man's place. As usual, he and his old wife gave us hearty welcome, and the latter passed us a dish of dried servis berries, and another of pemmican made of the choicest dried buffalo meat and marrow grease: "We will take them home with us and eat later," Natahki told her, and set the food at the back of the robe guest seat that we occupied.

As we came into the lodge Red Eagle was leaning against the slanting willow back rest at his end of the couple's couch, and singing, keeping time to the song by tapping a small, one head drum all painted in deep red, the medicine—the sacred color. He ceased only long enough to greet us, and then went on and finished the song.

"You seem to be happy tonight," I ventured.

Manuscript in the Special Collections Library, Montana State University, Bozeman.

"Ai! That I am," he replied. "And why shouldn't I be? I loaned Medicine Owl my black mare runner this morning, and lo! for my share of the days' chase he has brought me three fine buffalo cow hides, and much fat meat."

Natahki and I congratulated him, and she offered to help the next day in cutting the meat into sheets for drying. And then said I: "Uncle, listen: You have told me about the first gun the Blackfeet ever had, the first steamboat they ever saw, now, one thing more: tell me about the first horse they ever had—where, and how they got it?"

"Ha! That is another story," the old man exclaimed. "Wait. Let me fill my pipe; good tobacco and l'herbe smoke freshens one's memory of these old time tales."

"Well, it was this way," he began, after lighting the charge in the big stone bowl and drawing three or four cloud-like whiffs through the long stem. The Blackfeet first heard of the horse when they made peace with the Crees, after taking from them Is-so-kwo-i-na-ma, The Loud Mouthed Gun. You will remember that upon his return home from his mission of peace, a number of Cree families accompanied chief Na-mak-an for a friendly visit with the Blackfeet people. Well, on that visit to our fathers the Crees told some astounding things. They told about white skinned men who had come westward to the Assiniboines River, and there, with sharp, wooden handled, hard rock instruments, cut down great trees and with them built a number of homes of four walls, and a covering of poles and earth, with, inside, a stone place for fire, and its smoke. They told how these men were clothed: in very soft material that was neither leather, nor grass. They told, too, about the very many strange things these men possessed, and the use of them. And, lastly, and most interesting of all, they said that the white skins had animals as big, and bigger than elk which they used for carrying heavy, heavy burdens, just as the Blackfeet and Crees used dogs, and that they even themselves sat on the animals and were carried over the country as fast as an ordinary dog can run.

"Describing these animals more particularly, they said that they had jaws and teeth like the buffalo, or elk, long hair all along the top of the neck, and long haired tails, and, strangely enough, were no two of them of the same color. Also, that their hard hoofs were rounding, and not split, although they were eaters of grass. And, again, that they were very gentle, and could be guided in any direction by the rider by means of a piece of rope fastened to the lower jaw.

"Our fathers questioned and re-questioned the visitors about these elk-dogs, as they called them. Day after day they had them describe over and over the appearance and size of the animals, and the uses to which they were put. Our fathers were not fools: they realized at once what the possession of such animals would mean to them: relief from walking and burden carrying; ability to go long distances quickly; a wonderful aid in hunting and bringing home heavy meat and hides: 'We must have some of these elk-dogs,' said our fathers, 'and—how are we to obtain them?'

"Ai! How were they to get them? The Crees said that, for some reason unknown to them—the white skins had burned the log lodges in which they lived and then moved east, and that they came no more to the country. This was bad news; our fathers said that they would at least have liked to see the medicine animals. In due time the Crees returned to their country, but the Blackfeet continued to talk about the elk-dogs. Night after night, moon after moon, the medicine men tried to get dreams about them. So time passed. It was two winters after the first visit of the Crees, following the peacemaking, that an old medicine man did get the wanted dream: his secret helper told him that if the young men would go to war to the south, they would find elk-dogs.

"On the morning after the medicine man told this dream, the chief called the clan chiefs together for a council, and after the pipe had gone the rounds he said to them: 'You have heard the dream of this wise old man. If you will just think a little you will see that it means more to us than anything that ever happened: it points the way for us, and for our children, and for the Blackfeet

131

forevermore, to get relief from the carrying of heavy loads. I say that this expedition into the south is to be the most important of any that our tribe has ever undertaken. Its success will be more to us than the wiping out of a whole tribe of our surrounding enemies. Now, to my mind it is not well for young men to undertake such an important quest; none but the most experienced warriors should go, so, I say that I, myself, will lead the party, and I ask you all to go with me, each of you to select such men from your clan as you know are the right ones to accompany us.'

"The clan chiefs all agreed to do that, and many young men sitting and standing around outside the lodge and listening to the council, at once got heavy hearts: 'It is always the way,' they said. 'The old men keep all the good things, all the big things, for themselves.'

"One of the chiefs inside heard the complaint: 'Never mind,' he called out, 'young men, your time will come soon enough. Be glad that you are young and carefree.'

"Said another chief to the council: 'There is no knowing how far this search for elk dogs will take us. Farther than the Yellowstone, no doubt, and beyond that none of us have ever been. Now, there are our brothers, the Gros Ventres. We should invite one or more of their chiefs to go with us, because somewhere south of the Yellowstone live their kin, the Arrapahoes, who would be useful to us in this quest if we could only go into their camp as friends.

" 'Ha! Our brother is wise; his words are good,' said the head chief. 'We will send word to the Gros Ventre camp at once for one or more of their chiefs to go with us.' And that very day some young messengers were started for their camp, which at the time was only a short distance off. And then, after more talking and planning, the council broke up.

"Three of the clan chiefs of the Gros Ventres soon arrived to join the expedition. Some had to come, for the Gros Ventres, not themselves a strong tribe had long been under the protection of our people. Driven hither and thither by the Crees, the Crows, the

Assiniboines and others, the Blackfeet had taken pity on them, had helped them fight their enemies, and had given them equal rights in the great hunting grounds of the Saskatchewan country. The three chiefs said that in their lifetime their tribe had seen nothing of the Arrapahoes, nor had any word from them, but for all that it would not be difficult to find their country and them, as they were located near the Rocky Mountains, on the first really big river south of the Yellowstone and its tributaries.

"On the day following the arrival of the Gros Ventres the medicine men gave the party about to start a sweat bath, and prayed for the success and long life of all. And, following that, the whole party made the round of camp, Na-mak-an leading with the big mouthed gun. It was he, you remember, who took this, the first gun the Blackfeet ever had, from the Crees. He was now a chief, and almost equal to the head chief in authority. The prayers that day were especially strong; the sacrifices to the sun more plentiful, and of greater value than ever before in all the years of the tribe. It was a very, very solemn time. If a child even laughed it was scolded by its mother. That evening there was no feasting, no dancing anywhere in the big camp. The people all stayed quietly in their lodges and continued to pray for those about to depart.

"They started early the next morning, sixty chiefs and warriors in all, and the people all stood in two deep lines to see them depart. Wives and mothers cried. Old men trembled and had hard work to repress their tears. Looking straight ahead of them, the war party of chiefs passed along between the two lines of their loved ones without a word and without once looking back. They crossed the level bottom land, climbed the long slope of the valley, and disappeared over the rim of the plain.

" 'Take courage, all you people,' the old medicine man cried, 'take courage. My dream tells me that you will probably all see your loved ones again. They will be away some moons, but they will all return. They will all return, provided they fail not in observance of the medicine they carry.' And hearing that, the women took courage, and went to their lodges with lighter hearts.

133

"At this time the camp was on the Two Medicine Lodge River, under the very cliffs from which, two summers before, Na-mak-an and his men had driven the Crows. No longer was this their country. The party now travelled for days through the rich hunting ground that they had taken from this enemy. Southward across the Missouri they went, down across the Yellow River and its mountains, on across the hills and plains of the Bear River to the Yellowstone, and their hearts were glad: 'Of all the people of the plains, we are the richest,' they kept saying. 'Who else has such a long, wide game country as this?'

"From the Two Medicine Lodge River clear to the Yellowstone the party found no signs—fresh nor old, of the enemy; Na-mak-an and the Loud Mouthed Gun had scared them clear out of the country. But they had no sooner crossed the big river than they came upon a recently deserted campground of hundreds of lodge fireplaces. In some of these, at the bottom of the fluffy ashes, were hot coals; a sure sign that they had been abandoned not more than two days. The trail from this campground ran southward, up the valley of a fork of the river, and the party followed it, sending a couple of scouts ahead.

"The two scouts sighted the Crow camp on the second day out from the Yellowstone, and early the morning after, the whole party was looking down at it from some cherry thickets on the rim of the valley. And suddenly as one man they cried out: 'Elk-dogs!'

"Yes, there they were, five of the animals, picketed in among the lodges, and just as the Crees had said, they were larger, much larger and much heavier than elk, and no two of them were of the same color. One was black, with white spots here and there. Another was all white; the others were brown, and gray, and yellow haired. The Blackfeet stared and stared at the animals; watched them graze, and walk about here and there as far as the ropes by which they were tethered would permit them to go. Said the chief: 'Brothers, we must have those elk-dogs. We must have them.' And they began to plan; to try to determine the best way to take them. Some were in favor of going into the camp at night and leading them out of it. Others objected to that: 'We do not understand these elk-dogs,' said they. 'They are powerful animals; it may be that they will, like dogs, fight strangers, and should they choose to do so, they would quickly bite and trample a man to death. I say that it is safest to wait for the right chance to capture them in the daytime.'

"While they talked and argued the sun came up and the camp began to stir. Smoke rose from the lodges; women came out for wood and water; men presently appeared, and some of them led the elk-dogs to water, and back to the picketing places. Four of them went quietly enough; the black pinto was different: he ran around and around the man who led him; kicked up his hind feet, and again stood almost straight up on them. The Blackfeet held their breath, expecting to see the animal kill its leader. But the man did not seem to be at all afraid; he kept yanking the rope, and at last took a stick and beat the jumper, and it at once became quiet. Again the Crees had been right: the elk-dogs were gentle animals; unquestionably, men were their masters. Said the chief: 'We do not want a fight with these Crows. We are after elk-dogs instead of scalps. We will quietly take the five animals from the camp tonight, and go on our way south after more of them.'

"The Crows seemed to have plenty of meat in camp, for after the morning meal the men remained at home instead of scattering out to hunt. Soon after the elk-dogs had been watered their owners again went to them and moved them to fresh grazing. Four were led; but the owner of the black pinto sprang up on its back and rode around and around the bottom, now fast, now slow, and the watchers in the brush stared and stared at the strange sight. It was a great sight. Never in all their lives had they been so pleased, so interested. The inside of their bodies just ached with the desire to possess such powerful and useful animals.

"The black pinto owner rode around the bottom a long time, and finally stopped the animal, got off from its back and picketed it right at the foot of the slope from the top of which the Blackfeet were watching. A chief of the party remarked that it would be a very easy thing, and a good joke on the Crows, if someone were to go and ride it away before their very eyes, and everybody laughed: 'That would be a good trick,' they said.

"But one of the Gros Ventre chiefs did not take it as a joke. Said he: 'I am going to do that very thing. I am going to sneak down through the brush to that elk-dog, and get on it and ride away.'

" 'No, no. You must not do that,' the Blackfoot head chief told him. 'By so doing you would spoil everything, especially our chances for tonight. Knowing that enemies were about the Crows would so closely guard the other elk-dogs that we would not be able to get anywhere near them.'

" 'But listen. You did not wait to hear me out,' the Gros Ventre told him. 'There is no use of our remaining here in the hot sun, and thirsty, all the day when we can get all five of the elk-dogs now. Here is my plan. You will all of you back out onto the plain and circle to the rim of it up there at the end of this bottom. I will then go down and mount the black pinto and ride straight to you. The owners of the other elk-dogs will mount and follow me, you will kill them, and then we will make off with all five animals. All the Crows will follow us, of course, but one shot from the Loud Mouthed Gun will start them running back to camp.'

" 'But you don't know how to ride; you don't know how to guide an elk-dog,' the head chief objected.

" 'Ha! Anyone can do that,' the Gros Ventre laughed. 'Didn't you notice that man—how easy he did it? One has but to spring upon the animal's broad back and sit there, and with the rope guide it to the right, or left or straight ahead. Yes, I know I can do it.'

"Others now took part in the talk. Some were in favor of the plan, more were against it, and so it was dropped. But the sun rose higher and higher, the heat from it became almost unbearable; and when the Gros Ventre again said that he was going to take the elk-dog, no one made objection. One by one the chiefs and warriors slipped out over the rim of the plain, and around to the edge of the slope at the upper end of the bottom, and waited for the Gros Ventre to come to them.

"The man was a long time getting down to the animal. The slope was not all brushy, and in the open places he slid along like a snake; and so slowly that the movement of his body could not be detected by any chance watcher in the camp. None saw him. He safely reached the edge of the bottom and slowly walked out, as though he were a member of the camp. Nor did he hurry when he unfastened the end of the rope and coiled it as he approached the pinto. It paid no attention to him and kept on feeding; and the Blackfeet, eagerly watching, said to one another: 'He is doing everything just right. He will soon be with us. We will soon have those five elk-dogs.'

"Said the head chief: 'Na-mak-an, you are ready with the Loud Mouthed Gun? You are sure that its ear is full of powder?'

"'Level full, and freshly put in. It will not miss fire,' he answered, as with the others he anxiously watched the Gros Ventre. Ai! That was an anxious and exciting time of waiting.

"The Gros Ventre was now close to the elk-dog. Another step and he stood beside it and put out a hand and stroked its back. And then, just as he had seen its Crow owner do, he grasped its mane and sprang up and sat astride on its back. Even as he was getting seated the animal had commenced to move, and now it broke into a swift trot, then into a lope, and headed for the other elk-dogs, all four of them picketed just at the outer edge of the big camp. First with one hand, and then with both, the Gros Ventre yanked and yanked the rope, trying to turn the animal toward the hills and his comrades, but the harder he pulled the faster it ran in the direction it wished to go. Shouting arose in the camp and broke into a roar like thunder as hundreds of men, bow in hand, charged out from it, and still the Gros Ventre sat on the flying, hard-minded animal and yanked and yanked its rope: 'Oh, why—why does he not fall off and run toward us?' the Blackfeet watchers cried, and with straining eyes and fast beating

137

hearts they stood there in the brush watching the fearful scene, powerless to help—to save.

"Ai! Why didn't he jump while there was yet time, and break for the hills and his waiting comrades? Perhaps he was afraid to get off the swift running animal; perhaps, even to the last, he believed that he could turn it; perhaps the strangeness of it all so confused his mind that he thought of nothing except to keep his seat. Anyhow, all too soon elk-dog and rider, and crowd of Crow warriors met, and pierced with many an arrow the Gros Ventre went down and was lost in the yelling, surging crowd. The watching Blackfeet bowed their heads and mourned. Their comrade was dead. Bad luck had come to them. They took account of themselves to learn wherein they had failed in prayers and sacrifice, and observance of their medicines, and could find no fault. They knew not what to do.

"The Gros Ventre was dead. The body had been taken through camp and cast into the river. The five elk-dogs had been re-tethered, this time close to the lodges. The Crows, all excited, swarmed about in their camp like a swarm of angry bees, but none came out from it; they were afraid of what might be lying in wait for them in the timber and brush of the valley. For a long time none of the Blackfeet party spoke. Then: 'Well, what now?' asked one.

" 'We have come south for elk-dogs and we will, we must have them,' the head chief answered. 'I propose that we go back down the river and remain there a few nights, long enough for the Crows to quiet down. Hundreds of them will guard their elk-dogs tonight, but after several more nights have quietly passed they will believe that there is no enemy in the country, and become careless. We will then enter the camp, take the animals, and go on south.'

"As he said, so the party did. When night fell they sneaked away and went clear back to the Yellowstone, there killed meat and rested. All but the two Gros Ventres. One of them had bad dreams the first night there, and could not be induced to remain.

138

They left for home and that was hard on the Blackfeet; without an interpreter they could not well go on to the Arrapahoe country. On the sixth night thereafter they slipped into the Crow camp, but search as they would from one end of it to the other they could find only one elk-dog, the black and white pinto. That they took and at once turned homeward, and in time led it into the great camp on the Two Medicine Lodge River. Hai! How the people did crowd around to see the strange animal. And when one of the party got on it and rode swiftly up and down the bottom, they laughed, and shouted and were so pleased that some of them actually cried, and others embraced and kissed one another.

"But the party of chiefs felt differently. Said the head chief: 'Right when everything was most promising, we failed. Our Gros Ventres deserted us, and out of five elk-dogs we got but the one. We must try again.'

"Every one of the party was anxious to do that, and in a few days time, with other Gros Ventres for helpers and interpreters, they started south again and went clear to the Arrapahoes, who received them kindly, and gave each one several number of elk-dogs, both male and female. The tribe had great numbers of the animals which they had obtained from the Spaniards, and the tribes farther to the south, and by breeding. Thus it was, my son, that the Blackfeet first got elk-dogs, and thereafter, through far raids, and breeding, winter by winter, their herds increased until many a man owned such a large herd that he could not accurately tell the number of animals comprising it.

"The elk-dog, my son, is the most valuable, the most useful of all the animals and things the whites brought to this country from their own country. More useful it is than the gun, and that is saying much. But, you see, with a good, fast elk-dog the hunter does not need a gun. With a bow and a handful of arrows he can ride and chase the buffalo and kill more in one run than he and his family can use in a moon. And when he has made the kill, then come the women with other elk-dogs, and soon the meat and the hides are all safe in camp, all without much work on the part of the hunter. Ai! Truly the elk-dog is a medicine animal."[1]

[1] For more versions of how the Blackfeet obtained their first horses, see John C. Ewers, *The Horse in Blackfoot Indian Culture* (Washington, 1955), 15–19.

10.

The Famine Winter

The talk paper

THE TALK PAPER. From a painting by Charles M. Russell.

(Courtesy R. W. Norton Art Gallery, Shreveport, Louisiana)

10.

The Famine Winter

On a bitterly cold night succeeding the Medicine Chinook, Jackson, Apsi, Red Eagle and I sat in old Hugh Monroe's—Rising Wolf's—lodge. The buffalo robe couches were soft and comfortable; the grateful heat of the fire made us drowsy; conversation became fitful, and finally ceased. Then, presently, came in with her little son, the wife of the young man who herded the old man's horses. The couple made their home with him, and relieved him of all domestic cares. Gladly would either of his sons, John, and Francois, have had him with them, but his was an independent nature: he preferred to have a home of his own; a lodge where he alone was master.

The woman took her place, a long, broad robe couch with willow slat back rests at either end of it, to the left of the doorway, the boy also sat down and snuggled close to her, and looked solemnly at the leaping flame of the little fire with unblinking eyes. The silence continued. I was wondering what the child could be thinking about when he turned, and looking up into his mother's smiling face, asked: "Mah-ma-yi, who made us?"

Manuscript in the Special Collections Library, Montana State University, Bozeman.

"Who made us? Why—Old Man, of course," she hesitatingly answered.

"Woman, is it possible that you have not yet instructed your son in the cause of things—that you have not told him the sacred tales? No? Well, come here my boy, and I will tell you a story.

The little fellow readily ran around the fire to him, being careful to circle past the doorway, instead of in front of the master of the lodge—that would break one's medicine—and nestled cozily in his lap: "Now. Now tell me, grandfather, tell me true, who made us?"

The old man fondly stroked his shining, parted and neatly braided hair, and answered: "Old Man made us. I don't know who made him. I guess he always was. And he was, and is, a god. He was not called Old Man because of great age. The gods can not grow old, they live forever. Our first fathers gave him that name because of his appearance: blue eyed he is, and white skinned, and his hair is the color of the morning sky just before the rising sun comes in sight. He is a very handsome, a very beautiful man—this god, this world maker of ours.

"Well, Old Man, having made the world, the plains, and mountains, the great lakes and rivers, and little streams, the trees and plants and grasses, and all the animals, having got everything ready, as you may say, then made us: that is, our first fathers and mothers. But it was not a very good place, there where he caused them to grow up and increase. It was in a small valley at the foot of great mountains; and soon the people became so many that they killed off all the game and began to starve. Anyhow, there were no food animals other than deer and birds in that country.

"Said an old man to his wife, and his three married sons, one day: 'I have had a talk with our Maker. He told me of a country he had made where game is plentiful, and pointed the way. Let us go find it.'

"They started, the four men and four women, and after climbing high, rough mountains for many days, and descending them for many more days, came at last to the edge of the great plains.

146

There they saw game of all kinds; many, many animals new to them, and oddest of all were those that later they named buffalo: 'Father,' said the oldest son, 'let us kill one of those high backed, long whiskered, black horned grass eaters, and taste its flesh. Something tells me that it will be good.'

" 'Very well,' the father answered, 'it shall be as you say,' and he rubbed a secret black medicine on his son's feet which enabled him to run right up alongside a band of the animals and kill a number of them with bow and arrow. Their flesh proved to be better than that of any of the other new animals. The hides were found to be best of all for making lodges and clothing, warm wraps and bedding: 'My son, you have done a great favor to us all,' said the father. 'I see now that we are to become a very numerous people; too many to all camp together and hunt together. Therefore, you and your children, and those to come after them, shall be known as the Blackfeet clan. In time to come you must leave us, and choose, and live in a part of this great hunting ground Old Man has given us.'

"Hearing this, the other sons became jealous of their elder brother: 'You make him first in everything,' they told their father. 'You give him the strong black running medicine, you give him a name for himself and his clan that is to be, and his choice of a part of this great plains country. Now, what are you going to do for us?'

" 'Go forth on discovery,' the father ordered. 'Go east, go south, into unknown-to-us country and learn what is there; and when you return I will give you names according to what you have done.'

"The sons departed at once and were gone a long time. The second son returned first, bringing some weapons, and some beautiful clothing of a strange people, enemies who had tried to kill him, and so the father named him Pi-kun-i: clothing, and from him are we, the people of this tribe, descended. The whites, knowing no better, call us South Blackfeet.

"Came home the third, the youngest son. He had gone farthest,

147

seen many strange peoples, and killed and scalped a number of their chiefs. Because of that the name Ahk-ai-na, or for short, Kai-na: Many Chiefs was given him, for himself and those to come after him.

"As the old father had predicted, the children of his sons, and their children after them, rapidly increased in the rich game land Old Man had given them, and soon the time came when they were obliged to separate. Having the first right, the Blackfeet clan chose the country watered by the North Saskatchewan River and its tributaries. Next, the clan of the Pi-kun-i had the say, and they took the lands along the upper Missouri River, and its feeders, which proved to be the richest region of all. There was left then, for the Kai-na, or, as the whites mistakenly call them, the Bloods, the country watered by the Belly, Old Man's, and St. Mary's Rivers, and that they chose. And that, my son, is the story of the beginning of things. Having made us, and given us the best of all the game lands, he went away to the west, saying that he would return some day. We look for him to arrive at any time."

"Yes, grandfather," the youngster piped, "I understand it all now. Old Man made us, and gave us, the Blackfeet, Kai-na, and Pi-kun-i, the richest country of all the world for our very own. Yes. He was very good to us, wasn't he! Tell me more about him."

"Not tonight. I see you are getting sleepy," the old man answered, and sent him to his mother, and within five minutes he was sleeping the dreamless sleep of healthy childhood.

There was silence again in the lodge except for the occasional popping of the burning wood. Going over in my mind the just concluded story of the creation of the world, and man, I spoke my thought: "Red Eagle, friend," said I, "Old Man made the world; made you. Now, then, who made, for instance, the Crees?"

"Why, their god made them, of course," he readily replied," one they call Great White Rabbit. Listen. Old Man made the world, made us, and gave us the best country of all for our hunting ground. Then came other, and lesser gods, and made the Crees, the Sioux, the Crows, and so on, and wherever was unoccupied

148

country, there placed them. Each tribe of them, of course, coveted, and still covets, our rich game land, and so it is that we have ever been at war with them, and ever must be. Ha! they fear us. Every head of game they have taken from our plains and mountain country has cost them dearly.

"Now, just to show you what a miserable country some of them have; the Crees of the Forest especially:

"At times these people were at peace—and exchanged visits with the North Blackfeet. At one of these friendly gatherings—it was in the long ago, before the white men came, a Cree told of a strange kind of bear that lives in the Far North. Their fur was as white as snow, he said, and very long and soft.

"A Blackfeet medicine man named Old Sun was much interested in this; he had recently seen just such an animal in a dream, and his secret helper had advised him to get the skin of one for a sacrifice to the sun. He therefore questioned the Cree about the best route to the north country, determined to start for it in the spring.

"Spring came and Old Sun started off, taking with him his wife, his son, Two Bows, and the latter's wife, Lone Woman. The young couple had a son of three winters, named Otter. Of course they took him with them.

"All was well with them for a time. Buffalo were plentiful and easily killed, so they had plenty of good meat. Their horses, winter thin, soon became fat and strong from feeding hugely upon the young, green grasses. Every day they travelled from early morning until nearly sunset, and were pleased with the rapid progress they were making.

"As they went on, and on, the country began to change. They left the great plains and entered a region of much timber, and great swamps. The buffalo disappeared, and in their place were moose and caribou, and black and grizzly bears. Neither deer, nor antelope, nor elk were found after they came to the swamp lands. And now as they went farther and farther into the swamps, travelling became more and more difficult. The horses were con-

149

tinually sinking belly deep in the soft mud, and huge moose flies and mosquitoes drained their blood and made their hides a solid mass of festering sores. But in spite of these difficulties the little party kept up its courage, and in the second moon of the quest came to a great lake where conditions favored a rest. There the steady west wind kept the flies back in the timber, and along the shore was fine feed for the horses. They remained there many days, feasting upon moose meat. The horses recovered their strength.

"Starting again, they followed the rocky shore of the lake for three days, and upon leaving it entered the worst swamp country they had yet encountered. It soon became so bad that the horses could go no farther, so Two Bows led them back to the lake and turned them loose in the rich, fly free pasturage. No doubt they would remain there until wanted, he and his father thought.

"Afoot now, and carrying nothing more than their weapons and fire making drill, and a couple of extra robes for bedding, the party made better progress; and in the third month out from the Saskatchewan they gradually left the wooded swamps and entered a country of broad, mossy plains where the few trees and brush were very small. Here they found a few bands of animals new to them, and easily killed several, their dogs holding them at bay until they could walk right up to them. They seemed to be a relative of the buffalo, but were much smaller than that big wanderer of the Blackfeet plains. Their dark coat was very thick, and long, and their sharp, black horns were set differently on their heads. Their flesh was eatable, but strong with the odor like that of the muskrat. The Cree had also spoken of these animals, and said that where they ranged, there also ranged the white bears.

"Father and son now kept a sharp lookout ahead, and carefully noted the tracks in moss, and bare ground, but not a bear did they see of any kind, nor even old signs of them. On and on they went, Old Sun keeping count of the days and the moons by making notches on an arrow shaft with his stone knife. There came no change in the appearance of the country; ever in front of them stretched the deep mossed, almost treeless plains. And presently thin ice formed on the still waters in the summer nights. Sitting around the fire one evening, the old man and his son councilled together: Said Old Sun: 'I have just been counting the notches on my arrow shaft. Our trail from the Saskatchewan is one hundred and five days—almost four moons long. This is just about the middle of the summer, yet we see a little ice every morning; I don't understand it.'

" 'There's nothing remarkable about that,' Two Bows answered, 'ice sometimes forms in our country in the summertime, and if you will just remember, ten summers back there came a snow storm that killed about all of the little birds.'

" 'True enough,' Old Sun agreed. 'I do remember it. This is probably an unusually cold summer here. But what I was thinking is this: the summer is half gone; we will be as long on the back trail as we have been coming out; dare we go farther, or must we here turn toward home?'

"Two Bows thought a long time before he answered, and then said: 'Some summers are longer than others. This may prove to be a long one. Anyhow, let's take chances. If possible you must get a white bear. It is bad luck for you if you fail to accomplish that which your secret helper has told you to do.'

" 'Ai! I do not need to be told that,' Old Sun exclaimed, and after some thought took his son's advice: 'We will go on for fifteen more days, and that must be the utmost limit,' he said, and early the next morning they were lengthening their trail.

"Day after day they breasted the north and saw no change in the country, found no bears nor signs of them. Came the evening of the fifteenth day and again they councilled, and decided to go on for four more days. When the end of that time came they made their farthest north camp, there killing another of those strange little relatives of the buffalo. They had much difficulty in collecting enough fire wood with which to cook some of the meat. The

151

next morning they started on the long back trail with heavy hearts: 'I had a bad dream last night,' the old man said. 'I have been warned that great misfortunes are to befall us.'

"But, although Two Bows and the women plead with him, he would not tell them what the dream was.

"All was well with the little party for some time. Meat was plentiful, the weather continued to be clear and sunny; and now that they were turned toward home the women were so happy that they joked, and laughed, and sang, and bade solemn Old Sun cheer up: 'Forget your bad dream; laugh with us,' they told him. 'We will soon have our horses, and with them the rest of the way will be quickly travelled.'

"He did his best to do what they asked, and at times was really good company at the evening camp fire; but more often he would have never a word to say, and sitting apart from the others pay no attention to what they did or said. Frequently now he would get out his medicine pipe and pray, and make sacrifice to the gods, begging them to have pity upon the little party and allow them to return safely to Blackfeet land. And to his secret helper he would cry: 'Hai-yu! thou wise and swift creature of the great mountain forests! Help me now, oh, help me. Come to me in my dream. Show me the way to save these, my loved ones here.'

"There came no answer to these prayers. The gods seemed to heed not his sacrifices, and after a time his sadness, his fierce anxiety to press on and on from break of day to fall of night, had its effect upon the others and laughter became a stranger to their lips.

"While still a long way from the big lake and the horses the weather became colder and colder. Ice formed on little ponds, and where there was shade from the sun, never melted. By day and by night great flocks of the web feet tribes passed southward over their heads, flying low and uttering sad cries that filled their hearts with dread: well enough they knew that Cold Maker was not far behind the swiftly fleeing birds: 'But I can't understand it,' said Old Sun one evening after carefully counting the notches

152

on the arrow shaft. 'I have made no mistake in marking the time. This is only the second day of the sixth moon of the summer;* the tree leaves in our country are still green; it is too early for the web feet to be heading for Always-summer-land, but of a surety they are on their way to it.'

" 'Oh, well, I don't think that these south-flying, sad-calling flocks are cause for alarm,' said Old Sun's woman, she the only always-hopeful one of the party. 'Perhaps you all never noticed, but I have many times, that flock after flock of the web feet come south to feed and play in our prairie lakes long before the leaves turn yellow.'

" 'Ai! But not the big-white-coats, woman mine, not they. The red feet, the white jaws, yes. When the big-white-coats go, winter is ever close behind them.'

" 'Perhaps they go now only to the big lake where our horses are,' Two Bows suggested. 'Let us hope so, anyhow. Let us try to be more cheerful. Father, take courage.' He said that for the sake of his woman, who was crying. In his own heart was a great fear.

"The old man did not answer. That very night a windless snow storm set in; at daylight the amount fallen came halfway to their knees; it was very light and dry, however, and did not much interfere with their progress. They travelled steadily all day, the storm continuing at intervals, and ceasing at dark, when, with a clear sky, the night turned very cold. The birds had not lied; winter was upon them.

"That first snow never melted, and now and then more came until, at last, further progress became impossible without snowshoes. The men had never made, never seen, such walking instruments; they had only heard of them through the Crees, and had but a faint idea of the size and shape of them. However, they made bows of willows, and strung them with strips of a hide of one of the caribou they had killed, and after four days work completed a pair for each one of the party. They did not go very far on them the first day, finding them awkward, and heavy, and very

* Equivalent to our September.

153

tiring, especially to the muscles of the leg below the knee. And many a fall they had, tumbling head first into deep snow, before they learned to move their feet widely apart.

"Some days later they crossed the southern edge of the moss grown plains and entered the timber, scattering at first, but soon becoming a forest of fairly large trees. Meat had been scarce for some time, but here they expected to find the great number of moose and caribou seen on the northward journey. To their surprise not a track of them was to be seen; they had left the country; gone to their winter range—wherever that might be, south, perhaps, or west to the slopes of the Back-bone-of-the-world. The Crees had told of the immense numbers of rabbits inhabiting the forests of this, their country. When other game could not be found they were sure of an ample supply of the long-eared jumpers— except that every seventh summer they became diseased and practically all died off. Old Sun had counted on them for food if worst came to worst, and now there was no more sign of them than there was of the large meat animals; undoubtedly this was a seventh year. His despair was now complete: 'There is no hope for us. Here I give up. Here I die,' he told the others one evening, and it was with great difficulty that they persuaded him to take the trail next morning.

" 'No, I am not a coward,' he said in answer to his wife's scolding. 'Look at my war record; it speaks for itself; few men in all our tribe have a better one. It is that I know it is useless to go on. My medicine is somehow broken. We shall starve to death.'

" 'Take courage, father, oh, do take courage,' Two Bows entreated. 'It is not very far from here to our horses. We will kill them. Their meat will last us all winter.'

"The horses were indeed their one hope now, and they struggled toward them, weak and starving and fast becoming weaker. One day Two Bows killed two grouse; on another day a rabbit, and one evening sent an arrow through a great white owl that was hooting over their heads. The greater part of the meat of these was fed to the child, the others trying to sustain life by chewing caribou rawhide. It could not be done, and so they were forced to do what they had all along feared must come to pass: one by one they killed their four dogs and ate them, begging the gods for forgiveness for taking sacred life. The animals were very thin, more skin and bone than meat, but there was sufficient, used with care, to last them to the lake and the horses.

"They built the fire one evening on the site of one of their outbound camps, and knew that by noon the next day they would arrive at the lake, so for once they ate heartily, consuming the last of the dog meat, excepting enough for the morning meal. And then they made plans for the winter: they would kill all the horses, dry the meat, and with the hides, and the caribou skins they had, make a small lodge to live in until spring. Old Sun, however, took no part in the talk. 'We will see what we will see,' he said, and told his woman to spread the robes.

" 'Now! now for the horses,' Two Bows cried when they came to the big lake and its windswept grasslands the next day. But no horses were in sight, and leaving the others to rest, he ran from open park to open park in search for them. It was not long before he returned, walking slowly now, and watching him, the others held their breath; bad news was surely coming: 'Well, let us hear the worst,' the old man demanded, when he had arrived at the fire, and was standing dejectedly before it.

" 'Very well, you shall hear it,' the young man cried. 'I found the bones of the horses. Wolves have killed all of them.'

" 'Ai! It is just what I expected you would find; I was sure of it,' said Old Sun. Well, here ends my trail. Here I lie down to my last sleep.'

" 'Oh, no, father. No.' Two Bows cried.

" 'I have said. Nor all your talk shall change my mind,' he declared.

" 'It shall never be said that I deserted my father. I shall remain and die with you.'

" 'Oh, my son, my foolish son,' the old man wailed. 'Don't you see how it is? I order you to go that I may live. Not in this old

155

body of mine, but in the child there. We caused him to come into the world, and in him we live again. It is our duty to give him every chance for long life and happiness. How much greater that chance will be if I remain here. You will have one less mouth to feed—'.

" 'Two less, for here I remain with you,' his old wife cried.'

" 'Ah! I thought you would say that. I am glad,' said Old Sun. 'Ai! my son, you heard her. You will have two less to care for. The little game you may find will perhaps support the three of you; there is the chance that it will. Go, then. Start at once and take the chance. You have to go. You have no choice in the matter.'

" 'Two Bows, man mine, father is right. You have no choice. Come. Let us start; we must at least try to save the child,' said Lone Woman. She was crying.

"At that Two Bows himself began to cry, hoarsely, gaspingly, as men always do, truly a heart rasping sound. And presently: 'Father, Mother, I take your word,' he said, and embraced them, as did Lone Woman. And when the old couple had bid farewell to the child, they took it and started on, never once looking back lest what they should see might break their none too strong resolution. And as they went they heard Old Sun, brave to the last, singing the victory song.

"Day after day the thin and weary couple trudged over the deep snow, by turns dragging the child on a caribou skin. By hard hunting the man managed now and then to kill a grouse, or an owl, and rarely indeed a rabbit, no more than enough to enable them to stagger slowly southward. And of the meat he killed the hunter took the least portion, ever insisting that he had not the hunger feeling.

"Thus they travelled all through two long, cold winter moons, and a part of another, and then, one day Two Bows killed three grouse. Right there he built a fire and told his woman to cook them, and started out after the remainder of the flock. She roasted them nicely, fed the child, ate half the breast of one, and waited for her man to return and eat his share. She waited and waited;

the short day passed; he did not come. When the moon arose she took the child and the remainder of the cooked birds, and followed his trail. Not far, however. She soon found him, lying by a little fire that he had built. The fire was nearly out, and he was dying. She knelt beside him, took his head in her lap. He opened his eyes then, and whispered: 'Press on. Press on. Save the boy. The way is not far now,' and having said, he died. For her sake and that of the boy, he had starved himself to death.

"Weak, and half crazed with grief, the woman did press on. And on the very next day she came to the edge of the buffalo plains and to a camp of Crees, and was saved, and later taken to the camp of her own people. And there, my friends; now you know how terribly unkind is that country of the Crees. Of little account, of poor medicine, is that god of theirs, else he would have given a better hunting ground than those barren swamps and deep mossed plains of the north.

"Kyi! I have said."

11.

A Bad Medicine Hunt

LAST TRAIL. From a painting by
Charles M. Russell, 1904.

*(Courtesy R. W. Norton Art Gallery,
Shreveport, Louisiana)*

A Bad Medicine Hunt

January, 1878, in northern Montana was a month of chinooks. The warm weather enabled Jackson, and Apsi and me to skin the several hundred wolves that had so long lain frozen around our strychnined baits, and Apsi's mother and sister were kept busy fleshing, and pegging the hides out to dry. In every direction from the Blackfeet camp on Cow Creek the plains were covered with buffalo—and antelope as well, so we all remained right there instead of moving down to the Missouri, as the chiefs had intended to do earlier in the season. All the hunters agreed that never in their lives had they anywhere seen the game more plentiful, and had anyone told them that in five years from that time the last of the buffalo would be exterminated they would not have believed it. None of us whites, even, at that time realized that the buffalo days were drawing to an end.

On the evening of January 28, according to my old notebook, Jackson and I were guests in Apsi's lodge. He had invited us to a little feast, and his mother and sister had cooked for us some buffalo boss ribs, some flour cakes fried in marrow grease, some

Manuscript in the Special Collections Library, Montana State University, Bozeman.

servis berries and a pot of tea. The meat was not fat and Apsi made complaint about it.

"Well, then, why don't you kill some fat meat?" his mother answered. "I am not the hunter, you know. Myself, I have for a long time been wanting some fat bighorn meat. It would be nice for a change from buffalo and antelope meat."

"Oh, yes, brother," his sister chimed in, "do kill a fat bighorn for us."

Apsi made a face at her: "Listen to that," he said. "They ask me to take the time to hunt bighorn when we have all we can do to look after our wolf baits.

"But what is one day—or two days?" I put in. "I too would like some bighorn meat. Let's go kill one or two of the animals."

"I'm willing," said Jackson. "Of course the old males are poor now, but a two year old male, or a female will make fine eating."

After some further talk it was agreed that we would go on a bighorn hunt the next day. There were some of the animals on the bare tops of the nearby Little Rockies, but as more or less of the hunters of the camp went up that way every day, we decided to go down to the breaks of the Missouri below the mouth of Cow Creek, where the game was still more plentiful, and undisturbed.

We rode out from camp quite early the next morning, taking with us two pack horses, some bedding, and a little food, and a pot for making tea. Our route was straight down the valley of Cow Creek, on the trail the Nez Perces had followed a few months before. It was actually a wagon road. In low water time the steamboats could only ascend the river as far as Cow Island, and from there their freight was hauled on to Fort Benton with bull— and mule trains. On our way down this day we passed the remains of Joe Pickett's bull train, destroyed by the Nez Perces. On the day they had fled from the river, attempting to get to the Canadian line before the soldiers could overtake them, the advance guard of the tribe had sighted this train, slowly wending its way along the dusty road, and swooped down upon it. Seeing the crowd coming, Pickett and his bullwhackers had mounted their ponies and fled. Nor were they pursued. From a far high point they watched the Indians slaughter the bulls as, fast bound in yokes and chains, they struggled to free themselves and escape. Every last one of them had been quickly killed for food for the on-coming rush of women and children, and then the warriors had tumbled the loads out of the nine wagons, broken open boxes and bales and taken such of the provisions and dry goods as they wanted. Pressed as they were for time, the young men in the party could not help having some sport in the looting of the train. Taking the end of a bolt of white goods, or bright patterned calico or gingham in hand, they would ride out full speed from the wagons, unrolling the bolt as they went and leaving the thirty or forty yards of cloth strung along on the tops of the sagebrush. Lastly, the wagons and piles of freight had been set on fire. What we now saw was bent and twisted wagon tires and irons, and charred bits of wood. Jackson said that Col. Ilges and his Fort Benton soldiery and citizens, hot upon the trail of the Indians, had here come upon Joe Pickett, sitting near the wreck of his train and crying. Crying like a child, big six footer that he was, but more from anger, than from sorrow for the loss of all he had. He later put in a depreda-tion claim for twelve thousand dollars against the Nez Perces, and the Government paid it years afterward.

We went on down to the Missouri at the mouth of Cow Creek, and then taking to the ice, which was mushy on top and good footing for the horses, we passed Cow Island and made camp in the bottom just below it on the north side. A considerable grove of cottonwoods afforded good shelter for us, and there was fair feed out on the flat for the horses. A large herd of buffalo ran out of the bottom when we entered it, crossing to the south side of the river, and in the timber we raised a number of whitetail deer, Jackson killing one of them, a dry doe, and fat. As the last rays of the setting sun painted yellow the tops of the black rock buttes and cliffs overlooking the bottom, we saw upon one of them a small band of bighorn, sharply outlined against the blue sky background. The sight augured well for the morrow: "Perhaps we

165

can kill what we want early in the morning, and get home before night," said Apsi.

"We sat late around the camp fire, talking, and roasting and eating ribs of the deer, and, the mild chinook wind continuing, slept warm under our none too plenty coverings. Apsi had the fire going again before daylight, and after a tasty meal of meat and tea we set out on foot for the badlands. The sun was just rising as we passed out of the timber and re-picketed our horses. Just beyond them four or five mule deer were travelling single file back to the breaks for the day, and at the lower end of the bottom were a dozen or more elk and several buffalo. Game of all kinds was, indeed, plentiful on the upper Missouri in those days. In the summer time Cow Island and vicinity was a notable place for grizzlies. The animals seemed to have a regular runway on Cow Creek along which they travelled from the Bear Paw and Little Rockies to the river, and back. An old American Fur Company man, Henry Kennerly, once told me that one autumn morning, while guarding some freight at the mouth of Cow Creek, he counted nineteen grizzlies here and there in the bottom. He was afraid of them, he said, and took turns with the two men with him in keeping a fire going all night long.

We separated after moving the horses, Jackson heading for the breaks at the upper end of the bottom, Apsi for those at its lower end, while I took a middle course. Soon after leaving the flat I lost sight of them both.

It was rough country that I soon got into, as bad as any I ever tackled in the Rocky Mountains. Here and there were treacherous trap rock cliffs to scale, and some of them were unclimbable. There was nothing to do then but to turn to the right or left, slide into wash after wash and climb their steep sides, until I could find a break in the wall. Where there was no rock the footing was bad. The badland, volcanic ash earth was crusted on top, and soft and powdery for all of six inches beneath the crust, and before I had gone a mile in it my steps began to lag. A plainsman is never much of a walker. Accustomed to going everywhere on horseback, when once set afoot he requires days of practice to make even an ordinary tramp in the hills.

It was mid-forenoon when, wet with perspiration and just about fagged out I came to the foot of a cliff well up toward the summit of the breaks, or, in other words, the level of the plain. I had passed many bighorn signs, single tracks and trails of bands of them, old and fresh, and here under this cliff was a hard beaten runway of the animals, with, above and below it, oval, pawed out depressions in the ash-earth where they had lain down to rest and sleep. I crossed the trail and sat down with my back to the cliff, also to rest, and had no sooner lightly leaned against it than rectangular pieces of the rock came tumbling all around me. I looked around and saw that I had broken down the walled up entrance to a small cave six or seven feet long, about three feet high and five feet deep. On the floor of it lay stretched out full length a human skeleton. I quietly laid down my rifle and crawled inside to examine it.

Judging by the inch or so of gray, powdery world dust on the cave floor and the coating of it on the bones, the grim remains must have lain there a long, long time; for several centuries, perhaps. It was so old that some of the ribs had fallen from place; and when I handled them they crumbled. I blew the dust from the skull, and found in the top of it a jagged hole. Of clothing, or of weapons or implements of any description there was not the least sign, but I thought that there might be something covered by the dust and I began to scrape it out with a straight edged piece of rock. Clouds of it arose and well nigh choked me, but I kept on scraping, removing bones and all, and presently uncovered a yellow flint knife about five inches in length, which had been deposited on the outer side of the remains, close to the hip. On the inner side, close to the shoulder, were sixteen black obsidian arrow points about three-quarters of an inch in length, very narrow and rounding, and slightly barbed. They had lain close together the points all one way, toward the head of the remains, and must have been attached to shafts when deposited there, but

167

so very long ago had that been that nothing remained of the wood except yellowish streaks of dust in the gray world dust covering every part of the floor. I laid the points and the knife on the ground outside the cave, and clearing the dust out of my eyes and nose, sat down to examine them. I had seen arrow points which the Blackfeet claimed had been made by their ancestors, and by the Crows, who, in historic times, about 1743–45, had been driven by the Blackfeet from the Missouri and its tributaries south to the Yellowstone, and I was satisfied that these had been manufactured by neither tribe.

I sat there a long time, examining the ancient weapons and picturing in my mind the life and times of their long dead owner. Could I only know who he was, I kept saying, what light it would throw on the migrations of the tribes of the country in far back pre-historic times. And I may as well state here that I have since found no arrow points like those I brought to light that day, except in a cave in the Superstition Mountains, Arizona, in which Apache Indians had deposited their dead; this proven by the peculiarly woven and designed baskets found with the remains. The Apaches, and the Navajos as well, are of Athabaskan stock, which had its origin in the region we call Alaska, and British Columbia. Did these people in their migration southward tarry for a time in what later became Crow, and then Blackfoot territory? I wonder.

My musings were broken by a shot, and then another, not far east of me, and a little higher than my position. I stuffed the arrow points and knife into a coat pocket and picked up my rifle and listened. Apsi, of course, had done the shooting and I was sure that he had killed, else why the second shot so long after the first one? I was about to arise and work over his way when I heard the thud! thud! thud! of jumping feet and an instant later a dozen and more bighorn came flying toward me along the trail by which I sat. A big ewe led the band. I blatted loudly and she stopped short, the others crowding close behind her, and then I fired at her brisket, well up, and with a tremendous leap she pitched out off the trail, struggled to regain her feet, and rolled on down the steep to the foot of a boulder and lay still. The rest whirled and tore back the way they had come. I did not fire again. The ewe was all the meat I cared to handle. I soon had her dressed and ready to drag down to the edge of the bottom.

I had not gone far with my quarry, dragging it down slopes and tumbling it over cliffs, when I saw Apsi coming down the next slope to the east, and he too had a bighorn in tow. We signalled to one another, and a little later came together in the bottom of a deep coulee into which both ridges merged. Just below was another cliff, and we dragged the animals to the edge of that and sat down. He had killed his meat, a fine two year old ram, from the band out of which I had later picked the ewe; and as I surmised, had at first crippled it, and finished it with a second shot.

The hunt all explained, I then told of my discovery of the burial cave, and produced the flint knife and handful of arrowheads: "And here they are," I concluded, "the weapons of that ancient man."

At sight of them Apsi sprang away from me: "Take them back to the place and leave them there," he cried, and in his voice was real terror. "You know well enough that robbing the dead is about the most dangerous thing one can do; it never fails to bring bad luck; death even. Do you suppose the ghost of that ancient one will not take revenge for what you have done?"

"If he does, I will be the one to suffer—not you," I answered. "But I shall not suffer, never yet was a white person who saw a ghost, or was ever troubled by one."

"Oh, I know, I know," he cried, his face dark with misery, his hands tight gripped together. "You and your kind do not see the ghosts because you have no medicine and are blind to them. All the same, ghosts are; and they do to you just what they do to us: they steal to your couch in the night, and tap you with their unseen, unfelt hands, and give you dreadful sickness. They give you bad luck in many ways, especially if they be the ghosts of enemies. But, you, you whites, you can not see, you do not believe, and lay

169

your troubles to other causes. Oh, my brother. Take back the things, or, at least, drop them here." And with that he pushed his ram over the edge of the cliff, and descended somewhat to the right of it where the wall was broken down. I did likewise and soon overtook him: "Did you throw them away?" he asked.

"Apsi, brother, I just can't do that," I answered, and explained to him as well as I could that I wanted to send the things to a great house—the Smithsonian Institution—near the Great Father's house, where were rooms full of ancient weapons, tools, pottery, and the like, which wise white men were ever collecting and studying in order to learn something about the peoples who made them. But it was as though he had not heard. He neither answered nor looked at me, and very soberly started on down the slope.

"But many of the Blackfeet have these ancient stone knives and arrow heads, and do not fear them," I said, when we again stopped to rest.

"Ha! That is different. Those that they keep came not from graves. They have been handed down from father to son ever since they were made in the very long ago," he explained, and would say no more. Nor did he again ask me to throw away the knife and points, but the look that he gave me was intensely reproachful.

It was long past noon when we reached the foot of the slope with our bighorns. The long drag had pretty well denuded them of hair, especially along the back and thighs, but the hides were not damaged and I was glad of that as I wanted to tan them for a shirt. Bighorn leather—or so called buckskin, is the best of all for that purpose, as it is very light and of even quality, the neck part being very little thicker than the flanks.

After another short rest we left the animals there at the foot of the breaks and started across the bottom toward camp, wending our way among clumps of sagebrush and greasewood higher than our heads. This growth extended only half way from the river and timber, the rest of the flat being fine grass land. We presently came to the edge of the sage belt and Apsi, in the lead, stopped short: "The horses. They are gone," he exclaimed.

170

Sure enough they were gone. Only a short time before, as we neared the approaching slope, they had been in sight and quietly feeding. I suggested that Jackson had probably come in ahead of us and driven them to water: "That is possible, but we will just wait here and see if it is so," he said, and we drew back into cover of the brush.

We must have stood there all of half an hour, waiting to see the horses brought out of the timber. They did not come, and Apsi said that it was a sure thing that a war party had taken them. I was still of the opinion that Jackson had them, had them in the camp and all saddled, awaiting our arrival. But my partner shook his head: "No, Sik-si-kai-kwan is not there, else he would be cooking; we would see smoke," said he. "Anyhow, we must take no chances. The one thing for us to do is to sneak up through this brush to the upper end of the bottom, and then down through the timber until we can see our camping place—and whatever may be there. "But, oh, my brother, be wise. Take my words: for my sake, now, before we start, throw away those things that you have there in your pocket."

There was no resisting that appeal. Much as I hated to do so I took out the flint knife and the arrow points and tossed them down at the foot of a big sage; and as they clinked together on the ground Apsi straightened his shoulders with a shrug, as though he were casting off a heavy burden, and a bright smile lit up his face. He started on, and I, following, tossed my handkerchief into the bush to mark the place where my relics lay, and otherwise well marked the place. I had no mind to lose them; at some future time I would recover them. Apsi did not see me throw the rag.

We were not long travelling up the bottom to the river, where point of grove and belt of sagebrush met. There we slowed up and very slowly and cautiously started down through the timber. I still believed that we were doing all this circuitous sneaking and spying needlessly, that Jackson was in camp with the horses, when, not seventy-five yards ahead of us, a gun loudly boomed, a puff of smoke burst from a clump of willows, and with a low cry

171

of pain Apsi dropped his rifle, and reeled, and swung half around, clapping his right hand to his left shoulder. As he did so another shot was fired somewhat to the right of the first one and a bullet spatted into a tree behind which I was dodging. I saw the smoke from that gun also, and, more dimly, the man behind it, partially screened by willows. Once, twice, three times I turned my '73 Winchester loose at him as fast as I could work lever and trigger, and that was pretty fast. At the first shot he sprang from the willows and ran toward the larger and thicker clump from which his comrade had fired at Apsi. My second shot also went wild—I was terribly surprised and excited by the suddenness of the attack —but when the third cartridge slipped from the magazine into the barrel I had somewhat recovered control of my nerves, and when I pulled the trigger the man almost dropped, then straightened up for a couple of jumps, and finally smashed down into the willows he was heading for.

All this happened in a few seconds of time. While I was shooting, Apsi was recovering his rifle and circling around to give me free sweep at the enemy: "Ha! You hit him that time," he cried, as he passed me, "come on, there are more of them, our only chance is to make a stand on the island."

By the way he ran I knew that he was not badly hurt. And how he did sprint up to the end of the bottom, and up the ice on the river to the lower point of Cow Island. A half dozen shots were fired at us before we reached the thick willows, but all went wild. Once in the shelter of the brush, we turned and looked back: not one of our pursuers was in sight; but we well knew that they were lying somewhere along the bank of the shore from which we had come, and were trying to plan some way to safely overcome us and lift our scalps.

"How badly are you hurt?" I asked.

"Oh, it is nothing," Apsi bravely answered, and pulled his shirt out from the top of his shoulder. Between the point of it and the neck was a deep gash in the flesh, and the collar bone was broken. Some blood was trickling from the wound. I made him go to the far side of the point, where water was running on the ice, and wash it while I stood watch. He soon returned, cheerful as ever despite the pain and the fact that he could not use his left arm, and we began to discuss the predicament we were in. The enemy was, of course, a war party of Assiniboines. No other tribe made a practice of going on raids in the wintertime; and no other warriors of the wide plains were anywhere near as expert as they in sneaking around and taking their intended victims unawares. We dreaded the coming night.

And what of Jackson. Where was he? Would he come heedlessly down to the bottom and across it to camp, and fall into their hands? There was a chance that he wouldn't. Some of the enemy would be waiting there for him: there were three riding saddles and two pack saddles, and five horses in our outfit, and by that they would know that there were three in our party. But there was the chance from a point somewhere up in the breaks Jackson had heard the firing in the bottom and seen the enemy pursuing us. How we hugged that hope, for we could in no way aid him, in no way appraise him of what lay concealed in the apparently deserted bottom.

"Brother, I see one possible way for us to get away from the enemy," Apsi suddenly exclaimed. "Farther up, under the shelter of the grove at the upper end of the island, we may be able to reach the south shore without being seen. If we succeed we can work our way up the river to a point away above Cow Creek and then cross and strike out for home."

"Let's try it, let's try it," said I, and we fairly tore our way through willows up into the none too long grove. From there we backed out onto the ice, keeping the grove between us and the whole length of the bottom below, and on across the narrow south channel to the shore. There we halted in the brush for a few minutes, and seeing no one in pursuit, went on. By three o'clock we were again on the north side of the river, and at dusk walked into the Cow Creek trail certain that no one was following us. At midnight Apsi declared that he could go no farther, so weak was

173

he from loss of blood and pain. But he insisted that I should go on and arouse the camp, and I did so.

I don't know how I ever accomplished it, but I got within five miles of home without ever stopping; and there, as day was breaking, I met Jackson with about a hundred Blackfeet riding like mad to our relief. From the top of the breaks he had seen us running for the island, seen the Assiniboines shooting at us, and at once started out for help. I told them where Apsi was, and one of the party agreed to give him a lift home. Another turned back right there with me and I was soon home. Apsi came in at noon and Kipp dressed and bandaged his wound and shoulder. Then we slept, never stirring until the next morning. The shouts and victory songs of the returning party aroused us and we hurried out to see what they brought. They had every one of our horses, and the scalp of every one of the Assiniboines, who, the day before, had come so near getting our hair.

But we lost our fine bighorn meat. The wolves got it. Some weeks after, I recovered the flint knife and the arrow points—only to lose them in a flood the following summer. I did not tell Apsi about it. Apsi always insisted that if I had not thrown them away when I did, we would never have made our escape from the enemy.

12.

Laugher, The Story of a Tame Wolf

COVERING THE TRAIL. From a
painting by Charles M. Russell,
1906.

*(Courtesy R. W. Norton Art Gallery,
Shreveport, Louisiana)*

Laugher, The Story of a Tame Wolf

"When I was a young man my close friend was Nitaina," said old Red Eagle, as we sat around his lodge fire in the big camp on Cow Creek one evening in February, '78. I remembered Nitaina: Lone Chief, a tall, straight, fine featured, quiet and reserved old man. Only the winter before his shadow had gone forth to the Sand Hills, unhappy abode of the Blackfeet dead.

"Nitaina was of my own clan, the Small Robes," Red Eagle continued. "We were born at about the same time, grew up together, and always where one of us was, there was the other. Together was joined a party on our first war trail and were both successful, returning home each with a scalp, and some horses. The raid had been against the Assiniboines, away down on Milk River.

"In green grass time of the summer following the summer of this raid, there came a heavy rain that continued for five or six days and made rivers of small streams, and lakes in every depression of the plains. The whole country was under water; the roar of the floods was like steady and distant thunder. The medicine men had been praying for rain, that the berries might be

Manuscript in the Special Collections Library, Montana State University, Bozeman.

plentiful, and large and sugary. They now prayed for the rain to cease; so furious was the storm the men could not hunt. The horses had disappeared and there was no track of them. The camp ran out of meat and began to starve.

"I believe that it was the sixth night of the storm when the clouds broke away and we once more saw night light and her children in the clear sky. Everyone rejoiced at the sight of them. The hunters prepared to scatter out from camp at daybreak. Nitaina and I started before that time and were quite a long distance out when the sun came up. The long coulees were still running bank full but we did not mind that, and plunged across them, holding our guns and ammunition high above our heads to keep them dry. The storm had been from the east; we travelled west, and before midday found our horses, and many other bands belonging to the camp. We each of us roped a horse to ride, and arranged with an old man who had followed us to drive our bands home, we to go on and hunt and give him a share of whatever we might kill.

"Away out on the plain north from where we found the horses were many buffalo. We rode nearly to them, then made a sneak to the nearest of the bands and each killed an animal. It did not take us long to make double pouches of the hides, throw them across our horses' backs and fill them with meat, and then climbing on top of them we started home.

"We presently came to the edge of a very wide, long lake of rain water. The bottom of it was very soft and bad footing for the horses, but, rather than make a big circle around, we rode straight into it. Ahead, away out in the middle, was a small rise of ground, an island, not more than the width of three hands above the water, and on it sat two wolves watching us. As we neared them they became uneasy; they would walk and trot around and around the shore, go to the center of the grassy spot and lower their heads, and then, after a long look at us, trot around again. 'They have some young ones there. Let us kill them,' I proposed, and Nitaina nodded his head in assent.

"The old wolf and his wife did not leave the island until we were quite near it, and then they splashed only a little way out in the water, and stopped and howled. We could have killed them, but powder and balls were scarce, and only to be used for killing meat; and anyhow, at that season their hides were worthless. Splashing along through the lake and often almost miring down, the horses finally brought us to the island; and there, in the center of it, at the edge of a big, water filled hole, lay close to the ground and trembling a lone wolf pup. A little, fuzzy, fluffy tailed, weak eyed thing. And in the water, right in front of its black little nose, floated several of its drowned brothers and sisters: 'Oh, how pitiful. What a poor, scared, shivering little one it is,' Nitaina cried. 'We can't kill it, can we!'

" 'No, we can't,' I agreed. 'See how it trembles; how it looks at us and turns its head away. Young as it is it understands its father's and mother's cries. It knows that it is in danger.'

" 'I am going to take it,' Nitaina told me, 'take it home and feed it and make it grow fast. It may perhaps become a useful companion to us.'

"I made no objection and he jumped from his horse and taking the little thing by the neck, lifted it into his arms. It did not offer to bite. It trembled more than ever, and tried to hide its head between my friend's left arm, and body. It was a male pup.

"We rode on and the old wolves circled around and back to the island and howled and howled. All their children but one had drowned, and now that one was taken from them. They felt very sad, the father as well as the mother. Wolves are not like dogs, you know. A dog father knows not his own children. A wolf marries and he and his wife live always together until death. When children come he hunts for them, and brings food for them, and watches over them faithfully while the mother goes out to hunt and run around, and keep up her strength. Ah, they are wise, true hearted animals, the big wolves of the plains. And what hunters they are; they never suffer from want of food.

"We brought the wolf pup into camp and to Nitaina's lodge, and

181

set it down by the side of a big, old dog that herself had three pups of about its age; and strangely enough, she began to lick it and nurse it just as though it was one of her own ones. Other dogs around, getting the wolf scent, came mad and growling to kill it. She rushed at them so savagely, bit them so hard, that they all ran howling away. Nitaina's mother cut some meat into small pieces and held them before the wolf pup in the palm of her hand; it ate them quickly, every piece. It was hungry for meat and ate it every day for a long time before the dog pups of its age would touch it, and it grew very fast; very much faster than the others.

"Nitaina made a great pet of the wolf pup and it soon learned to love him, and follow him around wherever he went in camp. He named it Laugher, because it was fond of standing up and putting its paws on his shoulders and shaping its lips into a laugh, just as a person does when pleased. In many ways it was like a dog. It would wag its tail when pleased, and it was very playful; but unlike a dog, it did not bark, or, rather howl, when playing. At night it would stand outside the lodge and listen to its own kind howling away out on the plain, and answer them, and every little while run into the lodge to Nitaina and look up in his face and whine, as though it wanted its master to go with it out to those howling critters. It seemed to be afraid to go alone away from camp. Then Nitaina would say: 'No, Laugher, no. We can't go out there, lie down,' and the wolf would turn around and around and drop down on the couch beside him.

"Until Laugher was about ten moons of age he was afraid of the camp dogs and always ran to his master or his lodge when they took after him. They all hated him, all the males. The females liked him—and the young ones often played with him. But when he was about grown he one day fought—and tore a big dog so that it died, and after that he had no fear of all in camp. They could have killed him, would have done so but for one thing: these dogs ran in cliques. That is, the dogs belonging to one lodge were all friends, and partners in everything, but they were always at war with the dogs of every other lodge. Well, those of a certain lodge would get together and, watching their chance, fall upon Laugher; but the fight would no more than start than other bands would rush in and it would be dog against dog instead of all against wolf, and Laugher could outfight any one dog, or any two or three of them very quickly. He did not bite, and hang on; he had very long, sharp teeth, and was a slasher instead of a biter, and he never stood still. He would rush at an enemy's flank and make one snap as he passed, and often rip its whole side open.

"And another thing. While Laugher loved Nitaina and his mother, he was not friendly to anyone else, and many people he really hated, always ruffing forward his back hair and showing his teeth when they came near. He didn't do this to me, who was with his master so constantly, and would even take meat I offered him. On the other hand he showed not the least liking for me, and never would obey any order I gave him.

"During that first winter of Laugher's life Nitaina taught him many things. He taught him to help round up and drive our horse herd; to chase and pull down wounded game; to lead a horse by its rope; to carry a pack, and to sneak along behind us when we were approaching game. By the time green grass came he was more wise, more useful than any dog in the whole camp.

"Green grass time is war time. Nitaina and I decided to join a big party that was going on a raid against the Spotted Horses People,* but when the leader of it heard that Laugher was going with us, he said that we could not join unless the wolf was left at home.

"Now, if Laugher had been a dog, the leader of the party would have been right enough in his objection. About the worst thing a war party could do would be to have with it one of the animals, for dogs would be the same as though they climbed boldly to the top of every hill and shouted: 'Here we are. We have come into your country to fight you, and raid your herds.'

"Nitaina explained to the chief that Laugher was different; that he would in many ways be a help instead of a hindrance. That the

* The Cheyennes.

enemy, seeing him, would think nothing of it for wolves are everywhere. But still the chief objected, saying that he felt that the animal was bad medicine; and that made us somewhat angry: 'Oh, very well, we don't have to go with you,' Nitaina told him, and we didn't. We got ready and started out on our own war trail, Laugher, with head and tail taking up the lead. We went east, bound for the country of the Sioux.

"At this time our people were encamped on the Willows Around bottom of the Maria's River.[1] We followed the stream down to where it joins the Missouri, and there cut across the plains for the western end of the Bear Paw Mountains, travelling only at night. We were one night, and part of another from the river to the pines on top of the westernmost butte of the range. Night Light was shining bright in the sky, there was a cool wind, and so we made fast time. On the second night, as we approached the foot of the butte, Laugher suddenly stopped and sniffed the wind, and then ran up it with long, swift leaps, chased something that we could dimly see running, and knocked it to the ground. We went to the place as quickly as we could and found that he had caught and killed a young antelope. It was his first kill on the trip, and his very first one of unwounded game, and he was proud of what he had done. When we got to him he wagged his tail, jumped up against Nitaina and laughed, ran back to the antelope and licked its torn open neck, and then jumped again to his master, putting his forepaws on his shoulders and licking his face, as much as to say: 'Just see what I have done. I can kill meat for you.'

"We were glad that he caught the antelope. We were out of meat and did not like to fire a gun and so make known our whereabouts to any war party prowling in the country. And, besides, we had very little powder and ball. Life itself might depend upon a single charge of it. We dressed the little thing and packed it along, taking turns carrying it. When we reached timber

[1] Willows Around (Willow Rounds), two miles below the mouth of the Two Medicine River, was a favorite Piegan winter campsite.

on top of the mountain we hurried to build a little war house to hide a fire by which to cook the meat, and by the time we had finished eating the day broke. We then went out on a rock faced point, or cliff, and sat down to have a good look at the country between us and the Missouri River to the west. Nowhere was any smoke rising, nor game running—the plains were covered with buffalo, so we concluded that neither camp nor war party was anywhere out there, and moved across the butte for a look at the plains to the north of it. Conditions there were also peaceful, so we laid down for a sleep, Laugher stretching out beside his master.

"We were both light sleepers. Every little while one or the other of us would awake, and sit up and look out over the plains and all around, and then sleep again. So we passed the day until late afternoon, and would have slept longer had not Laugher aroused us by growling, and then rushing away from us down the timbered slope to the east of where we lay. We sprang up gun in hand, expecting to find enemies approaching, but saw instead a big grizzly bear and her two cubs, about fifty steps away. She had been pawing a rotten log, and was now sitting straight up watching Laugher, standing quite close to her and trying to get her scent. This was the first bear he had ever seen and he did not know what to make of it.

"We were not glad to see that grizzly. Let me explain: in those days the hunters always let them alone, unless mounted on a good, swift horse and in open country, for many had been killed by them. As you know, they are very hard to kill and will often keep coming and fighting long after a ball has torn through their lungs, or other vital parts. Also, some time was required to reload one of those old flintlock guns, and a wounded grizzly was certain to get the hunter before he could fire another shot. So it was that we stood perfectly still, hoping that she would soon go away. Apparently she had not noticed us. She kept staring at Laugher, and once in a while turned her head to look at the cubs, pawing and nosing the ground twenty or thirty steps off to the right.

Laugher did not see these—his eyes were all for the old one, until one of them bit the other and it squalled. Then he turned and looked at them, and sprang toward the spot where they quarreled. The wind, what little there was, was from the south, and so he had not caught the scent of the bears, nor had the old mother caught our scent. But when he was passing to the north of her and was almost to the cubs, he stopped short; there it came to him strong, the rank sickening bear odor, and it frightened him. He whirled around and started straight back toward us, and the old bear started after him. I was about to fire at her when Nitaina cried out to me: 'Don't shoot. Run. Climb a tree.'

"Just back of us were some low branching young pines. Thither we ran, and each climbed into a tree, just as Laugher caught up with his master, and tried to climb after him. I was obliged to drop my gun in order to reach the nearest branch of my tree, and safety. Nitaina's tree had lower branches; he carried his gun with him; but suddenly a branch broke from his weight and he tumbled to the ground just as the bear was coming under it. In his fall he struck Laugher, and he bounced out of the way, and the bear made a swipe at him and missed, and continued to chase him, passing with a big leap straight past Nataina there at the foot of the tree. When my partner tumbled to the ground my heart had almost stopped beating from fear for him there, right in front of the mad bear. But she no sooner passed him than he was on his feet and again climbing, and the expression of his face was so funny, his eyes were so big and wild as he tore his way up from branch to branch far higher than he needed to go, that my fear suddenly turned to laughter. Never had I seen a funnier sight than that. I laughed until I almost cried, and became so weak from it that I nearly fell out of my own tree. From a height away above me Nitaina looked down: 'Crazy one, you needn't laugh; you yourself would have done some quick climbing had you been in my place,' he said.

"The old bear chased Laugher around and around our trees for some time, he easily keeping out of her reach. She was very fat and soon began to froth at the mouth; but she was so angry that she kept after him until her wind gave out; then she left him and went back to her cubs, and with them on down the mountain and out of sight. We then slid to the ground, picked up our guns and went the other way, out to the south side of the butte. The country was still quiet. We descended the slope to a spring, drank, and ate the remains of the antelope meat, and went on.

"We went the length of the Bear Paw range, crossed the gap in which this Middle Creek heads, and went on down the length of the Wolf Mountains, out there, now keeping high up and travelling in the day time. On our last day on these in places bare, and in other places timbered peaks, we were crossing a rounding, bare rock butte when Laugher, in the lead, suddenly stopped and put his nose down to the rock and sniffed, and ruffed up his long hair on neck and shoulders; and then he looked at us and whined, and sniffed the rock again. Said Nitaina: 'Either a war party or a bear has recently passed that place. Let's be very careful how we show ourselves.'

"We crept on to where Laugher awaited us but of course could find no tracks of anything on the hard rocks. Nitaina patted Laugher on the back: 'Go on,' he told him, 'go on, find out what it is.'

"We were a little south and somewhat below the summit of the butte. Laugher started straight toward the summit, walking slowly and smelling the rock, and working his ears, often looking back at us creeping after him. He reached the top of the butte and stopped. We crept almost to him and little by little raised our heads until we could look down the north side; not a living thing was in sight. But on this north slope heavy pine timber grew well up it, up within shooting distance of where we lay, and looking into it we discovered smoke. Just a little; a thin fog of smoke that did not show above the tree tops; and by that we knew that a war party was there, cooking meat in a war house. The wind just at that time shifted and swirled, and we smelled the smoke; got even the odor of meat on the hot coals. Laugher sat down on his

187

haunches, pointed his nose straight up toward the sky and howled. Nitaina, whispering, scolded him. He paid no attention and howled again, and two men came to the edge of the timber and looked at him. They were Crows. That was certain by the way each of them wore an eagle tail feather at the back of the head. We did not, we dared not move: 'If they come we will kill them and then run,' I whispered.

" 'Yes,' Nitaina answered.

"But they didn't.

"But they did not come out of the timber. After looking at Laugher a short time one of them called out something to the others by the fire. Someone answered him, and he and his comrade turned and went back. They were no sooner out of sight than we drew away from the summit, and then ran down the south slope as fast as we could go, never stopping until we reached the shelter of some cottonwoods along a little stream at the foot of the butte. There we drank much water and rested, and Nitaina hugged Laugher. It had been our intention to go to the top of the butte and take a good long rest and a careful look at the country around. Had it not been for the wolf we would have done so, and right there would have been the end of our trail.

"We remained in the cottonwoods until night, keeping close watch on the bare butte, and two lookouts who had come up on it soon after our flight. Toward sundown they were joined by the rest of the party, twenty and more, and in the dusk we saw them start off to the west along the very way we had come. They were evidently heading for our own Blackfeet country. We had little fear that they would do our people harm: the young men were closely guarding the horse herds of the camp. We took our escape from them as a good sign, and went on.

"In the first light of a morning some days later, we looked out from a patch of brush on the rim of the plain and saw below us in the valley of the Little River, a great Sioux camp. Nowhere around it were there any loose horses; they had all been kept in among the lodges during the night, and now the guards were turning them out to graze. Each band following its leader, some on the run and some hungrily feeding, they scattered up and down the big bottom and up toward the plains: 'It will be useless for us to try to go into the camp and choose the best animals. As soon as those two bands pass us and go out of sight of camp on the plain, let's round them up and go.'

"I agreed with him that that was the only thing to do. As one of the bands passed near us we discovered that one of the animals was a big, fast buffalo runner that had been stolen from Nitaina's father the summer before. That made us happy. We would have it, and many others as payment for the killings the Sioux had made with it during the winter. We waited until both bands had passed out on the plain, and then, uncoiling our lariats, took after them. As we sneaked back out of the brush several early hunters were riding away from the camp: 'They will soon be after us. Hurry,' I called out to Nitaina.

"We had no trouble in catching each of us a good, strong horse, and then making a bridle of the rope, we mounted and herded the two bands into one and headed westward as fast as we could go. Laugher was a big help in this. The horses feared him. He kept running this way and that way behind them, snapping at the heels of the slow ones, and they did their best to keep out of his reach. On and on we went, and before long a couple of riders, then a big bunch of them, came in sight on our trail. A few of them slowly gained on us; we roped fresh horses and went on. There was where we had the advantage. The Sioux had each of them but one mount. We kept changing to fresh ones every little way, and by the time the sun reached the middle we were apparently free from our pursuers. But we took no chances. We rode as fast as we could all that day, and, after a short rest at sundown, all the following night. And after that we kept on day and night, with but more and more frequent short rests, until we again struck the mouth of Bear River.

"We now felt safe from pursuit and prepared for a good rest. Not in the timbered bottom, however. After a good feast of

189

buffalo meat that we had killed, we watered the horses, drove them up on the point of the plain between the two rivers, and picketing two of them laid down. We were to sleep by turns. It was my first watch, and without knowing what I was doing I also fell asleep. I was awakened by a shout from Nitaina: 'Mount! Mount!' he cried. 'See what is coming!'

"I sprang up and saw a number of men running from the breaks of the Missouri toward the horse herd. I ran to my animal, freed the rope and got on him; Nitaina was already astride. Away we went for the herd and started it, the war party now quite close and shooting at us. We didn't fire even a shot at them. We hadn't time. And by good luck we got away from them with the loss of but one horse, killed by a stray bullet. Again it was Laugher who had saved us. He had seen the enemy coming, and had whined, and nosed Nitaina until he awakened. Ha! He was a smart one, that wolf.

"Well, the next evening we rode into camp with our big band raising the dust ahead of us, and so ended that raid, successful only because of Laugher, as I have said.

"And that is all."

"What became of the wolf?" I asked.

"Ha! That is another story," the old man answered. "But not tonight. Go. Go home all of you. It is time to sleep."

13.

The End of Laugher

Apsi and Jackson had not been present the evening Old Red Eagle related the story of Laugher, the tame wolf, how his chum Nitaina had captured it when a little pup, and taught it many things, they at last taking it with them on a raid against the Sioux, on which occasion it twice saved them from the enemy. But while we were skinning some wolves at one of our baits down on Cow Creek I retold the story and they were as anxious as was I to hear more of the life of the truly remarkable animal. To that end Apsi told his mother one evening to prepare a little feast for us, and himself invited Red Eagle to come over and eat and smoke.

"Ha! That is why you invited me here; you want to hear more about the wolf!" the old man exclaimed, after the feast was over and Apsi had lit a big pipe for him.

"Well, you shall hear. I like to tell about the happenings in those long dead days. About the only pleasure old men have, you know, is to live over in memory the stirring times of their youth.

"Let me think. Where did I leave off the other night? Oh, yes. Well, when we came home with the big band of horses we had

Manuscript in the Special Collections Library, Montana State University, Bozeman.

taken from the Sioux, and told what a great help Laugher had been to us, Nitaina's mother fell upon the animal and hugged and kissed him, and so would have my mother have done had she dared. The news spread all through the great camp how Laugher had saved us from the enemy. The war party that had refused to let us go with it because of the wolf, returned home on foot defeated, and with three of their number missing. The leader felt worse than ever when he learned of our success, and offered to start right out again with us. A great many warriors, old and young, wanted us, with Laugher, to go with them on a raid. We refused to do so, and prepared to go, just we two and Laugher, into the country of the Cheyennes. That tribe had a fine breed of horses; most all of them pintos. We wanted some of them. My father had once been to war against the Cheyennes, and gave us directions how to go. Leaving the Missouri at the mouth of the Marias, we were to strike off southeast across the plains to the lower Yellowstone, and from there on to the headwaters of the Little Missouri, or some other stream not far beyond it. Somewhere in that vicinity, he said, we would find the enemy.

"At that time the people were preparing to put up the medicine lodge so we waited to take part in the ceremonies before setting out on our far expedition. On the first day of the lodge we made sacrifices to the sun, partook of the sacred dried tongues, and prayed the great god to have pity and give us long life and happiness, and success in all things, this coming raid in particular. Our mothers and fathers also prayed for us. On the fourth day of the lodge Nitaina and I stood before the people and counted our coups, not many at that time; we were but youths, and had been only twice against the enemy.

"When Nitaina counted his coups Laugher stood beside him. When he finished he called out its name and the wolf raised up and put its forepaws on his shoulders: 'No, no, not that way,' he said, 'turn around so all can see you.' He turned it around, holding it up by its forelegs.

" 'Friends,' he went on, 'Laugher is going to count his coups.

He does not speak our language so I shall be his interpreter. Now, then, listen.' And raising his voice he shouted: 'Laugher. That is me. That is my name. I went on a raid with Nitaina and Red Eagle. On a bare rock butte of the Little Rockies I discovered the trail of the enemy and gave warning, and saved the lives of my two men. Later, I helped them round up and drive off a band of Sioux horses. Still later, while I alone was awake, I saw the enemy running to kill my sleeping men and take the horses, and again I gave warning, and assisted them to escape. There. I have said.'

"Oh, how that great crowd of people shouted, and when he finished, and the waiting drummers whanged their big drums: 'Laugher! Laugher! A chief is Laugher, the wolf,' they cried, and the women longed to pet the animal and dared not. He seemed to sense what was going on. Nitaina released him and he ran around and around, wagging his tail and jumping up time and again to lick his master's face. The three of us soon left the lodge and went home to get ready to start out that evening.

"We left camp at sundown, well outfitted for the long trail. Each of us had six extra pairs of moccasins, and Laugher packed them and our lariats. We had plenty of powder and ball; some extra flints; and our guns were good guns for those days: at the distance of one hundred steps we could usually kill a buffalo or elk or deer the first shot, if it was standing still. No one at that time risked the loss of a charge by shooting at running game. Beside our guns we each carried a bow and arrows in bow case and quiver slung on our backs, these for silent killing of meat, and for use in all ways should anything go wrong with the other weapons.

"In three days time we arrived at the mouth of the Marias, there crossed the Missouri on a raft of driftwood, climbed out of the valley to the plain, and went southeasterly across it to Arrow Creek. The narrow valley of this stream, you remember, is mostly cut cliffed; from its head in the Highwood Mountains to its mouth are only a few places where one can cross it. We struck the rim of the deep cut before daylight one morning, and waited for the sun to drive the darkness away. We took the little pack off from Laugher's back and laid down for a rest. We were very thirsty; the sound of running water down at the foot of the cliffs made us even more thirsty and restless; we could not sleep. Laugher was even more thirsty than we were; he kept going to the edge of the cliff and looking down and whining. If there had been a way for him, he would have gone down to the creek. He was in such distress that he presently began to howl, oh, so sadly. This he did a number of times before light began to rise in the eastern sky.

"As the light grew we noticed three wolves coming toward us, one a very large one, and so old that his hair was almost white. Laugher went trotting out to meet them, and they stopped and watched his approach. The morning wind was from the west: from them to us. They could not smell us. Laugher went close to them, wagging his tail, wiggling his body, showing, puppy-like by all his actions that he was somewhat afraid of them. The smaller of the three advanced to meet him, and he playfully bounded off to one side, circled and ran to the far side of the three, and stopped. At that they all sudenly threw up their heads and nosed the air, went close to him and put their noses to his side, took a smell and then bounded away out on the plain as only frightened wolves can run. Not once did they stop so long as they were in sight. Laugher stood still and watched them go, and then came whining to us and looking very foolish: 'Now, what do you make of that—what think you frightened them?' I asked.

" 'Easily answered: Laugher carries the odor of man in his long, thick hair. Our odor; the odor of his pack, and smoke of campfire. It is no wonder that they ran from him,' Nitaina answered.

"He was right enough and we were glad that it was so. There was little chance of Laugher's brothers becoming friendly to him, and enticing him away from us.

"The canyon and breaks of Arrow Creek was the home of band after band of bighorn; to this day they are there very plentiful. As we descended one of their trails, three big males saw and smelled

us, and ran off to the right along a narrow ledge. Laugher ran
after them—we were carrying his pack down—and pressed them
so closely that the hindmost of the three sprang from the ledge up
on a little shelf just large enough for footing. It was a big leap it
had made; Laugher did not even try to follow; but he stopped
right under and raising up on his hind legs pawed the cliff wall
and whined, looking up at the bighorn and then at us. I handed
Nitaina my gun and got out my bow, and walking right under the
shelf fired an arrow clear to the feathering into the animal's body.
With one big leap it shot straight out over my head, struck another
shelf far below, and went bouncing and rolling clear to the bottom
of the canyon. The fall did not injure the fine, fat meat. We
stopped right there for two days, drying thin sheets of it in the
hot sun, and then went on. We saved that meat for a possible time
of need, and kept killing fresh meat from day to day, as wanted.

"From Arrow Creek to Yellow River [Judith River], from it to
It-Crushed-Them Creek,* and from there to Black Butte, at the
east end of the Judith Mountains, we saw no people, nor any sign
of them; but beyond that, down in the valley of On-The-Far-Side
Bear River,† we found some—and right there came very near
ending our trail. It was still night when we looked down into the
valley from the edge of the plain. Night Light, low in the western
sky, was broken in two and the small part of her in sight did not
enable us to see things at any distance. Great black patches below
were of course groves of cottonwoods, and lighter places were
open, grassy bottoms. We thought to stop right where we were
until daylight; a patch of young quaking aspens offering good
concealment; but thirst, intense thirst, drove us on; the far, low
call of the river drew us to it. We descended the hill and struck
out across the bottom for the lower point of a big grove.

"As we neared it there arose from the upper end of it a sudden

---

* It-Crushed-Them-Creek (Armell's Creek) was so named for some women
digging red paint who were killed by the falling of the high cutbank.
† On-The-Far-Side Bear River (Musselshell River) was so named to dis-
tinguish it from the other Bear River, the Marias River.

thunder of noise and we stopped to listen. It was coming toward us; the ground trembled from the pounding of hundreds of heavy hoofs; dead branches cracked and snapped; leafy branches and brush swayed and swished; a stampeded herd of buffalo was headed our way.

" 'Run! Run! Get behind a tree,' Nitaina cried.

"He had no need to do so; I was already running to shelter as fast as I could go. I passed through the outer brush of the grove; the first trees were very small; there was not time for me to go on to larger growth; I stopped at one not larger than the width of my hand, too small to climb, and pressed against it, Nitaina taking the one next to me on my right; and at that instant came the buffalo, an almost solid mass of them, hundreds of them, smashing past us. One lunged against my tree, struck my right shoulder, and though I was gripping the trunk with both arms and held on, the shock knocked me out to the other side where I was hit again, and so hard that time that I almost lost my hold. The hot, steamy breath of the big animals made me gasp for air. Flying pieces of hoof-spurned wood and earth stung my face. Again and again, now on one side and then on the other an animal brushed against me, and every instant I expected to be knocked from my hold and trampled to death.

"And then the the last of the big herd passed. It went thundering on down the valley. The air cleared and, wiping the dust out of our nostrils, we again breathed freely. Said Nitaina: 'Laugher is gone. Perhaps he is killed—'

" 'Your mouth, close it. Something comes,' I told him.

" 'Yes. Lie down!' he answered, and we threw ourselves flat on the ground. There had been a faint snapping of sticks in the distance; more sticks snapped; nearer and nearer; and then with soft tread came men; many men; one behind another, passing on our left, and very close. In the dim glow of Night Light and her children we could no more than make out their moving forms. One spoke, another answered, and several laughed. Their talk was strange in our ears. They could not see us, lying so near them on the ground, itself as dark as night. They went steadily on with hurrying step and were gone. Once more we breathed freely and our throbbing hearts slowed down. In the distance a wolf howled: 'Ha! There is Laugher. I feared that he had been trampled to death. He did not leave me until a part of the herd had passed,' said Nitaina.

"Said I: 'Our medicine is good; the gods have listened to our prayers; all this that we have safely passed through is a sign that we are to be successful on this long trail.'

" 'Do not boast. Keep on praying—'

"Laugher interrupted him by leaping up and licking his face. He had lost his little pack; our moccasins, lariats, and a part of the dried bighorn meat were gone.

" 'We can make new ropes and kill more meat, but without those moccasins right here we turn back,' said I.

"Nitaina did not answer. We went to the river and drank and drank of the cool water, then crawled into the thick willows lining the shore and laid down and slept until almost midday, when we drank again, and washed ourselves, and ate a little of the dried meat that we carried. I then went up on the rim of the plain and stood watch, and Nitaina hunted for the lost pack. After a long search he found it in thick sagebrush near the point of the grove, and signalled me to return to him. I had seen nothing of the war party that had passed us in the night. The whole country was quiet. At sundown we struck out for the Bull Mountains, a group of low buttes east of the On-The-Far-Side Bear River.

"On and on we went night after night, past the small mountains and across the big plains. Nothing happened; of buffalo and antelope there was no end, but of riders, or people afoot not even a sign. And at last, in the early part of a night, we descended a steep, but short hill, crossed a wide bottom, and drank from the waters of Elk River, or as you whites call it, the Yellowstone. There we camped for the rest of the night, and at daylight, putting our guns and clothing and other things on a couple of dry logs lashed together, we swam and pushed our way to the other shore.

197

"There were no trails, no signs of people in the big flat there, except some fire places of the past winter, rain beaten and grass grown. We climbed to the rim of the plain for a look at the country and saw that we had struck the river far too high up. My father had said for us to cross it midway between its mouth and the mouth of the Crow's Bear River—as you say, Powder River— and right below us was the Crow's Bear River. We crossed the wide point and went down into its valley, and there struck a fresh trail; a big, dusty, fresh trail of many travois and dragging lodge poles, and countless horses. A big camp of people had recently passed there, travelling up the valley. When evening came we followed the trail, hoping that the makers of it were those we sought—the Cheyennes, breeders of the spotted horses.

"In the early morning, just before daylight, Laugher began to whine, and sniff the air, and then leaving us was gone sometime. We didn't know what to think of his actions; we were alarmed; we stopped right there and waited for him and for daylight. When he returned he was quiet enough and laid down beside us in the tall sagebrush. Morning broke and we found ourselves at the edge of a recently deserted camp ground; in more than one of the many lodge fire places the ashes were still warm. We moved quickly through the trampled brush and fresh broken strong smelling sage toward a shelter in a grove, picking up here and there a cast off, worn out moccasin. The porcupine quill embroidery of the tops was of strange design; neither Sioux nor Crow; we were undoubtedly following a Cheyenne trail.

"Two nights later as we were following the big trail, Laugher all at once halted in front of us and howled. We could hear nothing and wondered what disturbed him. Farther on he howled again; our ears were quick to catch the noises of the night but still we could hear nothing except the hooting of an owl over by the river. Somewhat later he howled again, and then we knew that his ears were much more keen than ours; what he had long since heard we now heard: the distant howling of a multitude of dogs; where they were was of course the big camp we were trailing.

"Right there we took to the hills, first filling a couple of buffalo bladders with water, and some time before morning cached ourselves in some thick brush overlooking the bottom in which were the lodges. When the light came we saw about two hundred of them over against a belt of cottonwoods by the river. And horses, they were as plentiful as the grass, and they were pintos mostly. Band after band grazed in the bottom, and on the hills on the far side of the river, and in among the lodges were tethered the choice stock: the valuable stallions and swift buffalo runners: 'Those are the ones we want—the ones we must have,' said Nitaina.

" 'Right you are,' I answered. 'We have come far; only the best of them will pay us for the long trail that we are making.'

"We lay quietly there in the brush all day, sleeping by turns and watching the Cheyennes. Many of the hunters rode out early for the chase but none came near us. In the latter part of the day a lot of young men held a war dance. They were fine dancers; their drums were loud and deep toned; their singing was fine. But it made Laugher uneasy; Nitaina was obliged more than once to slap his ears to keep him from howling.

"Toward evening we made our plan to raid the camp. We would wait until the last lodge fire died out and then sneak in among the tethered horses and lead out one or two at a time until each had ten of them. That was the number we decided upon, ten big, swift pintos each. A small grove of cottonwoods at the lower end of the bottom was to be the place where we were to lead, and tie the horses as fast as we obtained them, and there, too, Laugher was to be hobbled until our work was finished: we well knew that it would never do to allow him to get in among the camp dogs.

"Some time after dark we went down to the lower grove. Then, waiting until every lodge was dark, Nitaina tied Laugher's four feet together with a moccasin string and we left him lying there on the ground and whining, and slowly advanced toward the camp: 'Before taking any animals let's go all through it and pick out the very best of them,' I proposed, and Nitaina answered that that was the right thing to do.

"Night Light was not quite strong; she enabled us to see our way some distance ahead. We did not sneak into the camp; we walked naturally in past the outer lodges just as though we belonged there, and so did not arouse the suspicions of the dogs and get them after us. But, once inside, we went more slowly, looking at this horse, and that one, deciding which of the many to take. And all the time we kept a sharp lookout all around for the enemy; someone might come out at any time and discover us. All was quiet enough, however. In several lodges people snored. In another someone talked in his sleep; we prayed that all would sleep until we got away with what we wanted.

"We had gone about half way up the length of the camp when some dogs at the lower end began to bark as though they were attacking something. More and more dogs joined them. They all seemed to be coming straight up among the lodges. Their howls and yelps and growlings grew until the noise was deafening, and wakened people began to call out to one another. And then, away ahead of the rush, came Laugher and jumped up against his master. He had gnawed off his hobbling string! Oh, how frightened we were. We ran; at first through a howling mass of dogs that tripped us several times. They passed on, hundreds of them, Laugher leading them out from the lodges and away off across the bottom toward the hills. We ran the other way; into the grove and down it, the shouts of the whole camp of aroused men and women and children ringing in our ears. None followed us, doubted that any of them had discovered us, but still we ran, out from the big grove and down the bottom to the small one from which we had started. There we stopped and watched and listened; there was still some commotion in the camp; one after another the lodges began to glow with the light of freshly kindled fires; but out at the foot of the hills the dogs had given up the chase; there was never one that could overtake a wolf. With occasional yelps they were going back to camp, and presently, panting loudly, Laugher came to us, wagging his tail, jumping around us and whining, proud of what he had done. We were very angry at him; our hearts heavy with our failure of the night; but we agreed that it was useless to whip him, to scold him: he could not know that he had done us wrong. We gathered up our things and went away back down the river, and remained in hiding for three nights.

"People passed down and up the bottom in front of us every day, so we knew that camp had not been moved. On the fourth night we again approached it and stopped in the small grove below. There I remained with Laugher while Nitaina went on, and after a time returned with two horses, I then took my turn and brought back two; and so we worked until we had ten each, the number we had in the first place decided to take, and with that many we were content. We had had no trouble whatever in getting them out of the sleeping camp; that was a good sign for the future. We each mounted an animal, and with Laugher helping, herded the rest up out of the valley and over the plain on a swift run for home. If any of the Cheyennes followed, we never saw them. On the whole way back we saw no enemies, and had no trouble of any kind; and how our people did cheer us when we rode into camp with our band of beautiful pintos.

"And now I come to the end of my story. In the latter part of the following winter Laugher began to absent himself from camp; at first for a day; then for several days; and at last for many days at a time. We knew why he went: his kind were calling him; he was looking for a wife among them, and we could not help it. It was useless to tie him—he would snap ropes in two as fast as they were put on, and to keep him hobbled was too cruel. And then came a day when he came home no more. Later on we saw him one last time. We were hunting, and away out on the plain noticed two wolves sitting on a low butte watching us. As we neared them one came trotting down to meet us, and lo! it was Laugher, oh, so glad to see his master. Nitaina got down off his horse and petted him, then remounted and called him to follow. He sat down and watched us starting on, and whined, and trotted back to the butte and the wife he had found. He jumped around her, wagging his tail, and then started toward us, looking back—by all his actions coaxing her to follow, but she would not move. Again and again he did that, and at last gave up and howled. He loved Nitaina, but he loved his young wife most.

"We had thought in the spring to capture several wolf pups and tame them, and saw that it would be only a waste of time and trouble. The call of kind to kind is stronger than any other love.

14.

The Fatal Sign

OFFERING TO THE SUN GODS.
Bronze by Charles M. Russell,
1902.

*(Courtesy R. W. Norton Art Gallery,
Shreveport, Louisiana)*

The Fatal Sign

The sun sank behind the snow-capped peaks of the great mountains, and as the shadows of night deepened in the valley where the long camp was pitched, more fuel was piled on the blazing lodge fires, suffusing the interiors of the cone-shaped skin structure with a cheerful, ruddy glow. There was song and laughter and jesting talk throughout the length and breadth of the camp this night, for the people were happy; game had been found in great abundance, buffalo and antelope on the prairie, deer and elk in the foothills, and the hunters had killed a large number of the fat animals. No wonder, then, that the men smoked, and feasted, and laughed together, consuming great quantities of rib meat and rich tongues, which their patient women broiled for them over the blazing hot coals.

Of all the great warriors and hunters, Raven's Voice was alone unhappy. He sat on his couch at the back of the lodge and neither spoke, nor touched the food which had been placed before him. His wives and children, grouped on the opposite side of the fire, seemed to share the mood which possessed him; their faces were very solemn and they spoke but little, and then in the lowest of

Published in the *Great Falls Tribune* (August 24, 1902).

205

tones. Raven's Voice had good cause for not joining in the gaiety which pervaded the camp this night. Mighty hunter as he was, for three consecutive days he had gone forth on the chase, and had failed to kill a single head of game. Shot after shot he had fired at buffalo, elk, and deer, but had drawn no blood, had not even touched a hair of the quarry. Such an experience, as he and everyone else well knew, was a sign, a warning, that some dread misfortune was soon to befall him, or those dear to him; it had proved true time and again. There was the case of Lone Chief, for instance. One day he fired sixteen shots at buffalo, missing every time. Soon afterward his son was killed by the Crows. Only the previous winter Heavy Breast had missed everything he shot at for a couple of days, then became sick, took to his bed, and died. Yes, this was a sure sign of death's approach, discovered long since by the ancient people and handed down in the traditions of the tribe for untold generations to the present day. At first Raven's Voice had thought that his ill-luck was due to the fault of his rifle, but, tested at a mark, it sped the bullets as accurately as ever, so there was no doubt but what the evil spirits had chosen him or his for their victim. This evening he looked sorrowfully at his wives and the little children hushed in their arms. Could it be that one of them was to be taken from him? He groaned at the thought and prayed the sun to protect them. "If misfortune must come," he cried, "let it fall upon me. Shield my family, oh Ruler of the Day, Life of the World."

"Friend," he said to the white man who was living in his lodge and trading for the tribe's robes and furs, "Friend, you white skins are very wise; but we, even the oldest of us, are simple children; out of your wisdom surely you can devise some way to avert this calamity which threatens me?"

"I told you," I replied, "that my people do not believe in signs and omens, in ghosts, spirits good or bad, nor in dreams. Your nerves are out of order, and therefore you have failed to take a steady aim when shooting. In a day or two you will hunt as successfully as ever, and the racks outside will bend under the weight of fat red meat."

Once more there was silence in the lodge. The warrior stared absently at the dancing flames of the little fire. It was not quite dark outside, and the women covered their heads with their ample robes and bent over in fear, for with the night came the evil spirits, unseen and noiseless, to prowl about the lodges in search of victims they had marked for their own. The mirth and merrymaking throughout the camp increased; there was dancing and song to the steady boom! boom! of the drums, and the rising and falling chant of the gamblers here and there. The roar of the river just back of our lodge was drowned by the din and life of the village.

"Husband, protector," said one of the women after a little, "let me ask Morning Eagle to come to you; he is very old, very wise and perhaps may be able to save us from the danger which threatens."

"Go," Raven's Voice replied, "tell him to come over, if he will."

The old man came in a few minutes, and with a cheerful word of greeting took the seat of honor at the host's left hand. He was bent with age, his face was wrinkled, his hair the color of last year's bleached grass, but his large, clear, piercing eyes seemed to retain all the fire and sparkle of youth. Everyone of the occupants of the lodge visibly brightened under the influence of his presence and his ready flow of cheerful talk. The host brought forth tobacco and "l'herbe," and began to mix a pipeful of the fragrant weeds. When the great black stone bowl had been filled, fitted to the long stem and lighted, he handed it to the old man, and as the latter blew great clouds of smoke to the gods of the sky and earth, began to recount the misfortunes of the past few days. Morning Eagle listened attentively, occasionally muttering a long-drawn "Ah-h-h!" of surprise as the narrator told of some particularly near and easy shot he had missed.

"Ai!" said he, at the conclusion of the tale, " 'tis true; it is the warning that death approaches you, your wives or children. But let us think a little; let us plan a bit. I believe that, perhaps, we may devise some way to avert this pending calamity. I remember hearing my grandfather tell of a great hunter who suddenly began to miss game, even the buffalo, at closest range, but who escaped the snares of the spirits through the intercessions and power of the Wolf Chief. That, of course, happened very long ago, when men and animals understood and conversed with each other. But even if in these late days the old gods, Chief Wolf, Chief Bear and others, no longer come and talk with us in person, we know that they still roam the earth, that they live in some far part of it which the white men have not yet found and desecrated, and we have the assurance that they still visit us in the spirit, unseen and unheard except as they appear to us in our dreams. Yes. And we know that they still heed our prayers and intercede for us with the sun, ruler of all, for his mercy and aid. Therefore, tonight, before you sleep, you will pray Wolf Chief to beg the sun's favor, that he may break the power of death, which you have been warned is coming near. Tomorrow, early, you must take some of your most valuable property, even your war shield, and sacrifice it to the sun, leaving it tied on a tree where he will be sure to see it. Then, a little later, we will build a large sweat house, and calling together all the old and wise medicine men, we will enter it, sing the sacred wolf songs and pray the gods to protect and save you."

"As you have spoken," said Raven's Voice, "so shall it be done. My wives shall build the lodge, gather the rocks and the wood to heat them, as early as possible."

Again the great stone pipe was filled and lighted, and after smoking thoughtfully for a time the old man said: "Ai-yah! Those ancient times when the gods were very near to the people. I would that I had been born then, and lived my life. It was a great privilege our forefathers had, to associate with them and learn the things they have handed down from father to son, and father to son, even to this day. How I would like to have been that great

208

hunter and warrior Bear-Skin, who met and lived with the Wolf
People and learned their medicine songs and mysteries. This is
how it happened: the tribe had camped for a long time at a place
on the Big River [Missouri River] and from constant hunting in
the vicinity, game became rather scarce and wary. One morning
Bear-Skin ordered his family to take down the lodge, pack up and
prepare to move. 'Where are you going?' the people asked,
crowding around.

" 'On discovery,' he replied. 'Game is no longer plentiful here-
abouts, and, anyhow, I am tired of this place and want to see
something of the world. I am going to travel far, far. Perhaps even
to the jumping off place, to the very edge of the earth where, it is
said, these plains and mountains end abruptly at the verge of a
great cliff, beyond which there is nothing but the blue sky.' (The
Blackfeet believe that the world is flat and circular like a wheel,
with a sharp cut edge all around its circumference.)

"The people shook their heads and entreated him to remain
with them, warning him he would be likely to encounter great and
unknown dangers which he, alone, would be unable to cope with.
But he paid no attention to them and soon the little family trailed
out of camp, their dogs packed, and dragging travois, loaded with
their few robes, their lodge and various household goods. Besides himself there were his two wives, a grown daughter and a
son not yet old enough to bend a hunter's bow.

"After the first day's travel over the great plain they began to
pass great herds of buffalo and other game, but somehow Bear-
Skin could not kill anything, although he shot arrow after arrow
at different animals, at very close range. On the third day they ate
the last of the dried meat and pemmican they had brought along.
On the evening of the fourth day they camped on the open plain
far from any wood. The buffalo chips were wet and soggy from a
recent rain and would hardly burn. It was early spring and everywhere the plain was covered with the water of the melting snows.
The little family was very miserable. Bear-Skin had been unable
to kill anything, his strange ill-luck continuing. Hungry, weak,

209

they sat, huddled around the smoky lodge fire in silence. A drizzling rain began to fall, and the drops coming in through the smoke hole still further dampened the smouldering fire. All at once the door curtain of cow skin was suddenly thrust to one side and a young man, a stranger, entered and sat down, startling the little family by his abrupt and unexpected appearance. He was a very handsome person, and very beautifully, very richly dressed; his long, heavy, neatly braided hair fell far below his hips. But what they particularly and immediately noticed was that his moccasins were perfectly dry and clean. How had he traveled over the prairie, wet and muddy, and kept them dry? There was something mysterious about that and at once they conceived a great fear of him. Bear-Skin had to summon all his courage to address the stranger. 'Friend,' he said, in a low trembling tone, 'we welcome you to our poor lodge and a seat at this smouldering fire, but, alas! we cannot give you food; none of our little store of meat and pemmican remains; we are starving.'

" 'Starving?' cried the stranger. 'Starving in the midst of great herds of game? That is strange. I never lacked for food in my life, but I think it must be very unpleasant to be real hungry. It is lucky for you that I happened to come around this way and see your lodge, for I can help you. I will go and bring some meat.'

"He hurried out; they listened with suspended breath and open mouth for the sound of his retreating footsteps, but nothing was to be heard after the door skin dropped back to its place with a click of the cross pole. Their fear increased. Would he return? they wondered. Had he really been there in their lodge? or was it an enchantment which had taken possession of them, a vision caused by the pangs of hunger? While they were hurriedly, excitedly talking and questioning one another, the door curtain was again raised, and again the stranger entered, handed one of the women a heavy, woven grass sack, and sat down. His moccasins were as dry as ever. The sack was filled with rich meat, boss ribs flaked with streaks of white fat, some kidneys, a large piece of tripe and several tongues. There was also a quantity of dried tallow. The women placed some of this in the fire, and the damp buffalo chips soon blazing up, they began to cook large portions of the meat. The stranger began to talk, asking many questions, learning where the family had come from and of Bear-Skin's strange misfortune, his inability to kill any game. Then the stranger talked a little about himself: 'I am one of the wolves,' he said. 'We live on the river, not very far north of here. Tomorrow I will come over here and guide you to our camp, where you and your family shall stay as long as you please and live on the meat we kill. You will find us a peculiar people, our ways not as yours; but do not be afraid, for you will be well treated. I will now go home. Prepare to break camp early, for I shall be here soon after sunrise.'

"When he had gone, as silently as before, the hungry family broke their long fast. They were so hungry that they could not wait for the meat to properly cook, but ate it half raw. Then, before they slept, they talked about the mysterious stranger and wondered whether his friendship was real, or a cunning snare to lead them to utter destruction. 'Be it for good or evil,' said Bear-Skin, 'we must do as he says. We could never escape from that man; he has more than human power, I am sure.'

"The next morning the Wolf man came, came early as he had promised. They had already packed up, and he started out with them over the plain. It was a pleasant, sunny day and the sunshine in a measure cheered their hearts, dispelling their gloomy fears and forebodings of the night. The ground was still wet and muddy, but the moccasins of the young man remained perfectly dry, and his foot-falls moreover were perfectly noiseless. This peculiarity, as Bear-Skin and his family later learned, was common to all the Wolf people.

"Before the sun had traveled half of his daily trail through the sky, the party came to the verge of a broad, deep valley seaming the plain. Down in it, sheltered by large groves bordering the stream, were the lodges of the Wolves, a great camp of many hundred homes. They descended the hill and passed through a part of it to the lodge of the great chief, who proved to be their friend and benefactor's father. As they went, on all sides, the well-dressed and pleasant-faced people greeted them pleasantly, one after another of the warriors saying some kind word to Bear-Skin. It was a rich camp, the lodges of clean, new, white skins, every one of them surrounded by scaffolds of drying meat. The chief at once had a feast prepared for the newcomers, and they had barely finished eating when a neighbor called him and Bear-Skin to another one. And from that place they were asked to go to another lodge. There was a continual round of feasting in the camp during the day and far into the night, feasting, dancing, gambling, singing queer but beautiful songs. The Wolf people led a happy life. Wherever Bear-Skin went, the warriors greeted him kindly, and made him presents of strange and useful things, such as odd-shaped bows; fine-pointed arrows; flint knives; thick and heavy war shields; shirts and leggins trimmed with weasel skins, and embroidered with the colored quills of the porcupine.

"On one side of the valley, not far from the camp, there was a large semi-circle corral at the foot of a tall rock cliff. It was made of large tree trunks, driftwood from the river and boulders of varying size. The cliff itself formed the back part of the structure. The Wolf chief told Bear-Skin it was used to capture buffalo. 'We lure and drive them over the cliff into it,' he said, 'and then shoot those not killed by the fall. Tomorrow we shall make a drive and you can see how it is done. But let me caution you and your family now about one thing: You may take all the meat you want, when the kill is made, but you must be careful not to touch, or pick up any bow, arrow, knife or any implement whatever you may find in the corral. Be sure to remember this, and caution your family about it.'

"During the day women prepared a great sweat house, making the frame of willows and covering it tightly with lodge skins. Nearby, in a big fire they heated rocks, and then the medicine men went inside. The rocks were passed in, and rolled into a hole in the ground in the center, one of the men sprinkled them with water, and as the hot steam filled the place, prayers were offered and the sacred pipe smoked to the sun, and his favor asked to insure a successful take of buffalo on the morrow. Bear-Skin was one of those who sat inside, and he found that this sweating and purifying of the body renewed the energies of youth. When he came out he felt as if years had rolled off him and that he was again a lively, active, hardy young man. That night until late in many lodges prayers were continually offered to the sun for his favor, and many Wolf songs were sung, which Bear-Skin repeated over and over until he knew them perfectly. They were the songs we sing today, and none are more potent than the Wolfs' hunting song which every hunter repeats ere he starts out in search of game.

"When Bear-Skin arose and went outside the next morning, he saw the men and youths of the village hastening up the side of the valley on each side of the corral bluff; so, without stopping to eat his morning meal, he hurried after them, and after a steep climb arrived at the rim of the valley, where he could see far out on the plain. From the verge of the cliff Bear-Skin saw that two lines of rock piles and brush extended far out on the flat prairie, ever diverging to the right and left until, where they ended, they were very far apart. Behind each of these piles, which were half a bow shot apart, crouched a man or youth. Beyond the lines a large herd of buffalo was feeding, and presently a swift-footed man, covered with a buffalo robe, hair side out, approached them, bawling in imitation of one of their calves when frightened. Hearing him the buffalo began to make toward him, first at a walk, then running, then on a hard lope. The man kept retreating before them until he had led them into the space between the two lines, when he suddenly dashed to one side and hid behind a rock pile. The herd kept on; behind and on each side people sprang up from behind their places of concealment, waving their robes, and the now frightened animals bounded on faster and faster toward the cliff. Bear-Skin hurried down to the corral at its foot just in time to see them come plunging over it. There was nothing else for the

213

animals to do, for the pressure of vast numbers in the rear pushed them over the precipice. Some were killed by the fall, some crippled; others, unhurt, dashed madly around, trying to jump the barrier. Arrows were whizzing, cows, calves, young bulls falling one after another, and soon all were slain except the unhurt old bulls; a part of the corral was removed and they were allowed to escape. Then the skinning and cutting up of the animals was begun by the women, and Bear-Skin's wives did their share of it. While all were busy, his little son saw an arrow lying on the ground and picked it up; he had no sooner touched it than all the people in the corral instantly changed into wolves and came snapping and snarling at him. Terribly frightened, the little fellow dropped the arrow and the wolves immediately changed back into their usual forms. 'There,' said the Wolf chief to his father, 'I warned you; if he had not dropped the arrow he would by this time have been torn to pieces. These weapons and implements here are sacred; and no one but we wolves may use them; they were loaned to us by the sun and we dare not let even one of them pass into other hands.'

Bear-Skin remained with the Wolf people and learned their ways of hunting, their medicines and mysteries. All this he taught to his own people when he finally returned to them, and ever since the Blackfeet never lacked for meat until the white man came and destroyed the game.

"But above all, most important was the medicine, the ways of prayer and sacrifice, which Bear-Skin learned from these people. They taught him that his sudden failure to kill game was the sign of approaching death, but their medicine men saved him in the way which I have said we will intercede for you tomorrow.

"Well, the night is far gone and I will return to my lodge. Sleep well, fear not; we will save you from this impending danger."

The old man departed, and we turned in, Raven's Voice in better spirits, and looking to a release for himself on the morrow. But when, soon after daylight, he was called to arise and eat, he

214

made no response; he was dead, and there was mourning in that lodge. "Heart disease," I said to myself.

"The fatal sign," said the people. "Alas, that such a kind man, such a brave warrior, should have so early been death's mark."

We were camped in a narrow, rock-rimmed valley, close up to the summit of the main range. Early one morning, Yellow Fish, a noted Blackfoot hunter, started out in quest of goats, and a little later his shots rang out and reverberated from crag and rock-wall with a dull, continuous roar. We counted them; thirty-seven in all, and concluded he had slain a whole band of the animals. In less than an hour, however, he was back in camp, pale, trembling, a hunted, terror stricken expression in his eyes. "There were thirteen goats," he said, "I was very close to them and they stood while I fired all my cartridges at them. But I never touched one of them. It is the sign, the fatal sign; death calls me, or some of my family," and without another word he caught his horse, saddled it, and started out of the mountains for the Blackfoot camp many miles away. Ten days later we followed him, having killed all the mountain game we could pack, and a Blackfoot war party arrived home at the same time we did. They had been on a raid against the Crows and one of their number, Black-Face, Yellow Fish's brother, had been killed. Counting back, it was found that the Crows shot him the very morning that Yellow Fish missed the goats. I don't believe in omens, or anything of the sort, but, well, strange things happen in this world.

15.

Medicine Fly

RETURN OF THE HORSE
THIEVES. From a painting by
Charles M. Russell, 1887.

*(Courtesy R. W. Norton Art Gallery,
Shreveport, Louisiana)*

15.

Medicine Fly

It was a warm, sultry night in August. The moon and stars were obscured by the great volumes of smoke which for days and weeks had been pouring over the summits of the Rockies, caused by forest fires on the other side. We were camped for the night in the apex of a sharp bend of the creek. The only timber in this bottom was two or three cottonwood trees, and one of them, a very giant, had long since been blown down, and from its bare, dry limbs we now and then replenished our fire. Across the little creek, from the water's edge rose a steep bluff, on the top of which grew a few stunted pines.

It was long past our usual bedtime, yet still we lingered by the little campfire, talking of the happy days when we hunted buffalo, and of adventures which can never again be experienced.

"This place reminds me," said my comrade,[1] "of the death of Medicine Fly. We were camped in just such a place as this, and it

Published in *Forest and Stream* (August 11, 1900).

1 Schultz's comrade is William Jackson, grandson of Hugh Monroe and Apahki. For a biography of Jackson, see James Willard Schultz, *William Jackson, Indian Scout* (Cambridge, Mass., 1926).

was from the top of such a cutbank as that across the creek that the Assiniboines fired down on us."

"Tell me the story," said I. "Who was Medicine Fly?"

"Well," he continued, "as you know, I enlisted under Custer as a Government scout in 1874, and remained with the army in that position until in 1879, when everything had quieted down. In January, 1877, Yellowstone Kelly and some other scouts captured seven Cheyenne women in the Big Horn Mountains, and they were held as hostages. In March Scout John Bruyer was sent to the camp with two of these women, and they returned with twenty Cheyenne warriors. A conference was held, and the whole camp surrendered and came in. No sooner was this done than the Cheyennes asked for guns and ammunition, expressing their desire to join us against the Sioux. Many of the officers laughed at this, saying it was only a play to get a stock of ammunition, when they would again join the Sioux. But the Cheyennes said, 'No; they liked to fight, and didn't care much whom they fought with; and now that they were with the whites they would fight for the whites.' Finally, after considerable talk, it was concluded to grant their request, and a limited amount of ammunition and guns was issued them, and they were enlisted as scouts, with a salary of $10 per month.

"In the spring of '77 I was sent down to Fort Buford with dispatches, and in June I boarded the steamer *Far West* to come back up the Yellowstone. General, then Colonel, Miles was also on board. At the mouth of Powder River we were hailed by three Indians, and on landing found them to be Cheyenne scouts with dispatches from Col. La Selle, who had left that point three days previous in pursuit of a large camp of Sioux. After reading the papers, Gen. Miles called me aside and said, 'Jackson, I have here some dispatches from Col. La Selle; and it is very important that I should communicate with him at once. I wish you would try and overtake him.' I hesitated. I was only a boy, remember, and here I was asked to go alone through a hostile and to me unknown country in pursuit of a party already three and a half days away.

The General noticed my hesitancy, for he put his hand on my shoulder, and said, 'My boy, I know it is a dangerous undertaking, but it is very, very important that I should communicate with Col. La Selle. I will not—I cannot—order you to go; but I wish you would.'

" 'General,' I replied, 'write out your papers. In the meantime I will get my horse off the boat and prepare to start.'

"As I stepped ashore, one of the Cheyennes, a small, wiry, bright-looking fellow, came up to me and asked where I was going. I replied that I was going to overtake the command. 'We will go with you,' he exclaimed; 'the prairie is covered with Sioux. Let us join you and you will find us true friends. We will fight for you, and if one is to die we will all die, fighting like men.'

"Again I hesitated, for I distrusted them. Yet I reasoned thus: If they want to kill me they will follow and kill me anyhow; as well let them go along, then. So I went back on the boat and told the General what they said. 'Bring them in here,' he replied, 'and let me see them.'

"Well, after some talk, the General said to me. 'We will let them go. I think they mean well, and you know the whole camp is up at the fort. If they should harm you, you will be amply avenged. They know this, too. I am sure they will stay with you.'

"The papers ready, we were about to start, when the Cheyennes asked for ammunition. 'See' they said, pointing to their belts, 'we have not ten rounds apiece. We cannot fight with a brave heart when we have so few shots.'

" 'Help yourselves,' the General said, pointing to an open case on the floor, and help themselves they did, each one taking 200 cartridges or more.

"At last we were ready. The boat pushed out from her moorings and disappeared around the bend. I watched her out of sight with a heavy heart, and then we mounted and rode away on the trail. My companions were a happy set of fellows. Of course, we could talk to each other only by signs, but as you know signs among Indians take the place of words, and we managed to keep up a pretty lively conversation, at the same time riding ahead at a surging gait. We kept on the open ground as much as possible, and stopped on every hill and rise of ground to reconnoiter. At sundown we stopped and ate supper, and after dark we moved on a couple of miles and camped.

"I didn't sleep much, for I still distrusted my companions, and lay all night with rifle in my hands and pistol handy, prepared to kill the first one who made a break; but with the morning light all my doubts and fears gave way, and from then on I felt that I could trust them.

"Toward the close of the second day we were approaching a broken country, and were nearing the head of a timbered coulee, when suddenly Medicine Fly—the Cheyenne who first proposed they should accompany me—who was ahead jumped from his horse, and said he saw a war party coming up the coulee. We all dismounted and prepared to fight. I never saw such a happy fellow as Medicine Fly. He danced about and grinned, and said we would have lots of fun. 'I saw the war bonnet of the leader,' he said. 'We will now have some scalps. Maybe we will be killed; but if they kill us it is good.'

"Well, we waited a little while, and presently a great bull elk came up out of the coulee, followed by twelve others. They were the war party. I felt greatly relieved, for from the first I had tried to get them to go on at full speed, for I was thinking of my dispatches, but Medicine Fly would not remount, and we could not go off and leave him. One of the Cheyennes shot a yearling, and taking what meat we wanted we rode away.

"About sundown of the third day we overtook the soldiers, already camped for the night. I went to Col. La Selle's camp and delivered my dispatches. He thanked me, and telling us to all come back to his tent by and by sent us to the mess for supper. After a while we went back to the Colonel's tent. He found seats for us, passed around a package of cigarettes and then said:

" 'Jackson, I have got the worst lot of deadhead scouts here you ever saw. They will not go far enough ahead to get out of sight of the command, and it seems as if I never would catch up with these Sioux. They keep just ahead all the time. When I camp they camp. When I move they move. Now, I wish you would go ahead with your Cheyennes and find out where they are camped, and if possible we will fight them tomorrow. I've heard a good deal about you, and believe you are just the man for this business.'

"Boy that I was, I still realized that the Colonel was softsoaping me, and I was fool enough to be pleased. I told the Cheyennes what he said, and they instantly signified their willingness to go if the Colonel would give us fresh horses. He agreed to do that, said the guard would call us at 1:30, and sent us off to bed.

"Prompt to the minute the guard awoke us, and showed us the horses the master of transportation had selected for us. There were two mules and two horses—none of them very good, but the best they had. We saddled up, and by 2 o'clock were on the trail. There was bright moonlight, and the heavy trail made by the Sioux camp was easily followed. At daylight we were within a few miles of Sentinel Butte. On the south side of this, at a place called Ash Springs, as we subsequently learned, the Sioux were camped.

"Most of the warriors were out hunting whitetail that morning, but a number of them were left to guard the camp, and some of these from the top of the butte saw us coming and laid a trap for us. At a place where the trail passed between two quaking asp groves they ambushed, but by some misunderstanding, or before they had time to surround us, a warrior suddenly rose up behind us and gave a warwhoop. We instantly dismounted, and at the same time a dozen men came over a little ridge ahead and charged down on us. Medicine Fly's mule was instantly shot, and the bullets whistled all around us. One fellow, mounted on a fine black horse, charged right down on Medicine Fly. The boy stood his ground, smiling, and taking deliberate aim fired. The ball pierced the Sioux through the heart, and he fell almost at our feet. Medicine Fly instantly caught the rope which was trailing and stopped the horse, and then he scalped his man. The other

225

Sioux wheeled and turned back up the trail, and we gave them another round, and killed one man and a horse. Then we all mounted and dashed into the quaking asp grove at our right.

"Here we found a coulee, followed this down, turned up a fork of it, and so out onto the prairie again, and were at least 600 yards away before the Sioux knew what had become of us. Had we stayed there a few moments more we would have been surrounded and killed. As it was, they gave us a sharp chase, and it is a wonder they didn't kill some of us, for they kept up shooting a long time. After going three or four miles, we came in sight of the soldiers, who were coming up as fast as they could, and then the Sioux quit us. An hour later we were all back at Ash Springs, but the camp had gone. From this place they scattered out in bunches of three or four lodges, and the chase was abandoned.

"From that time on Medicine Fly was my constant companion on scouting trips. I never saw a man who so enjoyed a fight. At the least prospect of a scrimmage he would dance about, smile and say, 'Now for fun. If we are killed we will die like men. What is the use of growing old and sick?'

"At one time four of us were out, and we saw seven persons on horseback whom we thought to be Sioux. Medicine Fly got off his horse, threw the saddle off and waited for the rest to follow suit. The others threw their saddles off and stripped for fighting. I did not. I had a big, powerful horse, and felt more secure with a saddle under me. As usual Medicine Fly was impatient.

" 'Come on! Come on!" he said. 'Why so slow? Are you afraid? I believe you are. Hurry, hurry! Let's fight them.'

"Away we dashed. Four to seven was big odds, but we could do no less than follow Medicine Fly. The seven persons seeing us coming got down and prepared to fight. We were getting pretty close, when one of them held up his hand and asked who we were, and then we saw they were whites. Medicine Fly was disappointed and wouldn't speak all the rest of the day. The whites proved to be a scouting party from Fort Keogh. One of them was my brother Robert, and another Lieut. Casey.

"Five of Medicine Fly's brothers and his father had been killed in battle. But one relative was left now, an elder brother named Starving Elk. One day this man walked up to another Cheyenne and said to him, 'I heard you had called me a coward. Here I am now. If you do not shoot I shall think you a coward.' The man pulled a pistol and pointed it at Starving Elk. He never flinched nor raised a hand. Crack! went the pistol, and down fell Starving Elk, with a bullet through his heart. This happened while Medicine Fly and I were on our last trip together, or that would not have been the end of the affair.

"In March, 1878, we were sent from Keogh to Fort Peck with dispatches. We had been paid off a few days before, and Medicine Fly had $30 in gold. This he squandered at the traders' store at Peck, buying, among other things, a pair of fine boots and an accordion. He had no use for either of these, for he never wore anything but moccasins, and knew nothing about music.

"On our return trip along toward evening of the second day we were nearing a creek. I saw a band of buffalo not far off, and told Medicine Fly to go on and make camp and I would kill some meat. So he went on with the pack mule and I went over and killed a young cow, and took as much of the meat as I thought we could use. Instead of sneaking up as I should have done, I chased the band, and had quite a run before I got a shot. Well, I went on and found Medicine Fly had camped, as I said, in a place like this. I didn't like the looks of it, but said nothing for a while. After we had had supper I said, 'Let us pack up now and go on a few miles. There is a place near here called Crow Hill where the Sioux once killed a whole war party of Crows. There is a queer rock fort there, and I would like to see it.'

" 'This is a good place,' said Medicine Fly. 'Here is wood, water and good grass. Let us stay here tonight, and tomorrow we will go and see Crow Hill.'

" 'But,' I said, 'this is a bad place. We are shut in here. We can't see anywhere. The enemy might come to the top of that cutbank and kill us.'

"It was no use, I couldn't get him to move; so I was obliged to stay. It seemed as if the very devil was in him that night. He sang war songs, yelled, and made a noise with his accordion, as if trying to attract attention. Finally we made down our beds. Medicine Fly made his by the fire, but I made mine between the forks of a fallen cottonwood. I couldn't sleep, however. I felt uneasy.

"It might have been an hour or more after lying down, when I heard some gravel fall off the cutbank and rattle down into the water; then there was a shot. Medicine Fly immediately jumped up and fired back, and then there was a fearful flash, and twenty or more shots were fired at him. The horses were frightened and running about on their ropes. I didn't get up, but kept hallooing 'Whoa, Billy. Whoa, boy.' It was no use to call. They either broke their ropes or pulled the picket pins and stampeded. There was no more sound from the cutbank. I could hear Medicine Fly groan occasionally, and knew that he was wounded. After a while I got up and went over to him. 'Oh,' he said, 'I thought you were gone. Leave me now and get away if you can. I shall never go. They have killed me.'

"I replied that I would not go. In fact, I couldn't go, for the horses had stampeded. I fixed a bed for Medicine Fly, got him as comfortably placed as possible and then went off a little way and waited for daylight. That was an awful night. My old friend and companion was mortally wounded, I knew, and felt as badly about it as if he had been my brother. I couldn't think what had become of the war party. I wondered why they did not come in and finish us, and I made up my mind that if they did come I would kill enough of them to avenge us both before they took my hair. At last day began to break, and I sneaked out and took a look around. Not a living thing was in sight. I even went up on top of the cutbank, but could see no trails on the hard, dry grass. I went back to my friend. His eyes lighted up when he saw me, and he said, 'Still here! Our hearts are the same. I like you.' And presently, 'I am not afraid to die. This is the way to die; shot down by the enemy. I am glad.'

"After a while he asked for water. I got a cupful, raised him up and held it to his lips. He took only a swallow, shivered and died in my arms. For the rest of that day I must have been crazy. I remember nothing until about dark I found myself at the fort, forty miles from where Medicine Fly was killed. I told my story, and lay down and slept. Next day, with some others, I went back and buried Medicine Fly, and got our saddles and other things. And while we were burying him, I told the boys what a friend he had been to me, and how brave he was. Then one of the boys made a little speech. I can't remember all he said. He said something about everyone doing their best according to their lights, and how Medicine Fly had always done the best he could; that he had always done more than his duty, and that if there was any hereafter Medicine Fly stood as good a show to be happy as the next one.

"And then we got on our horses and rode away.

"I found out afterward that it was the Assiniboines who killed him. They told me about it themselves. They saw me running buffalo and heard Medicine Fly singing, and thought we were Crows. But when they heard me halloo at my horse they recognized my voice and went off. I did not tell them that they killed the Cheyenne. I wouldn't give them that satisfaction. I only said that they wounded him a little, and that he got all right in a week or two. I have often thought about that night. I shall never forget it, nor Medicine Fly. I wish for no better friend and companion than he was."

16.

Lone Elk's Search

INDIAN BEAUTY PARLOR. From a painting by Charles M. Russell, 1899.

(Courtesy R. W. Norton Art Gallery, Shreveport, Louisiana)

Lone Elk's Search

"Dec. 20, 1879. A clear, windless, exceedingly cold day." My old note book reads under that date: "We traded for fifty-two buffalo robes and some deer skins. This evening we were invited to a feast in Lone Elk's lodge. Berry pleaded fatigue, but I went and had a very interesting time. The talk was of the relation of men to the supernatural—to the gods. For the sake of argument I took the ground that, if there were any gods in the heavens above, or on earth, they had no communication with men. Lone Elk promptly took issue with me, and the result is that I got a story from him.

Then follows the story; in places the faded ink is quite undecipherable, but my memory supplies the missing sentences:

"I do not understand the white people," said Lone Elk. "Like us, their knowledge, their ability to do things was given them by the gods, but with this difference: Their gods are greater than ours, have given them power to do many things which would be impossible for us to undertake. We cannot make guns, nor powder, nor steamboats, nor matches; why, our women can't even tan leather as well as they do, thick and strong, yet very soft. Our gods compared to theirs are very poor, but they gave us

Published in *Forest and Stream* (March 9, 16, and 23, 1907).

all they could; the game of the plains and mountains, the art of making bows and arrows with which to kill, the power to build a fire with which to cook flesh, and to keep our bodies warm. We are thankful for what they have done for us, and we pray to them, make sacrifices, asking to favor us with good health, prosperity and long life.

"But the white men: They give no thanks for all that has been given them. Most of them deny even that there are any gods. True, there is a Black Robe here and there who teaches that there are, but the white men do not listen to him. Now, hear me: Gods made us, the prairie people, and gave us what knowledge we have. Gods then must have made them too, for they are no different from us except in color, and in greater knowledge. Is not that good and true reasoning, friend Spotted Robe?"

"Many long days and nights have I read sacred writings," I replied, "and much have I thought about this. Yet after all I can only say: I do not know. I do not know if it were gods, or what, that created the world and us. I know not whence we came, nor where we go, nor if there is any part of us, our shadow, as you call it, which survives the death of our bodies."

"Then are you indeed poor!" Lone Elk exclaimed. "And very forgiving must be your gods, for although you pray not to them, nor make sacrifice to them, nor even believe that they are, that they live somewhere in the great outside, they continue to prosper you in all your undertakings. You shake your head. I tell you friend, that the gods live. I can prove it. Listen:

"For two winters I had lived in a lodge of my own, just my good woman Pit'-ah-ki and I. We were happy. No one ever heard us speaking loud, angry words; in our lodge was always peace, and plenty and cheerful talk. I hunted not only for us, but for my father and his people, for he had grown old. But hunting was no longer the pleasure to me it had been; the only place I cared to be was at home with Pit'-ah-ki. It never was any fun to hunt on a cold winter day when the frost hung like fog in the air, or the

236

wind drove the dry, stinging snow in your face, and the hide of your game as you skinned it froze stiff in your numb fingers; but I endured it, thinking of the warm lodge awaiting me, of the bright fire, and the brighter laughing eyes of the little woman as she would hurry out to care for the meat and skin, and then hurry to set before me hot soup and other food. That made all things endurable, to know that some one cared for you, and awaited your return.

"It was the ripe-berry moon of the third summer that we had lived together. We were about out of meat; so very early one morning I saddled a horse and rode out on the plains to kill something. Luck was against me from the start. There were buffalo and antelope, plenty of them, but to none could I get near enough for a fair shot. Either the wind changed and gave them warning, or some sly old he antelope saw me and led his band away to safety. It was late in the day when I finally killed a cow buffalo, and almost dark when I arrived at my lodge with the meat. I noticed that there was no fire within, and for the first time my woman failed to come out and say in her happy voice: 'My hunter has returned.' So I called out for her: 'Pit'-ah-ki,' I said, 'I am very tired, and very hungry; come and help your old man unpack.'

"There was no reply. I slung the meat and hide off, unsaddled and turned my horse loose, and went inside. In the center of the fireplace was a little mound of cold, white ashes which Pit'-ah-ki had heaped up to keep life in the bed of coals. I raked them off, threw some fire wood on the coals and soon had a blaze. Everything was in order as usual. Just then my mother came in and I asked her where my woman was. 'Why,' she said, surprised, 'Didn't she go with you? I haven't seen her this day.'

"Then a great fear seized my heart. I knew at once that something was wrong. Indeed, I had felt ill at ease all day, as if some misfortune was about to befall me. 'I will go and see if she is with her parents, or her sister,' said my mother, 'and if she isn't, I will have the camp crier call out about her.'

" 'Go, if you will,' I said to her, 'but I know that it will be useless, for Pit'-ah-ki would be right here, right now, were it in her power. Something terrible has happened to her.'

"I put more wood on the fire and lay down. In a little while I heard the camp crier repeating over and over. 'Pit'-ah-ki, Lone Elk's woman has been missing since sunrise. Who has seen her? Who can give news concerning her?'

"My mother returned and began to cook food for me. 'Put the stuff away,' I told her. 'I cannot eat now.'

"Then friends began to come in and I had to sit up and fill pipes for them, and listen to their talk and their views regarding my missing one. My mother, after some search, found that a woven grass sack, made by beyond-the-mountains people, was missing. It was the one Pit'-ah-ki always used when she went to gather berries. She had gone berrying then, but why alone? And what had happened to her? Some said that a bear had probably killed her; others that she might have been bitten by a rattlesnake and died before she could get home. And one man, with a mean, cruel laugh said: "Oh, the women! You can never trust them, can never tell what they will do. More than likely she has run off with some pretty young fellow.'

" 'Say that again,' I cried, 'and I shoot you where you sit. If I ever hear of you repeating it, be sure to prepare yourself, for I shall hunt for you. Now, get out of my lodge and never again enter the doorway.'

"He went, but he never made the evil talk again so far as I know. He was mean to his wife, allowing her nothing but the coarsest food, the poorest scanty dress. And so, after many hardships and many beatings, she had run off with a man who loved her and was good to her. Who could blame her?

"When all my visitors had gone home I lay down, but it was nearly morning before I fell asleep for a short time. I had prayed long for help in my trouble, for some sign to be given me. In answer, a voice came to me in my dream, a loud, clear voice, and it said: 'Your woman lives; keep up your courage; seek hard for her and you shall find her.'

"I was going to ask the voice where I should seek, but just then I awoke, and then it was useless to do so; for the gods talk to our shadows (souls) only when our bodies sleep and they are free to wander as they will. Nor could I sleep again; morning had come, and the camp was astir. After the morning meal the whole camp turned out to search for my woman. We were then located where the Big River and the Bear River join (the Missouri and Marias Rivers). Some went up the Bear River, some up and some down the other one, through the timber and willows, the berry thickets, and among the breaks of the valley slopes. But the search was without result; not a trace could be found of the missing one, nor were there any signs that a war party had been near. I was satisfied though. I was sure that the enemy had been around and had captured her, for had not my dream said that she lived? And if she was alive would she not be at home with me, unless she were held a captive? That was plain enough, and I was to seek for her; but where? Where should I go? I left it to the gods; they would advise me, I felt sure. I sacrificed to the sun first of all, hanging in a tree some of my most prized property, also my woman's beautiful elk-tusk-strung dress. I got a powerful medicine man to unwrap his sacred pipe and pray with me to the sun, to Old Man, to all the gods of the air, the earth and the deep, dark waters. High up on the back of my lodge he painted the sign of the butterfly, the silent winger who gives us dreams. And then for four days and four nights I fasted, sleeping long and often while my shadow self went forth on adventure. Thus I met and talked to the ancient ones. 'Have you seen my woman?' I would ask them. 'Can you tell me where to go to find her?'

"Although I met and talked with most of them—the buffalo shadow chief, the wolf, the coyote, badger, lynx, wolverine, none could give me any news. I began to despair. 'My medicine is weak,' I thought. 'What evil have I done that I must suffer this great trouble and find no way out of it?'

239

"On the fourth night I slept and waked, slept and waked many times, a kind of half sleep it was until nearly morning, and then, at last, help came. I was walking along the shore of the Big River and came to a broad, smooth trail which led from the water up into a deep cave in the bank. Back in its depths there was singing, a low, slow, dreamy song. I entered the cave and felt my way along the dark passage for some distance and then came to a big, wide, high place which was lighted dimly by a willow-covered hole in the top. At the rear of this queer home sat an old, white beaver; on either side of him clear around were other beavers, also white and aged looking, and all were singing the beautiful song, beating time to it with cuttings of willow which they lightly tapped against the couch rails. As I stood looking and listening, four of them arose, standing on their hind legs, and danced out to the center of the place, danced slowly in time to the slowly sung song. When they were all met in the middle of the space they stopped and then danced four times as they were, after which they all turned short around and danced back to their seats. The singing ceased and the old chief beaver, motioning me to a place by his side, said: 'Welcome, man person, sit you down with us.'

"I took the seat he pointed to, and we talked together for a time. At last he asked me where I was traveling, and for what purpose. So I told him what was my trouble, and that I could get no trace of my missing woman. 'Ah,' the beaver chief exclaimed, when I had related my story. 'Ah!' he exclaimed several times; and 'Hah!' he said, scratching his white, smooth head with his little front paw. 'Hah. I think I can help you.' And with that he told me to follow him, and we went out to the shore of the river, all the other ancient ones following us. 'Call our people,' said the chief to one of them. Whereupon that old one slipped into the stream and struck the surface of the water four loud slaps with his broad tail. Again he struck it four times, and yet again four times. In answer we heard the slaps repeated away up the river, and away down it, and out near the further shore. That was the call of the ancient ones, the signal to gather at the chief's lodge; and soon they began to come, swimming in swiftly from all directions until a large number were gathered there before us, some on the shore and some in the shallow water. Then said the chief to them: 'Listen, my children. Did I not hear some of you say that some men persons had gone down the river lately? I seem to remember that you did. If there be any here who know about it let them speak.'

"Then spoke one who sat near us: 'True, chief,' he said. 'You speak true. It was I who gave the news. I saw them, a man person and a woman person drifting down the river on a raft of two logs which were covered with brush. The moon had not yet arisen and I swam close to them unperceived as they floated along. They were a man person and a woman person, and the woman was crying. She was bound to the logs with many turns of rope, and although she strove and struggled she could not free herself.'

"I was about to speak to the chief when I suddenly awoke. My shadow had returned to my body, and my mother had come in. 'You were dreaming?' she asked; 'was anything revealed to you?'

"She was glad when I told her what I had learned. 'The gods have been good to us,' she said. 'We must sacrifice to them; to the Ancient Beaver especially.'

"We did so, with many prayers, and I sung over and over again the song I had heard the beavers sing, until I was sure that I would never forget it. The song has always been good medicine to me. I have sung it whenever in danger, or great trouble, or sickness, and have mostly come safely and happily out of it all.

"It had been made plain to me that my woman was a captive in the camp of one of the down-the-river tribes, and there I must seek her. Many young men asked to be allowed to go with me on my quest, but I refused them, one and all. I had my mother build me a good strong skin boat,* and putting into it one evening the few things I wished to take, my weapons, some dried meat, a couple of ropes and a robe, I pushed out into the current. You

* "Bullboat" we used to call them. They were made by stretching a large green buffalo bull hide over a circular flat-bottomed willow frame.

241

know that such boats are different from those the white people make. You cannot do much in them, but try to keep them from turning bottom side up, and instead of rowing you have a paddle which you thrust in the water ahead and draw toward you. It is not of much use to paddle though, except enough to keep in the deep water and clear of snags. When the wind blows hard you cannot do anything at all, but drift ashore and stay there until the wind dies out. But I felt as I drifted on with the current that this was the best way for me to travel. It was better than going on foot because I would not become tired; better than riding horseback; at the risk of being discovered by an enemy through sight of the animal while it grazed and I slept.

"The moon had risen soon after sunset and gave plenty of light for me to see my way. It was so light that I could see the deer and other animals that came to the shore to drink. I saw too a beaver now and then swimming along, and sometimes when I startled one it would slap the water with its flat tail and dive down into the dark water. 'Do not fear me, little brother,' I would say. 'Your ancient father, your great chief has given me help and I will never harm any of you; no, not if I starve.'

"I floated on and on until the first light of day, and then I hid my boat on a little green willowed island, spread my robe in the deep shade and slept until night. That is the way I traveled, always by night, silently and with good speed down the Big River. If there were war parties prowling along the shore they never saw me. For some days the country was familiar to me and I knew where I was all the time. Below the mouth of the Yellow River (Judith) between it and Middle (Cow) Creek,† I had a mishap and nearly lost my life. I heard a loud roaring ahead and knew that I was approaching a rapid, so I looked to see that my gun and other things were securely tied to the willow frames of the boat. Not that I expected to be up-set, but one should never take any chances of losing his weapons. The roar of this rapid as I

† Undoubtedly Dauphin's Rapid, the worst one on the navigable part of the river.

came nearer and nearer to it was truly terrifying, so loud and angry was it. And I tried to make the shore and wade along down the edge of it; but I was too late. I could not get out of the strong current, and all at once I was going up and down, whirling this way and that way over big and hissing white topped waves. And then, suddenly, a bigger wave than any I had gone over, picked up the boat and pushed it against a large, round rock. Over it went, and I was thrown head first into another wave. When I came up to the surface I could not see the boat, so thinking that it was ahead of me, I swam on with the current. It was easy work; almost without exertion. I kept well up on the surface; then I came to the end of the rapid; a back moving upper current of water suddenly struck my breast, and the current I had been in seized my legs and dragged me down. Struggle as I would I was pulled down, down, I knew not how far, in the dark water, and then as suddenly I was cast up on the surface, only to be forced up-stream and dragged down again. Three times I was thus whirled around, a fourth time I was sucked down. I was about out of breath. I was getting weak. 'Oh, Ancient Beaver,' I prayed, 'pity and help me now or I drown.' He did help me. When I came to the surface again I found myself floating downstream away from that terrible place. Then my feet struck a gravelly bottom; I waded ashore and fell down, weak, trembling, almost strangled.

"Where was my boat? Even as the thought came to me I saw something drifting along close to shore. It was the boat sure enough; just one edge of it sticking up in sight. I arose and staggered out to it, dragged it to the land, and again laid down to rest. It was a hot night, the gravel I lay upon was still warm from the day's heat. So, although very wet I was not chilly, and I quickly fell asleep. Not for long though, but long enough to dream, and in the dream my shadow found my woman. She was sitting under a big cottonwood tree, all alone, and she was crying. That was all I learned. I hadn't time to approach her, nor even to speak. When I awoke I tipped the water out of my boat, unfastened my gun and cleaned it, drawing out the charge and ramming in a fresh one.

It was a good, grooved barrel caplock rifle. Again I went upon my way, both thankful and angry. Thankful that I had escaped drowning and that my boat had been held in that whirling water longer than I had, and then floated right down to me. Oh, but I was angry. I had been angry all these days, and when one cannot satisfy his anger, cannot crush and destroy the one he hates, his anger becomes something terrible, stifling him, burning him, wearing away one's flesh. How I longed to meet the one who had stolen my loving woman. I imagined meeting him; I thought of what I could do to him to most pain him, both in body and in mind. And that short dream, what did it mean? Where was the place I had seen her, alone, crying sadly under the big tree? And would I ever succeed in my search? There was a big country before me, inhabited by many tribes. In which camp was she held? Worst thought of all—what of my dream of the beavers— had my shadow really entered that home of the ancient ones— had they really seen my woman bound to a log raft floating down the river? It might be a mistake; perhaps she was a captive in some camp far to the south, or the north or west. 'I will not doubt,' I cried out, and the rock wall opposite answered: 'Will not doubt.' I sung the beaver song, sung it loudly, regardless of the enemy who might be lurking over in the shadow of the trees and thickets.

"One thing I had lost in the rapids, my sack of dried meat, and now I was sorry that I had not brought my bow and arrow, the noiseless killers. I did not like to fire a gun in that enemy-infested country. When daylight came I again cached my boat and concealed myself on a small island. I was very hungry, and the sight of some buffalo coming in to water on the north shore made me more hungry. There were deer on the island. I saw a big buck drinking on the lower point of it and could easily have shot it, but I felt that I must not fire; something seemed to keep telling me that I was not alone there, that the enemy were also thereabout. I looked long and carefully up and down the river shores, at the valley slopes and breaks, looked for the smoke from lodges or camp-fire, but could see nothing suspicious. I spread my robe and laid down, but I could not sleep. I was uneasy, watchful, listening, and pretty soon I heard the report of a gun close by. I arose, crossed to the north side of the island and looking out through the thick bushes, saw a number of men standing or sitting on the shore near a buffalo which three or four of them were beginning to skin. There were forty-four of them, Assiniboines, as near as I could make out at that distance. They soon skinned their kill, cut what meat they wanted and disappeared in the timber where I soon saw the smoke of their camp-fire rising above the trees. They were such a large war party that they didn't seem to care to conceal themselves; they kept a scout out all day though. I could see him sitting on a little butte at the upper end of the bottom. Now, suppose I had heeded the craving of hunger and shot the deer! That war party would have learned that I was on the island and they would have lain in wait for me, as I drifted along in the evening; at some point in my course there would have been a lot of shots and I would have rolled out of my boat and made food for the things that live in the deep water. Then, you see, the gods protected me; they gave warning that an enemy was near, that I must not shoot, nor expose myself in any way.

"It was near sundown when I saw the scout leave the butte, and a little later the whole party left the timber and moved off across the bottom westward. As soon as it was dark I pushed out and landed near the buffalo carcass; there was still a plenty of meat on it and I took what I wanted, carried some of it over to the fire the party had abandoned, cooked and ate it. Then I went upon my way.

"As far as the mouth of the Dried Meat River (the Musselshell) I knew the country well; beyond that I knew it only in places, never before having traversed the whole course of the valley. I was familiar with it about the mouth of Little (Milk) River, and Elk (Yellowstone) River, and I had once been on a visit with my people to the Earth-house people (the Mandans), who live some little distance below the mouth of Elk River. On

245

that trip I noticed in that vicinity in the big timbered bottoms, there were generally some Assiniboines or Yanktonais encamped. I felt that it was none of these people who had captured my woman. They feared the water; had any of them stolen her they would have taken her away on foot or on horseback. But the tribes below them, the Mandans and the Lower Big Bellies** (the Gros Ventres of the village) are river people, always paddling about in their skin boats. The Mandans have ever been at peace with us, the Lower Big Bellies always at war with us. I felt, I had felt from the first, from the time I met the Ancient Beavers, that it was one of the last tribe who had captured her, that she was in his camp. So, after some nights' drifting, when I came to the mouth of the Little River, I did not stop to look for any camp, but drifted on and on, hiding on a big island before daylight. I had passed a camp though in the middle of the night, for I heard many dogs answering the howl of wolves.

"I was now again out of food. I awoke late in the afternoon and had a look at the country from both sides of the island. There were deer trails criss-crossing the island in every direction; its shores were all cut up by their sharp hoofs. As I could see no sign of the enemy anywhere, as there were buffalo quietly feeding on both sides of the valley, I felt that I could take the risk and fire a shot. I had to—or starve. In a little while, as I sat in the edge of the willows on the north side of the island, a big he swaying tail (white tail deer) came out on the shore above, drank from the river and then walked down toward me sniffing the tracks he crossed. When I fired he dropped right where he stood, never even kicked. I sat still for a few minutes, carefully watching the opposite shore, which was a long gun shot distant. Nothing appeared; the buffalo beyond on the slope of the valley seemed not to have heard the report, continuing to graze. I went out to my kill, drew

** Pi-nap Ut-se-na: Lower or down-river Big Bellies, as distinguished from the Ut-se-na, or Gros Ventres of the prairie. The Village Gros Ventres are really Crows, Dakotas. The Upper Gros Ventres are Algonquins. The Blackfoot name for them, however, implies that they are of common stock—a divided tribe.

my knife and commenced to skin it. I hadn't more than half ripped up a hind leg when some bullets zipped over my head, thudded into the sand, splashed into the water, and one struck the deer. I knew what they were before I heard the boom of the guns, and saw smoke lifting from the willows over on the main shore. I didn't let go the leg. I unjointed it, skin and all, and got into cover with it before the enemy had time to reload and fire again. As soon as I was in the shelter of the brush I ran down it a ways and looked out. I could see no one, but the buffalo were running up on to the plain, and others that had been in the bottom were following them. Then I knew that those who had fired upon me were a war party and had lain concealed in the timber all day. The water was very shallow between us, the main river being on the opposite side of the island where my boat was concealed. 'They will wade over here as soon as it is dark,' I said to myself. 'I've got to get away from here now.' I had cached my boat at the upper end of the long island. I hurried over to it, threw in my meat, and pushed off, paddling for the south shore as hard as I could. The current was not very swift and I reached the land some little distance above the foot of the island which had hidden my movement from the enemy. As soon as I was ashore I broke some brush and threw it over the boat, and then crossed the wide sand bar and got into the timber; passing through that, then crouching along in the high grease wood and sage brush, and lastly walking up a narrow coulee, I arrived at the top of a high point from which I could plainly see the opposite bottoms. There were four men slowly sneaking down it, and when they reached the lower end, straight across from me, they concealed themselves in the sage brush at the edge of the high cut bank overlooking the river. The stream was narrow there and the deep channel of swift water was right under them. No doubt they thought that I had a boat or raft, and right there they would lie in wait for me. They were not all of the party; I had seen the smoke of at least ten guns. I could see nothing of the others, however; they were concealed in the timber from which they had shot at me. From where I lay, peering through a low sage brush, I could see the four men on the cut bank very plainly, for I was high above their position. It was not so very far either. More than once I had killed buffalo and elk and deer at that distance by sighting my rifle a space of about three hands above their backs. One of the men lay flat on his belly, head to the river, and more than once I sighted my rifle at him. I thought that if I aimed at his heels the bullet would strike him somewhere in his back if I held true. The temptation to try it was great; my other mind was not to attempt it. 'Think of what you are seeking,' it said, 'and run no more risk than you can help.' And then the other one: 'Perhaps this very party belong to the camp where your woman is captive; they have already shot at you, tried to kill you. Try it.'

"The day was about ended. 'Hai′ yu, great Sun,' I prayed; 'make my aim true. Let my bullet drain the blood of this enemy. I give him to you; his scalp shall be yours.' Long, long I aimed, again and again measuring the distance with my eyes, and at last I pulled the trigger. Through the drifting powder smoke I saw my enemy spring to his feet, saw him stagger, saw him fall, limp on the edge of the cut bank and roll off it, splash, into the deep water in which he sank like a stone. Ai! but I was glad. I almost shouted. I was so glad. I reloaded my gun as quickly as I could and shot at one of the others as they ran back to the timber whence they had come, but that time my bullet sped wide of the mark.

"I remained where I was until it was quite dark, and then returning to the boat I pushed out noiselessly from the shore and drifted down-stream, keeping as close to the south side as possible. I saw nothing more of the enemy. Some time before midnight the moon arose, but I was then far from where I had shot the enemy, and felt that they were not pursuing me; that my appearance on the south side of the river had made them think that I was a traveler afoot. When daylight came they would probably try to pick up my trail. I ate some of the meat I had killed. It was not very good raw, but it satisfied my hunger. I did not wish to take time, nor the risk to stop, build a fire and cook.

248

"After some nights of drifting I came to the mouth of Elk River; from there three more nights and I knew that I was near the Mandan camp. The moon was rising now after midnight and I feared that I might pass the place in the dark. I kept close to the north shore now watching for the steps in the high cut bank which the people used for their water trail. I came to them not long before daylight, but if there had been no moon I could not have passed by, for the camp dogs were howling as usual. I tied my boat beside some others like it, took my rifle and robe and my ropes and ascended the steps. There before me was the camp, a lot of round topped mud houses surrounded by a high fence of logs stuck endways into the ground, and so close together that a prairie dog could not have squeezed through between them. I knew better than to attempt to enter the place then. I sat down on the edge of the cut bank and waited for daylight, and the people to come forth. It was not long before some early rising women started out for water, and seeing me they ran back through the passage way in the fence and aroused the camp. Some men appeared carrying their guns, and I arose, made the sign of peace, also the sign that I was a Blackfoot. At that they too made the sign of friendship, and asked me to approach. I went up to them and gave them greeting, and they took me to their chief's lodge. He was a kindly man, that Four Bears, and made me welcome. While we smoked together, and I told him why I was there, about my dream and everything, his women cooked a feast for us of meat and beans and corn, and other things. I ate a lot of it all.

"I stayed with the good chief four days, feasting and resting, and devising a way to learn if my woman really was in the Lower Big Belly village. It was, the chief told me, just like that of the Mandans, built on a wide, open bottom and inclosed by a high log house. There was no place near it, he said where one could lie concealed and watch the going and coming of the people. We finally hit upon a way that we thought would do. It was full of danger, but the only one that seemed likely to succeed, and in the evening of the fourth day I set off again in my boat to try it. Four

249

Bears had given me directions to enable me to know the place of the village when I came opposite it, but in the darkness, I would have missed it had it not been for the howling of their dogs. It was near morning of the second night that I heard them, and drawing into the shore I saw the camp's water trails cut in the high bank. I went on down the river until I came to a large cottonwood grove, and there, out in still water opposite an old log on the sand bar, I sunk my boat by the weight of many stones. Back in the timber I cached my rifle, my robe, everything I had except my knife. Then I unbraided my hair, wet it, and combed and combed it, rebraided it roughly in two large braids, one on each side of my head. My scalp lock had disappeared. I no longer showed that I was a Blackfoot. I wore a pair of plain cowskin moccasins; a pair of cowskin leggins, a cowskin (unpainted) toga that Four Bears had given me. Nothing about me was suggestive of any tribe, far or near, that I had ever heard of. My only weapon was my knife, stuck in a plain parfleche sheath at my belt.

"Daylight was near. I left the timber, followed up the bank of the river and sat down by the water trail of the village. The first risers, as at the other camp, were some women who aroused their men. 'Who are you?' they signed, coming forth guns in hand.

" 'I am from the far south,' I answered in signs, 'I am of the people who live in houses set one on top of another in the land of no snow. I come with peaceful intent.'

" 'Approach, then,' their leader signed. 'Approach us in peace.' We met and embraced, they looking at me hard, but kindly. It had all been easier than I had thought. I had been much afraid that they would kill me. They conducted me to the big earth lodge of their chief. He was just getting up, and sitting back on his couch he motioned me to a place beside him, filled a pipe and handed it to me to light. I smoked with him and the others who had come in with me and told the story that Four Bears and I had made up. I was far from the south, from the hot country, I said in sign language. I was of a tribe which lived on a flat butte overlooking a great plain, a people who lived in houses built one on top of

250

another. I knew that there was such a people. My father had seen and fought them when he went to war in his young days. I also said that I was alone in the world, that I had no lodge, and I was traveling around just to see the country and visit the different tribes along the way. The old chief asked why I had no gun, no horse, and I replied that two days before I had fallen in the hands of a war party who came upon me while I slept, and that they had taken my bow and arrows and set me afoot. That lie passed too. Presently the women placed food before us and I ate as if I were starved. All this time I was longing to go out, to look through the camp for the one I sought, and yet I feared to. If she were there, if she cried out and ran to me when she saw me there I would be killed. She too, perhaps. I made up my mind to stay close to the chief until I saw her, if she really was there, and I was sure of that. I had faith in my dream. Yes, I would stay close to the chief, and if things went wrong, I would at least draw my knife and kill him before I was killed.

"After eating we smoked two pipes, and then the chief dismissed his guests. Soon afterward a woman came in and spoke to him. 'We are invited to a feast,' he signed, 'let us go.'

"There were feasts all that morning for us, and we took a bite and smoked at each place, while I had to tell over and over again about myself, and answer many questions. In the last lodge, to which we were invited, that which I had expected happened. I met my woman. I followed the chief into the place, the host made room for me next to him on his right, and when I took my seat and looked around, there she was, sitting in the shadow of the place, near the doorway. She gave me one swift, sorrowful look, and then bent her head. My heart seemed to jump up into my throat. I nearly jumped up to run over to her. Then I began to grow angry. Here beside me was the man who had taken her from me. I had a look at him. A big, powerful man he was, good looking, I suppose, yet he looked hateful to me. How I did long to stick my knife into him then and there. But I bided my time. 'Have patience,' I said to myself, 'he shall not escape you.'

251

"I thought that feast would never end. It was almost more than I could endure to sit there and smoke and tell this man, who had so wronged me, my story of lies in answer to his request. From time to time I stole a look at my woman. She was watching my hand as I made the signs, but she would not look me in the face. At last we went out, and returned to the chief's lodge. 'This is your home,' he told me; 'that is your couch; my food is your food; my pipe and tobacco are also yours. Go and come as you will.'

"I walked about in the village, out to the river. I sat in the shade of the lodges and smoked, and told lies about the south country, all the time thinking about my woman, how to rescue her. Thus two days passed. I found that she was never allowed to go out alone, two of her captor's wives always going with her for wood and even to the river for water. In the afternoon of the second day I sat by the water trail where it descended the cut bank to the river's edge. Came my woman with her guard for water; returning she led the way up the steps, and before the others reappeared I quickly signed to her: 'Don't sleep; tonight I shall enter your lodge and take you away.' She nodded her head to signify that she understood.

"The village was very quiet when I arose and crept out of the chief's lodge. Not a dog was barking; not a fire was alight nor a single person moving about. A mere hand's width at a time I crawled past the curtain of the hated one's doorway and into his lodge. Putting out my left hand I touched my woman's head, and she reached up and grasped me by the neck, pulled me down so that her lips reached my ear and whispered so softly I could scarcely hear her: 'He is asleep beside me. I am tied to him. Be careful.'

"I had been angry, but these words filled me with the rage of a wounded grizzly, and that is the most terrible rage of anything that walks the earth. I felt that I had the strength of a hundred men in my arms and hands. Edging up closer to my woman I reached out carefully to feel with my finger tips, my enemy's position. He was lying on his side, back to me, breathing slow

17.

Last Years of the Buffalo

17.

Last Years of the Buffalo

Black Butte, in Fergus County, Montana, was, in the long ago, a favorite lookout place for the war parties of various tribes of Indians roaming that section of the country. On a day in August, 1880, Pinukwiim (Far-off-in-Sight), a staid warrior and hunter of the Blood tribe, and I, rode up the butte as far as our horses could carry us. Then we climbed on foot to its summit to see what we might see, and what we saw was plenty. Northward to the breaks of the Missouri, twenty-five miles away, and eastward to the nearer, timbered valley of the Musselshell, herds of buffalo were everywhere upon the plain. I can give no accurate estimate of the number of the animals that we could see from our lofty perch; but there were surely more than a hundred thousand of them.

Said my companion: "Puhts ikahkaiim, amoksi kitainowa anan.—How very many, those we see."

"Ah. Kitssemini!—Yes. True," I answered.

It was the mating season of the buffalo. The bulls were pawing the dry surface of the plain, raising thin columns of dust high in the still air; fighting one another and frequently causing a whole

Published in *St. Nicholas* (July, 1934).

herd suddenly, senselessly, to run for a mile or so. Distant though they were from us, the deep-toned moaning of the bulls was like far off, ceaseless thunder in our ears. They did not bellow like the bulls of domestic cattle. They were silent save during the mating season, and their mating call was all in one key, one tone, comparable only to a deep bass note of an immense organ.

Closely west of the butte, the Blood camp of nearly two hundred lodges was pitched at the head of a fork of Crooked Creek, named Sacajawea Creek by Lewis and Clark in honor of the heroine of their expedition. All was quiet in the camp; its several thousand horses were resting or grazing close around it. No riders were coming or going, for the council of chiefs had forbidden all hunting until a herd of buffalo should come close enough so that all could participate in the run. At the request of the council, Pinukwiim and I had come up onto the butte to look for signs of any enemy war party that might be prowling about to raid our horse herds. Although a party of enemies might themselves be invisible to the camp's lookouts, the running of a frightened herd of buffalo or band of antelope often betrayed their presence; but now, in this mating season of both species, their sudden dashings hither and thither were no evidence that they were fleeing from the sight or scent of man.

Well we knew that war parties of Crows, Yanktonais, Assiniboines, and Cheyennes were infesting this, the country of our Blackfeet tribes; but, as Pinukwiim said to me, the only way we could learn of their approach would be actually to see them. I was the fortunate owner of a three-joint English telescope of thirty-five diameters, and with it, by turns, we scanned the country near and far. I leveled it upon the plain running north from the Missouri up to the foot of the Little Rockies, or, as we called them, Mahkwiyi Stukists—Wolf Mountains. There too the buffalo herds were as plentiful as upon our side of the river.

Smoking a pipe by turns, we rested our strained eyes and Pinukwiim sang a happy little song of plenty—of plenty of "real-food," as buffalo meat was termed. And then spoke: "What liars are some white men! For instance, Spotted Cap, he who speaks so well our language, says that the buffalo are fast being killed off, will soon be gone. Ha! Does that look like it, off there? No. As we have ever had them, so shall we ever have them, plenty of buffalo upon the plains of our tribes." (The three tribes of the Blackfeet Confederacy: Pikuni, of Montana, Bloods and Blackfeet, or Alberta.)

"There are no more of them upon our northern plains," I ventured, meaning the plains of Alberta. The last of the herds there had drifted south into Montana in 1878, two years before.

"That has happened several times. Always they returned, and will again return, probably in this coming winter."

"Perhaps they will. Let us hope that they will," I ended, again taking up the telescope. I hadn't the heart to tell him what I well knew, that the end of the buffalo was near, that they could not last more than two or three years. That knowledge saddened me. I visioned the sufferings that my Indian friends must endure with the passing of the buffalo, at once their food, their clothing, and their shelter. Then must end this wild, free life with them that was so dear to me, that I so keenly enjoyed. I had had three years of it; could have but two or three years more, and then—.

It suddenly came to me that this was the twenty-sixth of August and my twenty-first birthday. I thought of the presents that would be mine were I at home, back there in Boonville, New York. Well, all that my people could give me couldn't compare with the privilege of sitting with Pinukwiim on top of Black Butte, gazing down upon this vast horde of buffalo, this endless expanse of plains and mountains—country of the Blackfeet tribes as guaranteed by their treaty with the government in 1855; and so also mine, for I had been adopted by the Pikuni, and was therefore perfectly at home with the two other tribes.

The sun was nearly setting when, happening to turn the telescope upon a long, timbered coulee running down into the valley of the Musselshell, I saw a small band of elk run up out of it onto the plain; and as they stopped and looked back whence they had come, I told my companion of my discovery.

"Ha! Not yet their time to mate; something frightened them. Let me have it quickly, your far-seeing instrument," he cried.

Reluctantly I passed it to him and, after adjusting it to his different vision, he muttered: "As I suspected—a war party. Coming toward us. Ten . . . fifteen . . . still more coming up in sight . . . Now all out from the coulee . . . . Twenty-seven of them. Here, look you at them quickly, and then we will go."

By the time I had focused the telescope upon them they were so closely grouped, as they came riding swiftly out upon the plain, that I did not try to count them. They were all of three miles away, but so powerful was the instrument that I got an intimate view of them; their fluttering blankets, worn as togas; their guns; buckskin cased shields; the fringed, parfleche cylinders at their sides, containing, as I well knew, their war bonnets.

In order to conceal themselves, or for protection from the wind, the scouts of some long-ago war party had built upon the summit of the butte a breast-high circle of rocks, behind which we now sat. We dared not chance being seen by the advancing raiders, so upon hands and knees we crept to the west side of the shelter, broke a passageway through it, and were soon leaping down the steep slope to our horses. Less than a half hour later we charged into camp, Pinukwiim shouting again and again: "Coming near, a war party! Take up your weapons, mount your swiftest runners. Hurry! Hurry, that we may soon wipe them out, our enemies."

At once every able man of the camp was shouting to his youngsters or herder to catch his fast buffalo horse, the while he painted his face and ordered his women to place before him his gun, shield, war bonnet, and sacred belongings. Old men gathered around us to learn just where the enemy were and the number of them. Old women ran to watch their fighting sons dress, and to pray for their safety and success. Little children bawled. Young sons pleaded to be allowed to go with their fathers, and their mothers scolded them, told them to close their mouths and keep them closed. Dogs howled, horses pranced and neighed. Here and there eager young warriors raised a song of battle, of enemies to be overcome. What a din and stir of excitement our discovery had raised in the camp!

Running Rabbit, head chief, mounted his big black war horse and shouted, "Hurry, hurry you fighters, gather you here before my lodge." His bare legs were striped with red and white paint. His war shirt of buffalo leather was fringed with ermine skins and enemy scalps. Upon his head was a war bonnet of horns and ermine skins; a bow-and-arrows case was slung at his left shoulder; his left arm was thrust through the loop of his feather-rimmed shield, and his right hand upheld a long, scalp-tufted lance, one that his grandfather had taken in a fight with Mexicans in the far-south country of continuous summer. It was of great power; it turned aside the arrows and the bullets of the enemy. For hunting, guns of course, but for fighting he would use only his Sun-powered lance, and his equally powerful and sacred shield. More to complete his fierce appearance than for use was his bow-and-arrows case. The slowness of the warriors in gathering annoyed him, and when forty or fifty were before us, well mounted and well armed, he would wait no longer. Telling Pinuk-wiim and me to ride beside him, he led off, shouting: "You slow ones, you fumblers, serve you right if we kill off the enemy before you can overtake us."

A number of the laggards overtook us before we arrived at the foot of Black Butte, a mile or more from camp, and looking back I saw many others of them strung out upon our trail. We struck up into the sparse timber and brush on the north base of the butte, and rounding it, sighted the war party about a mile out upon the plain and coming directly toward us. Cried one and another: "There they are!" "Not one shall escape!" "Soon shall they cry, the dog-faces!" Shouted Running Rabbit: "Now then, my children, take courage! Shoot to make sure kill! Come, we go!"

263

Instantly sighting us as we left the timber at the foot of the butte, the raiders quickly bunched up, stood staring at us for a little, and then, well knowing that they were about to die and determined to die fighting, formed into a line stretching out upon the short-grassed plain. I never learned how my companions felt as we raced on toward them, for a Blackfeet warrior would never confess to a lack of courage. But I know how I felt: I wanted to be elsewhere. My flesh crept in anticipation of the sting of an arrow or bullet. But I had to go on and to do my best in the attack, or else ever afterward be scorned and ostracized by these, my chosen people. Most of my companions were armed with Henry repeating carbines; I myself carried a '76 Model Winchester rifle. The fight would be over almost as soon as it began.

Pinukwiim, speeding along close on my left, began singing a war song, a shrill fierce song of enemies to be overcome, and our whole crowd joined in, Running Rabbit marking time to it with abrupt wavings of his long lance. Somehow it numbed my fears, inspired me to do my best. Suddenly we were speeding past our crouched enemies, fifty or sixty yards to the right of their line, shooting at them and they at us. During the few seconds of our passing I fired at one who was reloading his gun, and then at another who rose upon his knees to aim his long-barreled fuke at us. He never got it to his shoulder; it dropped from his hands and down he went, face first into the grass. I hoped that it was my bullet that had killed him. Anyhow, I would claim him as my kill.

We sped on for several hundred yards, and then Pinukwiim shouted: "Far enough. Back we go to finish them." As with difficulty we slowed up our excited horses to turn them back, I saw first that one here and there was riderless, and then that Running Rabbit had circled from us and was already riding full tilt straight at the survivors of our attack; alone, with but his lance for a weapon. Crazy; sure to be killed, I thought, as we did our best to overtake him.

There appeared to be but four of the enemy left alive. One was standing and the others were running to join him. All were lustily singing a song strange to my ears. When Running Rabbit was almost upon them, all four fired at him, but still he kept on. A thrust of his lance, and one went down. Checking his swift, hard-minded horse as soon as was possible, he turned back at them. They had no time to recharge their muzzle-loaders, so, raising them as clubs, they bravely, and still singing, ran to meet him; to attempt to knock him from his horse. When he was almost upon them they sprang apart, two to attack him at his right, the other at his left. His long lance went deep into the latter's middle; his shield met the impact of one clubbed gun, and the other struck only his horse's flank. By the time he had swung around again, the foremost of our crowd were up with him and chanting: "Ahah-chista Makan, ha! Nitap Inah Ahahchista Makan!—Running Rabbit, ha! Running Rabbit, ho! Real chief is Running Rabbit!"

The wounded enemy sat, glaring at us, both hands pressing his dreadful wound; the two others, singing, brave to the last, ran to meet us, their useless guns raised high. A dozen shots from us laid them low, and Running Rabbit, springing from his horse, tapped the wounded one's shoulder with his lance, then thrust its sharp point deep into his breast, thus making the highest of all *coups*: striking an enemy before killing him.

But now no more singing, for along the line of our attack four of our number lay dead—White Eagle, Ancient Man, Wolf Plume, and Black Elk. Running Wolf was dying, and Weasel Head had a broken leg. While some of us cared for them, others dispatched the six or seven of our enemies who were wounded but still living. Then there were some arguments as to who was entitled to the weapons, shields, and war clothes of this and that one of the twenty-seven that we had killed; Assiniboines, they had proved to be. I claiming the belongings of the second one of the two at whom I had fired; but soon relinquished them to one, Arrow Topknot, who loudly insisted that it was his bullet that had laid low this particular enemy. Of us all, Running Rabbit alone had indisputable proof of what he had done: in sight of us all, he had added two more to his many *coups*.

265

Leaving our mutilated enemies, some of them scalped, to disintegration by the elements, we turned back with our dead and wounded whence we had come. Running Rabbit sent two of our number ahead with word of what we had done; so, when we entered camp near midnight, we were greeted with loud acclaim mingled with the sad wailings of women and children for their dead. Running Rabbit's four wives vied with one another to get near him and reach up and stroke him as they chanted his name, praising him for the brave one that he was. And I fairly swelled with pride when Pinukwiim's three wives patted me as they chanted: "Apikuni, ha! Apikuni, ho! Strong, brave, is Apikuni. He has made our enemies to cry."

The next morning I was awakened by the wailings of women taking their dead for tree burial well above camp. For many a day thereafter, for months, even, we would hear them mourning, crying over and over the names of their loved ones. Gone to the Sand Hills their shadows, that dreary abode of the dead. In the Blackfeet belief there is no Happy Hunting Ground.

While the women prepared our morning meal, Pinukwiim and I bathed in a pool of the creek. Winter and summer alike, that was a daily, not-to-be-shirked rule for all the males of the Blackfeet tribes from three-year-olds up. It hardened them, enabled them to hunt, to butcher their kills in below-zero weather. When in the dead of winter no open water was to be found in river or creek, a plunge into the snow and a brisk rubbing with it answered the purpose. On this morning, as we were returning from our bath, the camp crier was making his round of the lodges, shouting: "Hear me. Hear me, you men. Say our chiefs: After eating, we are to make a run of a big herd, so hurry to bring in your fast buffalo horses and prepare for it. Red Bird's Tail is to be your leader."

Good news—news that we had been eagerly awaiting! While eating, we learned that the camp lookouts had sighted a large herd heading to water at the creek well below camp, and where the lay of plain and coulees was favorable for close approach to it.

Within an hour we were off, all of the able men of the camp, bareback upon the fastest, best-trained horses that we owned; and following us came the women and youths, with travois horses and pack horses, to help butcher our kills and bring home the meat and hides. Red Bird's Tail and two of the young lookouts rode well in the lead.

We followed the tortuous course of the creek valley for a couple of miles, and were about to round one of its sharp bends when our leader sent a youth back to halt us, for the buffalo were close past the bend and were moving slowly back up the slope to the plain. When all had topped it, we would follow and get right in among them. Twenty minutes or so later we arrived at the foot of the slope, and our leader, a little way up it and facing us, signed: "Spread widely out, keep in line so that all may arrive on top at the same time." Then, when we had formed to suit him, he signed: "Now! We go up!"

The wind was right for our horses to get the odor of the buffalo; as we slowly ascended the slope, we had increasing difficulty in keeping them at a walk; they well knew that we were to make a run and were impatient to be at it. The trained buffalo runner had keen delight in it. With ears laid back and teeth bared, he always did his best to overtake the particular animal toward which his rider guided him. He seemed to have great hatred for the shaggy-headed beasts; to enjoy the sight and odor of the torrent of blood that gushed from nostrils and mouth following his rider's shot that pierced the animal's lungs. We kept our eyes upon Red Bird's Tail. Nearing the top of the slope he rode more slowly. At last he peered out upon the plain, then signed to us: "Come on; they are near."

"Ah! Kyi!—Yes! Now!" we cried, giving our horses their heads, and up over the top we went at full speed and right into the herd. It was well scattered; some of the animals were lying down, others grazing; still others were being pestered, driven hither and thither by the rampaging, fighting bulls, whose incessant moanings had been in our ears for long. At sight of us, at the reports of

267

our first few shots, the whole herd—at least a thousand head—was at once rushing to a common center and off upon the plain. We were right in among them, vying with one another to make the biggest killing of fat cows, easily identified by the roundness of their rumps.

My horse was very swift and perfectly trained; I had only to head him toward the animal that I wanted and he would do the rest, take me right up beside it for a close and sure shot. I gave a big cow a shot in her lungs, and at once, with a rush of blood from nose and mouth, she slowed up, staggered, and soon went down. I chose next a two-year-old; my shot broke her back and she flattened upon the ground as though struck by lightning. Looking for another fat one, I saw old Four Horns a little way ahead and to my right, and turned all my attention upon him, for he was one of a few conservatives who followed as closely as possible the old-time ways of their fathers. He scorned the blankets, the clothing, the weapons of the white man. His shirt was of soft buckskin, leggings and wrap of buffalo-cow leather, the latter having in red and yellow and black paint the pictured record of his many raids upon enemy camps, killings of enemies, and encounters with equally dangerous beasts.

Gripped now in his teeth were four or five arrows that he had snatched from the otterskin case at his side, and one by one he was fitting them to his short bow and firing them deep into the lungs of the fat cows that he unerringly selected for his kills. So forceful, so graceful was he, so sure in making every arrow pierce a vital part, that I kept my eyes upon him alone, saw him kill seven cows, and was right at his side when we brought our winded but still eager horses to a stand, and for a moment watched the great herd go thundering on as swiftly and tirelessly as when, a mile back, we had begun the run. A few, a very few of our crowd were still with it, but not for long. And then Four Horns said to me:

"So. It is ended. But what happiness, a buffalo run. What satisfaction to our women and young, our killing of plenty of real-food.

Well, let us go back, show them what we have done. You, your-self, how many? Only two? What was your trouble?"

"No trouble. Watching you with your bow and arrows, you so sure with them, was more to me than the killing of many," I answered.

"Ah. Because of a long-ago vision, this bow is my only weapon. As I slept, came to me an eagle and said: 'Your bow is Sun powered. Use it alone and you will long live.' "

Looking back whence we had come, we saw the plain strewn with the dark carcasses of the many kills of the run, several hundred of them, I thought. And here and there stood a few cripples, gathered together in sympathy for one another in their misery. They were being killed off by some of the hunters. Others were already arguing as to the ownership of this and that particular animal. Said Four Horns, grimly smiling: "No quarreling over my kills, my own marked arrow in each of them."

The women and youngsters had come up from the valley and were joining their hunters. All were soon at work, chatting, laughing, singing as they deftly plied their knives. Within an hour the course of our run was red with piles of meat upon spread-out hides. I gave my two kills to a widow and her old mother, and helped Pinukwiim and his women butcher the four big, fat cows that he had killed. As we finished, he remarked that we had made a perfect run. Sun had been good to us, for no rider had been hurt, nor had a horse fallen or been gored. By noon we were all stringing back to camp, our packhorses groaning under their heavy loads of hides and meat.

Came into our lodge that evening the widow to whom I had given my kills, came with the tongues of the two buffaloes and a pair of beautiful, quill embroidered moccasins, and said to me, "Far-off White Robe, oh generous man, here are your two tongues, and here is faulty handiwork for you to wear." I refused the tongues, accepted the moccasins. Then the present of a fine blanket from Pinukwiim's woman overcame the widow, and she went out, softly crying.

With that, tired and sleepy, we all took to our soft couches of buffalo robe and blankets. For a little I heard Pinukwiim humming a sacred song, one of the songs of the Beaver medicine, and then no more.

Never again was I to see at one time so vast a number of buffaloes as those that Pinukwiim and I had looked down upon from the top of Black Butte, on that twenty-sixth of August, 1880. Four days after our run of the large herd of them, I returned to my duties in Joseph Kipp's trading post on the south bank of the Missouri, thirty miles above the mouth of the Musselshell River.

At this time, of all the millions of their kind that had once roamed the plains, but two bands of buffalo now remained. By "band" I mean many not-widely-separated herds varying in number from fifty or sixty up to several thousand head. One of the bands ranged from the Yellowstone River south into northern Wyoming, the other from the Yellowstone northward to the Canadian line. The Crows, Cheyennes, Arapahos, and several Shoshone tribes were decimating the southern band. The northern band was hemmed in on the east by the Assiniboines, Yanktonais, and several other tribes of Sioux; on the north by the Blackfeet, Bloods, Crees, and Louis Riel's thousand or so Red River mixed bloods, mostly French-Crees; and on the west by the Pikuni and the Gros Ventres tribes. But, more destructive to the two bands than all of the Indians, were the white hunters camped all up and down the Yellowstone, slaughtering the animals for their hides alone. A single one of these hunters frequently killed more than a hundred from one stand. Yellowstone Valley stank to high heaven from the odor of rotting meat.

During the summer the Indians and the Red River people killed buffalo for their meat, for making leather of the hides, for new lodge skins, and many other necessities. Their killing of them for robes began in November, the month in which the new coat of the buffalo was at its best, full-furred and very dark. Well-fed and happy, unaware of what the near future had in store for them, all winter long the Indians came flocking in to trade their buffalo

270

robes to us. When spring came, our big warehouse contained more than four thousand well-tanned robes and nearly as many hides of elk, deer, antelope, and wolves. As Kipp and I well knew, that was to be our last big trade, for the buffalo were going fast. During the winter of 1881–82 we obtained less than half that number of buffalo robes and of small skins, and our trade in the winter of 1882–83 came to less than three hundred robes. Save for a small herd of them, safe in Yellowstone National Park, the buffalo were practically exterminated. In 1886, Mr. W. T. Hornaday, in the interest of the Smithsonian Institution, got the very last of them, twenty-nine head, from the Musselshell River–Big Dry badlands.[1]

There are still living on the Blood and the Blackfeet reservations in Alberta, and the Blackfeet reservation in Montana, a few, a very few, Indians with whom I camped and hunted and traded 'way back in the buffalo days. I visit them every summer, and around our evening lodge fires we recount our various adventures in that long-ago time of plenty and of happiness. Then, as the hour waxes late, and we seek our couches, one or another of us is sure to mourn: "Haiya! Nahktau, ohmik? Oh! Why gone, those times?"

[1] For an account of this expedition as well as a history of the end of the North American buffalo, see William T. Hornaday, "The Extermination of the American Bison," *Annual Report of the United States National Museum for 1886–1887* (1889), 367–548.